THE BROOD

WALL STREET JOURNAL & USA TODAY BESTSELLING AUTHOR

DEVNEY PERRY

THE BROOD

ISBN: 978-1-957376-47-9

Editing & Proofreading:

Elizabeth Nover, Razor Sharp Editing

Julie Deaton, Deaton Author Services

Judy Zweifel, Judy's Proofreading

Vicki Valente

Cover:

Sarah Hansen © Okay Creations

OTHER TITLES

Calamity Montana Series

The Bribe

The Bluff

The Brazen

The Bully

The Brawl

The Brood

The Edens Series

Christmas in Quincy - Prequel

Indigo Ridge

Juniper Hill

Garnet Flats

Jasper Vale

Crimson River

Sable Peak

Clifton Forge Series

Steel King

Riven Knight

Stone Princess

Noble Prince

Fallen Jester

Tin Queen

Jamison Valley Series

The Coppersmith Farmhouse

The Clover Chapel

The Lucky Heart

The Outpost

The Bitterroot Inn

The Candle Palace

Maysen Jar Series

The Birthday List

Letters to Molly

The Dandelion Diary

Lark Cove Series

Tattered

Timid

Tragic

Tinsel

Timeless

Runaway Series

Runaway Road

Wild Highway

Quarter Miles

Forsaken Trail

Dotted Lines

Holiday Brothers Series

The Naughty, The Nice and The Nanny

Three Bells, Two Bows and One Brother's Best Friend

A Partridge and a Pregnancy

Standalones

Ivy

Rifts and Refrains

A Little Too Wild

Treasure State Wildcats Series

Coach

Blitz

"So you want me to show her around or something?" Considering the size of Calamity, that tour would take roughly fifteen minutes.

"Actually, I was, uh . . ." Danny blew out a long breath. "I was hoping she could stay with you."

"Stay with me? What do you mean?"

"At your house."

Not a chance I was hearing this right. "At my house?"

"Yeah."

"What?" I stood from my chair so fast it shot backward, banging into the wall beneath my massive whiteboard. "You want Iris to live with me for two months?"

No. Absolutely not.

"I know you don't have guests often," he said.

Or ever. I had a guest room. But unless those guests had the last name Abbott and were my parents, I didn't want or like having guests.

Teaching satisfied my quota for social interaction, and when I went home, it was for privacy. Home was my sanctuary, where I could quiet my mind. And when that was impossible, it was where I could dwell on my mistakes in solitude.

The idea of tiptoeing around Danny's sister for two months, well . . . I'd rather be buried under a mountain of illegible science reports *and* moldy cheese.

"Danny, I can't."

The line went silent.

I knew what was coming before he ever spoke the words. I'd been waiting fifteen years for them.

"I'm calling in my favor."

Fuck. I ripped my chair away from the wall and plopped

into the seat. "You've had that chip in your pocket for years. You're playing it now? Why?"

"Iris is . . . I don't know. She's changed. I'm worried about her."

"What do you mean, changed? If this has anything to do with drugs or—"

"No. No, it's not that. She's good. She just seems . . . lost. She applied to all these colleges and then just never went. She disappeared to Europe for months without telling any of us. When she does come home, she always cuts her visits short. She is twenty-five and has no career or home or responsibility. And she doesn't really talk to me. Not that she ever has, but the first call I've had with her in years was earlier today and it lasted a whole five minutes."

Their age difference had always stood between Danny and Iris. He loved her, but the few times when I'd gone home with him in college, there'd been no loving, older-brother teasing. No inside jokes at the dinner table. No sibling friendship. He seemed more like another parent than a brother.

Though I was an only child, so what the fuck did I know?

"I know this is a big ask," Danny said. "But I'm hoping that some of your levelheadedness will rub off. That maybe she'll pick a real path, decide to get a real job and grow up."

So not only would I be keeping a roof over her head for the next two months, I'd also be acting as a guidance counselor. *Fucking great.* "No pressure."

His quiet laugh sounded through the phone. "This might be good for you too. Have someone with you in that house for a little while. I know how much you miss Amie. And I worry about you too."

My teeth ground together.

No one spoke Amie's name. No one in Calamity knew she existed, part of this small town's appeal. Even Danny had stopped mentioning her in our conversations. But just one name-drop and the ache in my heart soared to life. My chest constricted, making it hard to breathe.

"Fine," I said, not because I wanted Iris to invade my house, but because I was done with this call. "Send Iris my address. When does she get here?"

"She left Utah this morning but mentioned stopping along the way to sightsee. So probably tomorrow. Maybe Sunday."

There went my weekend plans. Goddamn it.

"Thanks, Wilder."

"Yep. Bye." I ended the call and tipped my head to the ceiling. "Shit."

In the scope of favors Danny could have asked for, a room for his little sister wasn't much. At least, maybe not for most people. But babysitting Iris for months? Having another person crawling around in my space? Torture. Pure fucking torture.

The bell rang and the hallway beyond my open door flooded with students. The noise was deafening as kids shouted, footsteps shuffled and lockers slammed.

Was Iris quiet? God, I hoped so.

Two months. What the hell was I thinking? I should have fought harder. I should have told Danny no.

Except I'd owed him a favor for so long. After all he'd

done for me, I couldn't turn him down. We both knew I'd agree.

At least school was still in session. For the month of May, I could leave Iris at home and escape to work. But what about after school ended in June? What about summer break? Iris was definitely leaving after two months, right?

Emily Cain, the high school's principal, had come in the other day asking if I'd be interested in teaching summer driver's ed. I'd told her definitively no.

What was worse? Tiptoeing around Iris Monroe in my own home? Or teaching teenagers how to drive?

Guess I'd decide after this weekend.

"Hey, Mr. A." Liam tapped his drumsticks on the edge of my desk in quick succession. "Can we mess around with the Bunsen burners today?"

"No," I grumbled. "And put your sticks away."

Liam ignored me. That kid always ignored me. He rattled out a quick rhythm on every table he passed on the way to his seat in the third row.

More kids streamed inside, each finding their own seats.

My classroom wasn't full of traditional desks, but stools and lab tables. Each student was matched with a partner, and I rotated them throughout the year when I noticed kids weren't a good fit for paired work. I'd rotated Liam more than any other student this year.

But at least he was graduating. Next year, he'd be some college professor's problem.

"Hi, Mr. Abbott." Sadie Brown walked into the room carrying an apple. "Want this?"

I held out my hand. "Yes."

"Here you go." She tossed it over.

CHAPTER TWO

IRIS

two months in montana. #thelifeofirismonroe

GOOSE BUMPS COVERED my arms and legs. The air had a chill, but the shiver that raced down my spine wasn't from the cold. It was from Wilder's withering gaze.

His eyes were narrowed in a harsh stare. They were intensely dark, like the blackest of coffee, and the same color as his hair. That neatly trimmed beard didn't disguise the clench of his chiseled jaw.

If there was ever an expression that screamed UNWEL-COME, it was all over Wilder Abbott's face.

Shit. Why was I here? Why on earth did Danny think this would be a good idea?

I squared my shoulders and raised my chin, pretending to be immune to his intimidating glare.

"Hey, Wilder." I smiled and held out a hand, the stack of mixed metal bracelets on my wrist clinking.

His gaze dropped to my hand, then lifted to my face.

The scowl didn't waver. "Iris Monroe." A statement now, not the question it had been the first time he'd said it in that gravelly baritone.

"Yes." I gave him a single nod. "Iris Monroe."

He scanned me head to toe. When he reached my Gucci Peggy gold platform rainbow sneakers—my happy shoes—his nostrils flared.

Nice. It wasn't the first time someone from my youth had stared too long and too hard at my tattoos or my hair or my clothes. Considering Wilder was Danny's best friend, I should have expected this. Yet it pissed me off all the same.

I snapped the fingers of my still outstretched hand. "Now that my identity is no longer in question, are you going to shake my hand or just stand there?"

His jaw ticked again, then his large hand engulfed mine. "Iris Monroe."

"How many times are you going to say my name, Wilder Abbott?" I asked as he let go of my hand.

Wilder cocked his head to the side.

It was . . . sexy.

Wait. No. Absolutely not. Wilder Abbott was not sexy.

Even though he was, in fact, sexy. Damn it.

In my defense, any single woman with functioning eyeballs would struggle to look away from that handsome face.

Had he always been this tall? The last time I'd seen him was, what . . . thirteen years ago? Maybe fourteen?

He'd come home with Danny one random weekend from college, but I'd spent most of the time in my room reading *Twilight*—Team Edward forever.

Wilder swallowed hard and rubbed a hand over his beard. "Sorry."

Why did men always rub their beards? And why was it so attractive?

"Welcome." He jerked his chin to the house. "Come on in. I'll unload my groceries, then help you haul in your stuff."

"I can manage it," I said, moving to the Bronco to open the back.

This truck was my pride and joy. I'd splurged on a custom remodel of a 1970 Ford Bronco. The style was vintage with shiny white paint and a removable soft top. But the inside was a modern dream with all of the features of a new car.

Danny thought spending hundreds of thousands of dollars on a classic was a fool's expense. Mom and Dad reminded me regularly I could sell it and buy a charming house in my hometown of Mount Pleasant.

But there wasn't a chance in hell I'd give up this Bronco, whether they disapproved or not.

The back was full of my three large suitcases. Most of the items inside were for warmer weather, like today's body-suit and denim shorts. But as a breeze caressed my skin—this time the goose bumps were from the cold—I realized I should have packed more layers. With any luck, one of the down-town shops along First Street had a cute coat for sale.

I'd made my own stop at the grocery store today too, mostly to scope out the local fare, but also because Mom had taught me never to show up at someone else's house empty-handed.

Hopefully, Wilder liked charcuterie and wine.

I stretched past the grocery bags, about to haul out my first suitcase, when a muscled arm brushed against mine.

Wilder's spicy scent mingled with the smell of pine and earth on the wind. Sexy and masculine. Exactly how a man should smell. I stifled a groan.

Oh, this was bad. Very, very bad. The last person on earth I should find attractive was Wilder Abbott. Not only was he Danny's best friend, but he was unmistakably *un*available.

"I can get these." And he could take that intoxicating scent anywhere else.

But he ignored me, yanked out two of my suitcases and headed for the house.

"Okay," I drawled. Grumpy and not great at listening. Noted.

Since he seemed determined to carry my luggage, I went to his truck and collected his groceries. With the bags looped over my forearms, I hefted them across the gravel driveway to a massive flagstone patio that led to the house.

I spun in a slow circle, taking it all in.

Wilder had found himself a little sanctuary in the Montana countryside. The road to his house was lined with trees, so I'd expected his home to be in the middle of the forest. But his log cabin was situated in an open meadow.

The trees leading up to the clearing gave him privacy, while the house was turned toward the most magnificent view I'd seen in months.

In the distance, the indigo mountains were capped in snow. The clouds in the cobalt sky were a fluffy white. The rolling hills and vast meadows were mostly golden brown, but there were a few areas where the neon green of spring was coming to life.

I loved it immediately.

There was a bench on Wilder's covered front porch. Did he sit there in the evenings and get lost in the view? Or did he take it for granted like so many, accustomed to the beauty around them?

Everyone in my family thought I was unhinged for bouncing from city to city every two months. But knowing that my time in one place was temporary meant I appreciated it.

This lifestyle wasn't all perfect. After hopping around for years, weariness had crept into my bones. With every move, it became harder and harder to pack those three suitcases. But at least I could say I lived in the moment.

Two months at a time.

Wilder appeared in the doorway just as I stepped onto his porch. He frowned at the grocery bags. "I was going to bring those in."

"Too late." I gave him a saccharine smile and continued past him through the door.

The scent of wood and that spicy cologne, like leather and anise, infused the open-concept space. I passed a living room filled with cozy leather couches and headed for the U-shaped kitchen. Two hallways led deeper into the house, probably to the bedrooms.

After depositing the grocery bags on the butcher-block island, I glanced around for my suitcases, but he'd stashed them somewhere out of sight.

Wilder strode inside again, his gaze as hard as it had been outside. He moved straight for the nearest hallway, disappearing with my last suitcase. There was a thud, then he came marching out, eyes trained forward like he was scared to look at me.

Did his jaw ever unclench? Or was it stuck that way?

I rolled my eyes and worked to unload groceries, tackling everything for the fridge first. When he returned, it was with my own foodstuffs and the handbag I'd left in the front seat of the Bronco.

"Thanks," I said.

"Yeah," he grumbled. "I'll take care of this."

"I can help."

"I got it."

As in, *get the fuck out of my kitchen.*

"Okay." I held up my hands.

Wilder worked in a fury to empty the bags. He didn't throw his loaf of bread in the pantry, but he didn't not throw it either. And that poor refrigerator door. If the condiments loaded in its trays survived the slamming, it would be a miracle.

I dug my phone from my back pocket, seeing a text from my social media manager, Kim.

today's post is going to set a new record

Kim refused to use capital letters. According to her, mixing upper and lower case characters wasn't aesthetically pleasing. So everything posted on my social media accounts was beautifully lowercase.

Since she spent more time on Instagram and TikTok than me, I didn't care how she styled the feeds. Most of the time, I sent her my content to schedule or post. But there were times, like today, when I'd post a photo myself. And those times, I had to remember not to use capital letters in the captions.

Today's post was captioned *two months in montana. #thelifeofirismonroe*

Real-life Iris preferred shouty caps and exclamation marks. Her caption would have read *MONTANA!*

The *#thelifeofirismonroe* hashtag had been Kim's idea too. We added it to nearly every selfie.

In the picture I'd posted earlier, I was standing in the middle of a deserted highway. I'd dressed for comfort and a long drive in my black bodysuit, favorite denim shorts and gold sneakers, not having planned to take any photos other than the landscape. Normally I layered necklaces but today, I'd only bothered with my favorite compass rose that I'd had for years and wore almost daily. As far as ensembles went, it was on the demure end of my spectrum.

Still, it had looked perfect in the photo I'd taken.

About thirty miles from Calamity, the road had straightened and there hadn't been another car in sight. So I'd pulled over, thrown up my portable tripod, and, with it on the center line, taken a few quick shots of me on the road with the mountains in the background.

Normally, everything I did was edited. But I'd wanted today's to be raw and real. Like the landscape. Like Montana.

I'd only been here for hours and could already tell I'd be sad to leave after my sixty days were up.

"I wasn't expecting you so soon."

I whirled at Wilder's voice, tucking my phone away. He stood on the other side of the island, his arms braced on its edge.

"Sorry. I thought Danny called you."

"He did. Today. He said you were sightseeing."

"Oh." I gave him an exaggerated frown. "Sorry. That's my fault. There wasn't much I wanted to stop and see, so I just kept going." The sightseeing excuse had mostly been to get out of Utah in a hurry this morning.

Though at times, I would linger between destinations if I stumbled upon a town to explore. But not this time. My only stop on the seventeen-hour drive from San Diego to Calamity had been in Mount Pleasant, Utah, last night.

I'd stayed with my parents. Danny and Mary had brought their kids over for dinner. I'd hoped it would be a chance to catch up and reconnect, but after the third mention of me getting a real job, I'd lied and said I had sightseeing to do.

Then I'd woken up early and gotten on the road.

"Thank you for letting me stay here."

Wilder huffed. Or maybe it was a grunt. More of that sunny, welcoming disposition.

No way I was living with that for two months.

This man clearly did not want me in his home.

Last night at dinner, Danny had made it seem like Wilder loved having guests. That if I crashed in his guest bedroom, it would be no problem at all. My brother either didn't know his friend very well, or he'd guilted Wilder into this arrangement.

Probably the latter.

"It's been a long day." I sighed, then pointed toward the hall. "I think Danny was trying to be helpful, but I'm going to head to a hotel."

There had to be a vacation rental in the area. Anything was better than grunts and glares.

Wilder worked his jaw, his gaze shifting to some invisible spot on the wall.

He wanted to agree, didn't he? He wanted to carry my suitcases back outside. The way he pursed his lips looked a lot like he was fighting a yes. But he stayed quiet, his eyes aimed anywhere but my direction.

This was exactly why I shouldn't have told my family where I was going until I'd gotten here. They meddled.

Mom and Dad would have forbidden me from going to Europe after high school. They would have thwarted my plans and shipped me off to a tame, boring college.

Back then, I'd been different. Not as bold. Not as brave. I wouldn't have had the courage to tell them no. It had taken me those adventures in Europe, most good, some bad, to build my confidence.

Now when they asked where I was going, how long I'd be there, I was honest. Though I was regretting that honesty at the moment.

Danny had called me this morning when he'd learned I'd already left Mom and Dad's. Over dinner last night, I'd told them my plan was to get to Calamity and scope out the area. I'd find a place to stay after arriving.

The only reason I'd decided on Calamity was because of Danny. Ever since his first trip to visit Wilder here, he'd bragged about the charming, old-fashioned town. So it had been on my destination list for years.

But my decision to come here was less than forty-eight hours old. I'd loaded up the Bronco in San Diego yesterday and hit the road, planning a quick visit to Utah before choosing my next destination. Yet by the time I'd reached the outskirts of Las Vegas, my heart had been set on Montana.

My spontaneity annoyed my brother, so he'd taken it into his hands to find me a place to stay.

I'd balked at his initial suggestion to bunk with Wilder. But then he'd begged and pleaded for a favor. For a guy who rarely left Utah, my brother could loop the globe with his guilt trips.

Danny was worried about his friend. Since his wife's death, Wilder had pulled away. And since I was already coming to Montana, who better to check on his friend than his sister?

Well, I hadn't exactly failed my brother. Wilder looked perfectly fine, emphasis on perfect.

He stood four, maybe five inches over six feet. Those broad, strong shoulders and muscled biceps stretched the fabric of his gray button-down. The shirttails were tucked into the waistband of his jeans, accentuating his narrow hips and flat stomach.

Drop dead gorgeous.

Too bad he was my brother's best friend. Too bad he most definitely wanted me to leave.

"It was nice seeing you again, Wilder."

"Wait." He held up a hand, stopping me before I could leave. If his jaw had flexed before, now there was a very real chance he'd crack a molar or two.

Why was that still sexy?

Brother's best friend. Brother's best friend.

Grieving widower. Grieving widower.

Time to get those suitcases.

"Really, it's fine." I took off for the hallway. "I love hotels."

Did Calamity have a hotel? I hadn't noticed one on my way into town. If they didn't, then I'd find a new place to explore. Though that idea wasn't overly appealing. Somehow, in barely any time at all, this had become where I wanted to spend my two months in Montana.

Calamity.

And this house.

Kim would lose her aesthetically focused mind over this place. The log structure was an exact balance between rustic and moody. It was slightly dated, meaning it had character. It was cozy yet clean.

Wilder had a masculine style with the chocolate and cognac leather, but it was tasteful and understated. If Montana was a mood, it was this house.

Content ideas, pictures and videos, raced through my mind, but I shoved them all aside.

There had to be another charming log cabin around here, right?

All three of my suitcases were lined up in a neat row in the guest bedroom. They were against the foot of a bed with a plush, white quilt. The fluffy pillows were calling my name, and I couldn't stop a yawn.

After two long days of driving, I needed a hot shower and a long nap. Oh, please let there be a hotel in Calamity with a soft bed. I had no desire to drive to a different town tonight.

My hand was wrapped around the handle of a suitcase when I felt Wilder at my back. Not his heat. Not that solid, broad chest.

That dark, brooding stare.

"Iris."

Oh, I liked how he said my name. There was a bit of a rough edge, a scrape, to the *r*.

Ugh. Make it stop. I couldn't, wouldn't, be attracted to Danny's friend. This sudden attraction was just the result of my exhaustion. That, and my epic dry spell. I was simply sex starved and hormonal. The coil in my lower belly had nothing to do with Wilder Abbott.

NOTHING AT ALL!

"Stay," he said.

"Be honest. You don't want me here. Do you?"

Silence.

"That's what I thought." I hauled the suitcase away from the bed, but Wilder didn't budge from his spot in the threshold. That large, honed body filled the entire doorframe.

Before today, I'd never really understood the expression *climb that man like a tree.*

Good thing I couldn't climb trees, not in these shoes.

"I want you to stay."

I scoffed. "Liar."

He dragged a hand through that black hair, and my knees weakened. Sexy. So, so sexy.

Now it was paramount that I escaped. This man was far too much temptation, and while my ego wasn't in any way fragile—I had snarky strangers on the internet to thank for my thick-ish skin—I didn't need to be rejected by Wilder.

"This is just . . . I don't have guests," he said. "Other than when my parents come to visit, I am out here alone. I like it that way."

His escape from the world.

That was what Danny had called this house. His theory was that Wilder had moved to Montana to escape the world. To hide in his grief over his wife.

According to my brother, Wilder and Amie were soul-mates. Her death had categorically changed him and irrevo-cably broken his heart.

Danny was probably right. The Wilder I remembered from all those years ago had smiled and laughed. The man standing in front of me was, well . . . a brood.

If Danny was so worried about his friend, he could come up here and check on Wilder himself.

"I appreciate that you'd let me stay here simply because Danny asked," I told him. "That's sweet. But let me take that burden off your shoulders. I'm going to a hotel."

"I promised Danny."

Why? Why had he agreed to this? What had Danny told him about me? "Wilder—"

"At least for a night or two. Just . . . stay." He held out a hand. It was the exact same gesture my parents used with their dog, Max.

Max always ran away.

"Look, I apprecia—"

"Are you a vegan?"

I blinked. "Huh?"

"A vegan. Do you eat meat?"

"You mean a vegetarian. Vegans and vegetarians are different."

He closed his eyes. Summoning patience? He was a teacher. Did he do that with his students too? Maybe a teenager would find the silence that stretched between us intimidating.

I found it oddly adorable.

"I'm not a vegan or a vegetarian. I eat meat."

The air rushed from his lungs. Those broad shoulders slumped. But his eyes stayed closed. "Just stay. Please."

It was the please that made me loosen my grip on my suitcase. That, and I was too tired to argue. "Fine."

For just one night.

CHAPTER THREE

WILDER

WHAT A CLUSTERFUCK. I should have let Iris leave. I should have helped haul those massive suitcases back outside and stuffed them in her Bronco. Instead, I was begging her to stay.

All because of that goddamn favor.

If only I could rewind time to that night fifteen years ago. To not be the dumb fucking twenty-year-old who'd almost landed himself in jail.

"Do you need any help?" I waved at her luggage. *Please say no.*

"No, that's all right. I'm used to dragging them around."

How? The damn things had to weigh over fifty pounds each.

She had a slight frame, and that top left nothing to the imagination. Not the slender curves of her torso or the swell of her pert breasts. Maybe she was short. Maybe she was tall. It was impossible to tell with those rainbow-monstrosity shoes. Her hair was draped around her shoulders, but even those silky waves couldn't hide the outline of her pebbled nipples.

I gritted my teeth and kept my gaze locked on her suitcases. Was there a bra in one of them?

For my sake, I fucking hoped so. Each time I caught a glimpse of those nipples, my cock twitched.

Danny's sister. She was Danny's sister. He'd sent her here so I could be a positive influence on her life. Act as her guidance counselor. Hell, she was only twenty-five. She was closer in age to my students than me.

I needed to get out of this room. I needed to get away from Iris standing beside a bed. So I went to the walk-in closet, ripping the doors open. Just like it had been the last time I'd checked, the space was crammed full of boxes.

Amie's boxes.

The only people who stayed in this room were Mom and Dad. They knew what was in this closet, and rather than disturb the space, they just kept their suitcases in the corner of the room. No sweat for a weekend trip.

But if Iris was staying for months, I couldn't expect her to keep her clothes on the floor. So I moved some boxes to the top shelf, trying not to think about what was inside the cardboard as I stacked them as efficiently and quickly as possible. Except no matter how fast I worked, the walls of the cramped space crept closer and closer.

I hated this fucking closet.

"Just . . . move whatever you want in here." I set the box in my hands on the floor and left the rest behind.

Iris was standing exactly where I'd left her, beside those suitcases. Her clear blue eyes studied me, likely noticing too much.

I grabbed one of her suitcases and carried it into the closet, dropping it with a loud *thud* just inside the door. Then I did the same for the second. But when I moved for the third, Iris placed her fingers on the handle, guarding it at her side.

Three massive suitcases.

Amie had always packed light. If we were flying, she'd refused, no matter how long the trip, to check a bag. Even when we'd drive somewhere, she'd brag about how few things she needed to be comfortable.

Yet on every single trip, she'd forget one or two or ten things. She'd borrow my razor. She'd get a toothbrush from the hotel's front desk. And when she'd forget a swimming suit or flip-flops, we'd have to find a store.

Going to Target wasn't exactly what I'd wanted to do on my vacations just so Amie could say she packed light.

Iris, on the other hand, could probably stock an entire women's boutique from the contents of her luggage. And that boutique would have her sweet scent.

If she stayed here, the whole house would smell like her, wouldn't it? Vanilla and citrus. Goddamn it, why did she have to smell good?

"Bathroom is in there." I breathed through my mouth and pointed toward the open door. "There are towels in the cabinet. Laundry room is next door. Make yourself at home."

"Thanks." She gave me a rueful smile, like she knew that last sentence was a blatant lie.

"I'll let you get settled." I turned and strode from the room.

If she did end up staying, then at least there wasn't much for me in this part of the house. My bedroom, bathroom and office were down the other hallway. I could hole up there in the evenings and spend my weekends outside.

This was temporary. I'd endured worse than a houseguest.

Much, much worse.

It was easier to breathe once I was out of Iris's bedroom and her scent wasn't invading my nostrils. I walked straight for the fridge, yanking the door open to grab a beer. With a twist, the lid came off and the bottle was pressed against my lips, the cold, bitter liquid easing the thickness in my throat.

Was this wicked pressure in my chest because of Iris? Or was it because I'd set foot in Amie's closet?

Both.

I took another gulp of my beer, then set the bottle on the counter, closing my eyes. Two months. Iris would stay for two months, then I'd have my life back.

On a sigh, I took my beer and wandered to the wall of windows in the living room. This view was the reason I'd bought the house and stretched my budget to its extreme.

For most of my life, visiting Montana had been on my wish list, but with school and life, I hadn't made coming here a priority. But after the funeral, it had seemed like the perfect place to disappear. To a town where no one knew my name. Where no one knew Amie's. Where I could be alone.

I'd applied for every open teaching position in the state. Four days after I'd agreed to be Calamity High School's new science teacher, I'd been in a U-Haul truck, heading north from Salt Lake.

I'd come to Calamity to escape. From the grief. From the pain. From the guilt. Except those feelings had come along for the ride, three unwelcome and enormous burdens, much like Iris's three suitcases.

Going back hadn't been an option, so I'd started house hunting. My first day in Montana, I'd found this house. My realtor had gotten a tip just that morning that the owner was considering listing it for sale. She'd brought me out here, and I'd known immediately as I'd stood by these windows, as I'd taken in the vast mountains that towered over broad, rugged plains, that I was home.

It was the first time since Amie had died that I'd felt a sliver of peace. This view, this house, was worth so much more than the price I'd paid.

Something in Iris's room clanked.

I tensed, my grip tightening around the beer bottle.

The water turned on, the pump quietly humming from the utility closet.

"Son of a bitch," I muttered, loosening a long breath.

She wasn't going to be quiet, was she?

Maybe this would be easier if she resembled even a bit of her younger self. But the Iris Monroe I'd known all those years ago had had brown hair, like Danny's. She'd been shy and quiet, a timid girl who'd mostly avoided eye contact.

The Iris Monroe currently banging around in my guest bedroom was a stranger.

Who was *this* Iris? Her eyes were the same but otherwise, so much had changed. Her hair was lighter, the color of Caribbean sand. The tattoos were endless, beautiful and colorful. Tattoos a man could spend days, weeks studying. Gone was the girl. In her place, a stunning woman.

And still, my best friend's sister.

How could I have thought about fucking her senseless

after seeing her at the store? I shook my head, hoping that idea would rattle loose, but it was already ingrained. For fuck's sake, it was stuck tight.

Danny was going to murder me in my sleep.

I dug my phone from my pocket and pulled up his name, sending him a quick text.

Iris made it.

His reply came before I could finish my beer.

Good. Thanks again.

He wouldn't be thanking me if he knew my initial reaction to her had been sheer lust.

A throat cleared.

I turned to find Iris standing beside a couch. Those shoes of hers were surprisingly quiet on my hardwood floors.

"Got another one of those?" She pointed to my beer.

"Fridge." I jerked my chin toward the kitchen. "Help yourself."

She walked with grace and a subtle sway to her hips. Her fingertips skimmed the butcher-block island in a featherlight caress. With the fridge door open, she cocked her head to the side, worrying her bottom lip between her teeth as she surveyed her options—Coors Light or Blue Moon.

Did Iris have any idea how sexy she was?

I ripped my gaze away and turned again to the view outside.

"Want another one?" she asked.

"Please," I choked out. I made a quick adjustment to my dick before she came to stand at my side, holding out my fresh beer.

I took a drink of my Coors Light.

She took a drink of her Blue Moon.

I kept my eyes trained forward.

She shifted to stare at my profile.

"What?" My gaze flicked to hers before darting back to the glass.

It was her mouth that had snagged my attention in that brief glimpse. That pink, delicious mouth.

I'm fucked.

This was the problem with going so long without sex. My body was clearly in control here, demanding that I succumb to the rush of heat flooding my veins.

"This is awkward," she said.

That I was so attracted to her? Definitely awkward. "Yes, it is."

"Why?"

"Why is it awkward?" The answer would make this unbearable. Not that I'd tell her the truth.

"No, why did you agree to let me stay here?"

"Oh." That was a question I could actually answer. I took a drink and lifted a shoulder. "I owed your brother a favor."

"Ah. Now it all makes sense. I'm the favor." She took a drink, the corner of her mouth lifting. If she was irritated, it didn't show. "Do I want to know what you did to owe him this?"

"Probably not."

That slight smile widened. "That bad? Now I'm curious. How many beers does it take for you to become loose-lipped?"

"More than two."

"Bummer. After this one, I'll tell you anything and every-thing you probably don't want to know about me." She pointed her bottle at my nose. "But use this newfound information for the benefit of good, not evil."

I chuckled. Well, I hadn't expected to be laughing tonight. Maybe we'd survive this after all.

"You have a nice view," she said.

"I do."

"It's peaceful here."

"It is."

She hummed, a sound so natural, yet sultry it sent shivers down my spine.

It was torture. Pure fucking torture.

She turned to stare at my profile again.

When a few moments passed and she just kept looking at me, I gave in and met her blue gaze. "Now what?"

Her head tilted like it had when she'd been assessing beer choices. "You look different."

"Than I did in college? I should hope so," I said. "You look different too."

She stiffened, her gaze narrowing before she turned it to the window.

"I didn't mean that as a dig."

"You'd be the only one," she muttered.

Danny had warned me that Iris had changed. Granted, she'd just gotten here, but from what I could tell, her biggest change had been this incredible poise. She'd grown into a confident woman.

What was there to criticize? The tattoos? The blond hair?

Danny was the closest thing I'd ever had to a brother, but I wasn't blind to his faults. He could be judgmental at times. And he liked everything to fit.

One look at Iris and it was clear she was not interested in conformity.

But would that really be enough to worry him? What wasn't he telling me?

There was only one way to find out. I'd have to let her stay.

Damn it. It was almost comical. Almost.

"Let's start over." Shifting my beer to my left hand, I held out my right. "Good to see you again, Iris."

She eyed my hand for a moment before her palm fit into mine. Delicate, but strong. Soft, yet her long nails would undoubtedly bite.

"You too, Wilder. Thanks for letting me crash here tonight."

I was probably going to regret it, but I spoke regardless. "You're welcome to stay here while you're in Montana."

Her eyebrows lifted. "Because you owe Danny a favor?"

Because I wanted to know her.

Because this woman was an enigma, and I'd always had a thing for puzzles.

"Is doing this favor for Danny such a bad thing?" I asked.

"I guess not."

"Then it's settled." I turned away from the windows, walking to the kitchen. "How about dinner?"

CHAPTER FOUR

IRIS

glamorous #thelifeofirismonroe #twomonthsinmontana

WILDER WAS DOING DANNY A FAVOR.

I was doing Danny a favor.

If it was any other person than my brother, I'd think this was some elaborate matchmaking scenario. But not Danny. There was no way he'd ever consider Wilder and me as couple material.

No, this was simply my brother worrying over two people he cared about.

He'd probably asked Wilder to look out for me while I was here. It was patronizing and intrusive. Wilder and I were both adults. It irked me to no end that Danny didn't trust that I could run my own life without interference.

Still, Danny's heart was in the right place. And if I could just get my own self in the right place and stop drooling over Wilder, this whole situation would be fine.

First and foremost, I really needed to stop staring at his forearms.

He had great forearms, muscled and dusted with his black hair. A few veins snaked beneath the surface of his tanned skin. They were a man's forearms. Everything about him was utterly male.

Wilder was a far cry from the scrawny musician I'd dated in Berlin. Or the lanky artist from London.

The sheer size of him was incredible, but add in that handsome face and sinewed forearms, well . . . here I was, still staring.

"You don't need to cook for me," I said as he sliced a tomato on the other side of the island.

"We both need to eat."

"I'm happy to help."

He lifted a shoulder and kept on slicing.

"You do that a lot."

"Chop tomatoes?"

"Speak with a one-sided shrug."

His forehead furrowed, creating twin creases between his eyebrows.

"You do that a lot too. Scowl."

Wilder's gaze lifted to mine, that scowl unwavering, before he returned his attention to the cutting board. His grip on the serrated knife tightened and his forearms flexed.

Antagonizing him had its benefits.

I lifted my beer to my lips, taking a long sip.

He'd been so sincere in his invitation to let me stay. Should I? Two months wasn't a lot of time, but it wasn't exactly a weekend getaway either.

It must be quite the favor he owed Danny. What was it? If I pestered him enough, could I coax it out of him? Maybe I'd conjure an elusive smile too.

Wilder had chuckled while we'd been chatting, a deep and delicious sound, but it had only come with a twitch of his lips. What would he look like smiling?

With the tomato sliced into thin circles, he took the head of iceberg lettuce and began tearing off leaves. He'd already shaped hamburger patties on a plate. The grill outside was heating.

He was the master of his domain, so I took advantage of the quiet moment and spun in my stool, surveying the open space and the living area.

This house was . . . perfection.

Staying wasn't as horrible an idea as it had been an hour ago. But I'd see how tonight went first. Maybe search for another vacation rental in the area, just in case. I didn't mind hotels for short trips, but for extended stays, I wanted a kitchen so I wouldn't have to eat out every meal. And I was not about washing my clothes at a public laundromat, not anymore.

I just had to figure out how to suffocate this attraction to Wilder. Maybe all I needed was some time for his allure to wear thin.

He'd probably do something brotherly soon and douse the heat in my veins. Maybe he'd chide me about my tattoos. That was my sister-in-law's favorite pastime at family func-tions—*snob*. Or maybe Wilder would tell me to stop showing so much skin, like Dad.

Mom didn't criticize as much, at least verbally. No, her

disapproval was the silent type, present in each and every glance and pursing of her lips.

Wilder hadn't said anything yet, but it was just a matter of time.

So until he inevitably turned me off, well . . . I'd enjoy those flexed forearms and the jaw twitches.

"I love your house," I told him, leaning my elbows back on the island.

"So you said."

"It's worth repeating."

"I love it too." His voice was low and quiet, like a whisper against my skin.

"If I took a few photos, not of the whole house but different pieces or corners, would you mind?"

"No."

"And if I posted them online? They wouldn't have your address or any way to identify the location."

"It's fine."

I spun around again to find his attention firmly fixed on our burger toppings. "It's sort of glamourous here."

Wilder glanced up and arched an eyebrow. "Glamourous? Not sure that's the word I'd use."

"Why? It's exactly right."

I'd had a fuzzy picture of Montana in mind before I'd decided to make this my next destination. And while I'd been close in some regard—the rugged terrain and wide, open spaces—being in this house had given that mental picture firm edges. So had driving through Calamity.

Everything about the town, this house, felt practical. Safe. Comfortable.

"It's authentic." I took another drink of my beer. "I need more authentic in my life."

"Danny said you have a travel blog or something like that."

"Something like that."

Either Wilder hadn't understood or my brother hadn't explained it correctly. Given Danny's constant frown when it came to my job, I was guessing the latter.

"I'm an influencer," I said.

Wilder blinked. "What's an influencer?"

"Good question." I laughed, taking out my phone. With my Instagram account open, I held it out for him to see.

His gaze raked over the screen, taking it all in. Then he nodded once before turning away to go to the fridge. "Do you want cheese on your burger?"

"Please." I set my phone aside.

I had over two million followers on Instagram. Nearly three on TikTok. But if Wilder was at all impressed, he didn't let it show. I sort of loved that.

They were just vanity metrics. In the beginning, I'd obsessed over followers. But after years, the sparkle had worn off. I was incredibly proud of what I'd built, but these days, I was searching for balance. It would have shattered Wilder's allure if he'd gushed over my very small slice of fame.

"So you—what, take pictures as you travel?" he asked.

"Basically. Though I don't just post about travel. It's fashion and beauty products and books and whatever else I'm doing. I built up enough of a following that brands will pay me to post about them."

"Ah." Wilder nodded, setting a block of cheddar on the counter. "Influencing."

44

I touched the tip of my nose. "Now you're catching on."

"My students are always on their phones checking that stuff." He flicked a wrist toward my phone, like its presence in his kitchen was an annoyance. Another invader in his home.

"You don't have any social media?"

He shook his head. "Nope. I'm too old."

"Yes, you're ancient," I teased.

His aversion to social media didn't have a damn thing to do with his age. It was just . . . him, wasn't it?

Wilder seemed like the type who'd hate the idea of a following. He was too busy hiding away out here in his Montana paradise. Maybe he had it right and the rest of us screen addicts were the ones who had it backward.

"I'll admit social media has its challenges," I told him. "But because of it, I've got a career that pays the bills and gives me a lot of freedom."

Wilder looked up, studying my face. He stared for so long that I began to squirm in my seat.

Very few people unnerved me these days. But there was something about his dark gaze that made my heart race. Like he could see straight through my skin, to my very bones, and the insecurities I'd worked so hard to overcome.

Was this when he'd tell me to get a "real job"? Or maybe he'd be like Danny and deliver a lecture about my lack of higher education. Would Wilder be yet another person in my life to warn me that social media was fickle and not a viable long-term career choice?

If there was an opportunity to smother this lust, now was the time.

"What?" I whispered, unable to bear his silence for another moment.

"Nothing," he murmured. Then his gaze shifted to our burgers and without a word, he carried the plate out the door adjacent to the kitchen.

That door led to a small patio off the side of the house. Like the front walkway, it was made from flagstone rocks, their shape a perfect semicircle.

The moment Wilder stepped onto that patio, the tension inside diffused, like he'd taken it outside with the raw meat.

I took another gulp of beer, the bottle nearly empty, and slid from my stool, retreating to the living room with my phone. With my camera open, I lined up a shot, using the window frames as pseudo picture frames to capture that view.

The indigo mountains and forest beyond the glass weren't as majestic in the photo as they were in person, but this photo wasn't only for my feed. This one was mostly for me. A memory of this perfect house, so that if I left tomorrow, I'd have something to revisit time and time again.

I posted it quickly, adding a *glamourous* caption and a couple hashtags. Then I tucked my phone away, more than happy to ignore it for a while.

Some asshole online would probably comment about my definition of glamourous. As my following increased, so did the number of trolls and keyboard warriors. But that was why I had Kim. She did her best to shield me from the negative comments so I could keep my sanity.

The door behind me opened and Wilder came inside with the now empty plate. He set it in the sink and washed his hands.

"Are you sure I can't help with anything?" I asked.

He grunted and shook his head.

I fought a smile.

This man was so wonderfully grumpy. I didn't remember that about him. Granted, it had been ages since I'd seen Wilder. And I'd been so much younger. But I definitely remembered him beardless and smiling.

Maybe he'd stopped laughing after his wife had died.

My heart twisted.

The boxes in the closet of my room were hers. When I'd put my last suitcase away, I'd glimpsed her name written on one. *Amie.*

Before returning to my stool, I went to the fridge for another beer. Two was my limit because I'd meant what I'd told Wilder earlier. Two beers, and no force on this earth could get me to shut up. So I sipped it while he worked around the kitchen. As he opened cabinets and drawers, I took note of what was inside. Plates above silverware next to glasses.

He moved with a fluidity that I wouldn't have expected from such a tall, bulky man. It was mesmerizing to watch. And equally interesting and irritating that he tried so hard to ignore me.

"Is it the tattoos?" I blurted. Apparently I didn't need all two beers to lose my filter tonight. One and a half did the trick.

"What?"

"Mary hates the tattoos. As I accumulate more and more, she has a harder time looking at me. Is that why you're pretending I'm not sitting on this stool?"

He tore two rectangular paper towels from the roll

beside the sink to use as napkins. As he set them on the island beside our plates, he finally met my gaze. Those dark eyes were nearly unreadable. "No, it's not the tattoos."

"Then what is it?"

"I'm not used to having someone in my space. Not great at small talk either."

"Ah." I nodded. "You prefer awkward silence over idle chatter about the weather."

Something sparked in those eyes, like he was holding in a snarky comment, but he stayed quiet.

"Well, I am allergic to awkward silence. And I'm nosy. Consider this your warning."

He cast his gaze to the ceiling, shaking his head.

"How much do you regret letting me through the door?"

Wilder's lips pursed, not from annoyance but like he was holding back a smile. Then he shoved off the counter and disappeared outside with a fresh plate to collect our burgers.

I giggled when the door closed.

Maybe it would prove impossible to work Wilder out of his shell. I had no idea what it felt like to lose the love of your life. But maybe I could at least make him laugh a few times. Remind him what it felt like to smile.

Two months in Montana.

Two months with Wilder Abbott.

Two months to push a few of his buttons and boundaries.

Hmm. Maybe this would be fun after all.

He returned with our burgers, plating them on the buns he'd already laid out, while I went to the fridge and took out the ketchup and mustard. The dining room table stayed empty as we sat side by side on the stools at the island.

"What do you teach?" I asked. "Is it science? I want to say science."

"Science."

"What grades?"

"High school." The bite he took was so large that I had to wait before firing off my next question.

"Do you like teaching?"

"Yes."

"Were you good in science when you were in high school?"

A nod.

"How many students go to your school?"

Throughout the entire meal, I asked questions. Wilder gave short, succinct answers. He provided no extra detail. No added emotion.

It was like he wore his privacy as a cloak. Or a shield.

That sort of privacy wasn't even in my realm of possibility. My life, or the illusion of my life, was broadcast for the world to see. To celebrate. To criticize.

Chances were, Wilder would never open up to me. We'd spend the next two months as strangers. But I'd never know him if I didn't try.

Why did I want to try? Why was this suddenly so important to me?

I didn't try to figure out the answers to those questions, not with my head light from the beer and my belly full from dinner. The exhaustion was catching up to me fast, and that plush bed was calling. So I slid off my stool, holding up a hand when he tried to clear his plate. "I'm doing the dishes."

He set the plate down and gave me a nod. Then without

another word, he left the kitchen, disappearing down the hallway that must lead to his room.

I quickly cleaned up the space, loading the dishwasher and finding a plastic storage container for the leftover toppings. Then I wiped down the granite counters, leaving them gleaming under the kitchen's lights.

The sun was still streaming through the window when I retreated to the bedroom. I drew the blinds and changed into one of the oversized T-shirts that I wore as pajamas. It dwarfed my frame and slung wide on a shoulder, revealing my collarbone.

Sometimes, I'd wear it with my red bra to let the strap show while I filmed a video. A pop of color, not because I needed the support. My breasts were perky but A cups at best. But tonight, I didn't bother digging the bra from my suitcase and I let the shirt drape down my bare nipples.

Then I pulled up my hair and washed the makeup from my face, setting up my phone to take a nightly ritual video with a new serum I'd agreed to try and promote. With it finished and sent to Kim for editing and promotional language, I flopped on the bed, staring up at the ceiling.

The hem of my T-shirt rode up my thighs, a stray thread tickling my bare skin. This shirt had been washed so many times it was nearly threadbare, and I'd have to find a replacement soon.

How big were Wilder's shirts? I bet they were huge. Soft. Exactly what I preferred to wear to sleep.

And I bet they smelled incredible. Just like him.

God, he really was gorgeous. The age difference between us didn't seem so big, not like it had a decade ago.

Not that it mattered. And not just because of his friendship with Danny.

I glanced at the walk-in closet, where the light was still on.

Wilder was in love with his wife. I had no desire to come between him and his ghost.

No, I just wanted to make him smile. At least once.

And maybe steal a T-shirt.

CHAPTER FIVE

WILDER

"LIAM," I barked.

The drumstick he'd just thrown in the air clattered to the floor.

"Throw it one more time," I pointed at his nose, "and I'll break it in half."

He muttered something under his breath as he bent to pick it up, then shoved it in the backpack hanging from his swiveling stool.

"Don't push me today," I warned, and the kid had the smarts enough to drop the smirk on his face.

So far, I'd given three kids detention. Class hadn't even started yet, but I had a feeling Liam would leave here with a white slip of his own.

"Hey, Mr. Abbott." Sadie waved as she breezed in the room. "Did you have a good weekend?"

"No."

Her smile faltered. She stared at me for a moment, taken aback, then ducked her chin and walked to her desk.

Shit. That was the fourth student today who didn't deserve my foul mood but had gotten it anyway.

This was what happened when I didn't get a weekend to decompress. I'd been on edge all day, snapping at students and losing my cool. Mondays were usually the easiest day of my week. After a weekend away, I'd find my patience again. The kids would whittle away at it over the course of the week, but I was a man who'd always enjoyed Mondays.

Not this Monday.

Because instead of relaxing this weekend, I'd walked around my own fucking house on eggshells.

Iris hadn't left for the hotel. Not that I'd expected her to after my plea for her to stay. But I'd hoped she'd at least take a trip or two to town. Give me space.

Nope. She'd refused to avoid me. No matter how many one-word answers I delivered to her unrelenting questions, she just kept firing them off.

What's your favorite place to eat in town?

Are there any bears out here?

How do you feel about the color yellow?

Annoyed. The color yellow annoyed the fuck out of me simply because I'd had to answer a question about the color yellow.

If the questions weren't enough torture, then there was the noise. Even when we weren't in the same room, she was loud. Each morning, I'd hear her talking in her bedroom. Maybe to someone on the phone. Maybe to herself.

Though I had a sliver of curiosity, I refused to ask what she was doing—she asked enough questions for us both.

The questions and noise might be sufferable. Except on

top of my irritation, there was this undercurrent of unfiltered lust that was driving me mad. I didn't want to *want* her.

Saturday, she'd worn a pair of leather pants that might as well have been a second skin. Yesterday, she'd had on a pair of loose jeans but had paired them with a turtleneck tank top that had been cropped just below the swell of her breasts, leaving all of her midriff on display. I'd fought a hard-on for two miserable days.

How the fuck was I supposed to operate with my dick throbbing twenty-four-seven? Jacking off in the shower each morning and night only made it worse. Every time I exploded, it was with Iris's beautiful face in my mind.

This had to stop. How the fuck did I make this stop?

At least today, I could come to work and escape.

I pinched the bridge of my nose as I waited for the stragglers to shuffle in from the hall. My lesson plan for today was a simple lab on acids and bases. I had beakers of various solutions in the back of the room, each with different liquids. The kids would test them with litmus paper to measure pH, then guess at what each solution was. The options were all on a bingo card. First desk to get a bingo got five extra credit points.

It was a favorite lesson for the kids. Interactive and fun. This time of year when attention spans were nonexistent with the seniors, it was better than delivering a lecture no one would remember.

But the last thing I wanted was a raucous classroom. My temper was on a leash but I didn't trust myself to hold it tight. My students would likely suffer, all because I couldn't get Iris out of my goddamn head.

Ryan waltzed into class last, just as the bell rang. His slow, lazy stride grated on my last nerve.

"Sit down, Ryan."

The asshole veered off course and plopped down on the edge of my desk, grinning from ear to ear as the other kids laughed.

"Get out." I pointed to the door.

"Come on, Mr. Abbott. I'm just messing around."

"Now."

His expression hardened as he stood. "It was a joke."

"Tell Principal Cain. If she thinks it's funny, you can come back."

Ryan's lip curled as he marched for the door. "Dick-head," he muttered just loud enough for me to hear.

Wasn't the first time a student had insulted me. Wouldn't be the last.

Maybe Ryan would go to the office. Maybe he'd just leave school early for the day. At this point, I didn't give a flying fuck.

"Aprons, gloves and goggles," I said. "We're doing a lab."

Stools scraped on the floor. Chatter erupted. The students likely realized I was taking no prisoners today, so they mostly stayed on task.

It was no surprise that Sadie and her partner won the bingo game, though neither of them needed the extra credit.

By the time the bell rang, I was drained and a headache had bloomed behind my temples. When the school's hall-ways had emptied, I cleaned up the remains of the lab and tidied the classroom, enjoying a blissful two hours of peace.

I sure as hell wouldn't get it when I got home.

What had Iris done alone in the house? She'd been

asleep when I'd left this morning. What exactly did an influencer do all day?

Danny had said she needed a real job, but she had millions of followers. That had to count for something, right?

I might not have social media, but I wasn't entirely ignorant of the online world. If brands were paying her to post about their products, that had to bring in some cash. Enough for her to buy that sweet vintage Bronco and pay for those sexy-as-fuck clothes.

What would she be wearing today? I wanted to find out. I didn't want to find out.

But I couldn't avoid home forever.

A custodian wheeled his cleaning cart down the hall, stopping outside my room. "Oh, sorry, Wilder. Figured you'd be gone already."

"Just leaving." Offering to clean the classroom myself was tempting, but I couldn't avoid home forever. So I collected my bag, giving him a nod as I headed out.

The parking lot was mostly empty when I pushed through the exit. I headed for my truck and had just unlocked the doors when I heard my name.

"Mr. Abbott." Sadie lifted a hand in the air as she jogged over from a car parked at the very opposite side of the lot.

"What's up?" I asked as she stopped in front of me.

"My car won't start." She was wide-eyed and her chin was quivering. She looked on the verge of a meltdown. "Ryan just dropped me off and now he's not answering his phone. I can't get ahold of my parents and my grandpa said he'd come get me but it won't be for another hour."

"Whoa." I held up my hand as a tear streaked down her cheek. "Don't cry."

I did not do well with crying. The sad eyes. The sobs and sniffles. It reminded me too much of Amie.

She used to cry daily. Happy tears. Sad tears. Angry tears. There were always tears for me to catch.

"This sucks." Sadie wiped her face but another tear fell.

"Please don't cry. Hop in. We'll try to jump it. If that doesn't work, I'll drive you home."

It took all of five minutes to get her car started. The minute the engine turned over, she burst into yet more tears.

"Th-thanks," she hiccupped.

"Are you all right to drive home?"

She nodded as fat, twin tears dribbled off her chin.

Goddamn it. "Sadie, you have got to stop crying." For her sake. And mine.

"Sorry. I'm good." She forced a smile and nodded.

"You sure?"

"Yes." She nodded again. "See you tomorrow. Thanks, Mr. Abbott."

I stood back, waiting until she'd put her silver Honda into drive and eased out of her space. Then I let go of the breath I'd been holding, the twist in my chest loosening.

Crying was the one thing I did my best to avoid. There were girls who frequently came into class with red-rimmed eyes, having just finished up a bathroom bawl. But if they needed a teacher's shoulder to cry on, it wasn't mine.

With Sadie gone, I put my jumper cables away and hopped in the truck. At the very least, the crying had been a momentary distraction from Iris. But that reprieve was short-lived. The moment I walked through my front door, I found Iris on the couch.

Sobbing into her hands.

"Iris." My heart seized.

Amie used to do that. Cry into her hands so hard that her entire body would shake. She'd been crying that hard the night she'd died.

My entire body froze, torn between rushing to Iris's side, begging her to stop and let me fix whatever was broken, and running the other direction. She could have this house if it meant I didn't have to see that uncontrollable crying. My lungs couldn't drag in enough air. My vision blurred at the edges.

Was this a panic attack?

Iris looked up, her eyes watery. Her cheeks were splotchy and her nose bright pink. "Oh, hell. What are you doing here?"

I blinked. "What?"

"What. Are. You. Doing. Here?" she spat every word, furious and seething through the tears.

"I live here."

"Gah." She let out a growl as she sent me a glare. Then she worked furiously to dry her cheeks. "You could have called first."

"To come home."

"Yes," she hissed.

"I don't have your number."

Her lip curled. "I didn't expect you."

"To come home." What the actual fuck was happening right now? "I live here." Why did that need to be repeated?

Iris huffed and clenched her jaw, still wiping at her face as she did her best to stop crying. "Go. Away."

She wasn't sad. She was mad. Those tears were angry tears.

58

Iris wasn't upset and crying for me to take care of her. She didn't need me to fix a problem. Those tears weren't a punishment or guilt trip. She was crying and pissed off that I'd caught her.

Angry tears? Those I could handle.

My shoulders slumped from my ears. My head stopped swimming.

Dropping my bag by the door, I bent and unzipped the main pouch, fishing out my empty lunch container. I carried it to the sink, setting it aside, then went to the cupboard above the fridge. With a bottle of whiskey in one hand and a glass tumbler in another, I joined Iris in the living room.

"Is it okay if I stay in my own house? Or did you still want me to leave?"

Iris shot me a glare but it didn't have any steel. The scowl withered as she let out a long breath. "Sorry. Ignore me."

"What happened?" I took the opposite end of the couch, leaning my elbows on my knees.

"Oh, I just got my feelings hurt, and you stepped into the line of fire. But you can stay."

"Gee. Thanks." I reached for the liquor to pour a healthy shot in the tumbler. Then I tossed it back.

"I thought that was for me," she muttered.

"Nope."

"Gee. Thanks."

"That one was mine." I pushed the bottle closer. "*That's* for you."

"Ah." She swept up the bottle, lifting it to her lips, but hesitated before taking a sip. "Are you going to kick me out if there's backwash? Because I spent most of the day scouring the area for vacation rentals and it's slim pickings."

I stretched out an arm, snatching the bottle, then poured my glass nearly to the brim before handing it over again. "Backwash away."

"Excellent." She took a gulp, a bubble bursting in the bottle as she grimaced. "Ooof."

I took another gulp, savoring the alcohol's burn. I didn't drink much. Maybe a beer or two during the week. But with Iris here, alcohol might be the only way to take the edge off.

"Why were you looking for vacation rentals?" I asked. "I told you, you can stay here."

"We survived a weekend together. Two months is a whole other story. I wanted to know my options."

"And there aren't any?"

"Not unless I want to play musical houses. There's nothing available for the full two months. I'd have to bounce around ten times to fit in the open windows. Even then, there was one weekend in June when nothing was available, not even at the hotel. Either I'd leave town or sleep in my car. Which I've done before, by the way."

God, the idea of her sleeping in her car. If Danny found out that she'd crashed in her car instead of here, he'd murder me.

I'd let him.

There would be no . . . *musical houses.*

"So you're staying?" Most of me wanted that answer to be no. If this past weekend was any indication, two months would be much, much harder—literally—than I'd expected when I'd made her the offer in the first place.

But there was a flicker of hope that she'd say yes and stay. Apparently, I was hell bent on punishing myself.

"The problem is that I love your house." She took

another sip of whiskey, her nose scrunching up as she swallowed. "It's ruined me. Nothing lives up to it. Everything nice around town is taken."

"That doesn't surprise me."

Spring was a busy time in Montana. But summer? The minute schools began releasing around the country, tourists came to the state in droves. Calamity's proximity to Yellowstone made this a great stopping point and it had gained more notoriety over the past nine years.

Calamity didn't get as much tourist activity as some Montana towns, but we definitely saw an influx. Over half the cars parked on First during June, July and August would have out-of-state plates. And with only a small hotel, many locals had learned to capitalize, renting out their homes for select weeks of the year.

Iris took another drink and sank deep into the corner of the couch, drawing up her knees and tucking her bare feet beneath her seat.

"I want to stay but don't want to put you out."

"You're not," I lied.

The corner of her pretty mouth twitched. "You're a horrible liar."

I scoffed. "I told you I'm used to being alone. This is an adjustment. But you're welcome to stay."

"I promise you won't come home from work every night to find me wallowing on the couch in despair."

"Who hurt your feelings?"

"Oh, a random stranger on the internet." She pursed her lips and grabbed her phone from the end table, stabbing at the screen so hard I was surprised the glass didn't crack. Then she held it out so I could read.

I had to read it twice. "What the fuck?"

Some motherfucker had called her a trashy whore.

"Aren't people the best?" She rolled her eyes. "There's another one on this post from a woman who says my nose is huge. And some dude said my voice is like nails on a chalkboard. But it was the trashy whore comment that sent me over the edge. I fucking hate it when people call me a whore. It's just that one hot button, and when someone presses it . . . boom."

This was bullshit. And she put up with it regularly? "How often does this happen?"

"More often than it should." She swiped through the screen again, and once more held it out for me to see. "This one is my favorite."

This time I took it from her hand, bringing it close to read it more carefully.

what will it take to get your face off my feed

"The idiot can't seem to find the unfollow button." She shook her head, then took a drink, clutching the bottle as she rested her head on the back of the couch. "It's nothing new. My social media manager usually deletes the nasty comments before I see them and blocks the trolls. But I got ahead of her today. And I know I shouldn't let it bother me. People are assholes and say shitty things all the time. It just . . . it got to me today. I don't like being called a whore. I'm not. But because I dress the way I do, because I like showing off my tattoos, it's like the default insult."

"This is . . ." I shook my head, scrolling and scanning comments.

Most were positive, saying how beautiful she was—comments from the people who weren't blind. But there were a few that jumped out as rude. One woman said she wished Iris wouldn't show as much skin. Another left a subtle dig about her tattoos.

In the video she'd posted, Iris was getting dressed in my guest bedroom, trying on different outfits until she'd landed on today's. A pair of black leggings and a neon green sports bra. The color was the exact shade of her nails. And she had on the same necklace she seemed to wear every day, a gold and silver compass rose on a dainty chain.

She looked incredible. The leggings were high-waisted and came up to the base of her rib cage. Her hair was down in long, curled strands that had a golden sheen. And her lips were painted fire-engine red.

That same red was now on the rim of my whiskey bottle.

The image of it on the root of my cock jumped into my head, so I tossed her phone aside and scrubbed a hand over my face. Then I took another drink.

How was it I could go from a near panic attack to wanting to strip those leggings from her legs in under ten minutes? *Fuck.*

"Sorry I snapped at you," she said.

"Don't worry about it. I've been snapping at my students all day. Guess it was my turn to be on the receiving end."

She sighed. "I hate crying."

And I hated to see her cry.

Any woman, not just Iris. But especially over something like this.

"I'm just having an off day," she said. "I woke up with a headache and it put a cloud over my head. Do you ever have days where you feel like no matter how bright your clothes, you're walking around in black and white?"

"I don't wear bright clothes."

She frowned.

It was so damn adorable I tucked my elbow over the armrest of the couch so I'd stay firmly on my cushion and not inch toward hers. "To answer your question, yes. I have days where I feel like I'm in black and white."

Something flashed across her expression that looked a lot like guilt. "I'm sorry."

"Don't be. Everyone has bad days."

"What do you do on your bad days?"

"Dwell on it."

She barked a laugh. "I want to tell you to be serious, but you're not joking. You just dwell on it."

I sipped my drink. "Yep."

"Does it help?"

"Nope."

I'd been dwelling for years.

Though when your mistakes were as big as mine, nine years of dwelling seemed like a small price to pay.

CHAPTER SIX

IRIS

get neon with me

WHAT THE HELL was wrong with me? I'd just asked
Wilder if he had bad days. Of course he had bad days.

His wife was dead.

"Sorry. Never mind." I clutched the bottle. "I think I
might get drunk now."

"I won't stop you."

Drunk it was. I took another drink from the bottle. My
bottle.

Wilder wouldn't want to touch anything that had been
attached to my lips. He'd made sure of it by filling that
tumbler nearly to the brim.

Maybe if I was a bit tipsy, the insults from internet trolls
wouldn't bother me as much. And maybe it would help me
relax around Wilder.

This past weekend had been, well . . . awful.

He'd grunted and grumbled. He'd rarely made eye

contact. And every time I'd attempted conversation, he'd barely engaged, answering questions with short, clipped sentences.

I'd had such hope on Friday night. I'd been so naively optimistic that Wilder and I could coexist for sixty-ish days. But as much as I wanted to make Wilder smile, that task seemed impossible now. He'd escaped the house this morning before dawn.

And I'd spent the better part of my day searching for a vacation rental.

Either I bounced around houses in Calamity, I left Calamity entirely, or I stayed with Wilder.

The logical choice would be to pick a new, larger town like Bozeman or Missoula. But somehow, after just a weekend, my heart had chosen Calamity. I wanted two months to explore this little town, to wander along First and discover its hidden jewels.

And I was weary. Down to my bones. If I wasn't in a bustling city, surrounded by noise and chaos, maybe I could actually get some rest. This trip to Montana could be the reset I so desperately needed. Rental hopping wasn't the worst thing in the world, but it also wasn't my idea of relaxation.

But I wasn't making any decisions on accommodations tonight.

No, tonight, I was getting drunk. With every sip, I'd mentally flip off the asshole who'd called me a whore. And maybe tonight's attempt at conversation with Wilder wouldn't go haywire.

"How was your day?" I asked.

"No one called me a trashy whore. But I did have a student call me a dickhead."

"To your face? Brave kid."

"He's a shit." Wilder shrugged and took a drink. His large frame was pressed into the far end of the couch, as close to the armrest as he could squeeze himself.

Was sharing a couch with me really so terrible? At least he hadn't disappeared to his room or outside to the shop. That was progress, right? This weekend, whenever I'd found him in the living room, he'd invented a reason to leave.

"This is an excellent couch." I reclined deeper, sinking into the plush cushion and buttery leather. "I went into town today to explore. I picked up a take-n-bake pizza from the grocery store."

Wilder moved to stand.

"Don't. Move." I shot out my free hand, holding it palm out.

He'd cooked for me all weekend. When I'd asked to help, he'd brushed me off. When I'd offered to prepare a meal, he'd declined. So I'd let him rule the kitchen. It was the only time when he'd been in my company for more than two minutes.

It had seemed like such a victory I hadn't wanted to push it. But the whiskey was warming my blood and giving me courage.

"I'm making the pizza. And either you let me contribute with meals, or I'll hide pine needles in your bed while you're away at work."

He arched an eyebrow.

"I'm taking that as a yes."

His mouth flattened into a thin line.

"Good talk. Glad we could come to an agreement."

Wilder took a gulp from his glass, but he stayed on the couch. *Win.*

"You're not a dickhead," I said.

"You're not a trashy whore." He didn't look at me as he spoke, his gaze fixed on the windows.

So I gave his strong profile a soft smile. "I know."

And I knew better than to take those ridiculous comments to heart. Actually, I knew better than to spend so much time online. That was Kim's job. But I'd been curious about how people would react to today's post.

At least once a week, I made sure to film some sort of fashion content. Usually it was of me trying on a clothing haul or a Get Ready With Me video.

Kim's *get neon with me* caption had been fun, but I should have expected the savage comments. The video had gone wild, reaching people far outside my core following. And that was always when the vicious trolls came out to play.

I took another sip of whiskey, then uncurled my feet, setting the bottle aside as I stood. My head was already fuzzy as I made my way to the kitchen to preheat the oven. With it warming, I returned to the couch, surprised Wilder hadn't taken my brief absence as his opening to disappear.

He was still glued to the armrest, his arm hugging it to his ribs like if he let go, the furniture would split apart at its seams.

I plopped down in my seat, sitting sideways to stare at him. "What's your favorite sexual position?"

Wilder's face whipped to mine, his eyes widening.

A slow grin spread across my mouth. "I was worried

you'd get a neck cramp from staring so hard at the windows. Just checking to make sure your muscles weren't locked up."

His shock vanished. His eyes narrowed.

"I get that you are used to your own space, and I'm encroaching on your sanctuary here. But if you keep avoiding eye contact, I'm going to get a complex that maybe my nose *is* too big for my face."

"Your nose is not too big for your face." His expression flattened. "Let's just not talk about . . . that."

"Sexual positions?"

His nostrils flared. "Iris."

I giggled.

He really did think of me as a little sister, didn't he? Here I was doing everything in my power not to lust after that handsome face and rock-solid body while he thought of me as that shy girl he'd met all those years ago.

Bummer. Not that I would have pursued Wilder. Lately, when it came to men, I seemed to be cursed. It was always the wrong time and the wrong place. Crushing on Wilder was a rejection just waiting to happen.

"Tell me more about this influencer thing," he said.

Was he actually curious? Or was he feigning interest to make sure I avoided the topic of sex? Part of me wanted to tease him for asking a question for a change, but whatever this curiosity was, I didn't want to ruin it. Not yet. "What do you want to know?"

"How'd you get started?"

"It sort of just happened." I propped an arm on the back of the couch, letting it hold up my head. "I knew my senior year in high school that I didn't want to go to college. Mom and Dad loooooved that, by the way."

Never in all my life would I forget the looks on their faces when I'd announced at dinner one night that I'd thrown all of my acceptance letters in the trash. First, it had been shock. Then outrage. Then denial. And lastly, crushing disappointment.

Seven years later, that disappointment still lingered.

"I think they thought I'd change my mind after graduation. That all my friends would pick a college and I'd decide to go too. But instead, I secretly planned a trip to Europe using all the money I'd saved from babysitting and mowing lawns and working at H&M."

"What do you mean, you secretly planned a trip?"

"Danny didn't tell you about it?"

He shook his head. "Nothing in detail. He mentioned a few times you were in Europe, but he doesn't talk about you much."

Ouch. I wished that didn't sting. "I knew that if my parents or Danny had known I was planning to go to Europe, they would have objected. They would have talked me out of it or scared me into staying. So I didn't tell them. And after graduation, I just . . . left. I called Mom from France when my flight landed."

Wilder blinked. "You just left. For France?"

"It sounds awful. I realize that." I gave him an exaggerated frown. "Looking back, I know now that I should have handled it differently. But at the time, I was eighteen and felt trapped. It was the only way I could figure out how to break free."

Wilder stared at me, studying me. "I can't believe Danny never told me any of this."

"I'm not." I shrugged. "Compare me to Danny and it makes sense why he'd keep it to himself."

Danny was the poster child for responsibility. He didn't break the rules. He was a model son who mowed our parents' lawn every week of the summer and shoveled their driveway in the winters. He and Mary lived three blocks from our childhood home. Their kids went to the same school where we'd gone. They attended Mom and Dad's church.

That life—his life—was what he considered normal.

Meanwhile, the first chance I'd had to leave for another continent, I'd jumped.

"Do you think they're ashamed of you?" Wilder asked.

"No. I think I puzzle them. My parents and brother don't talk about me often with their friends because I don't think they know what to say. It's like the three of them had already formed this perfect familial unit, and when I came along, they didn't know where to fit me in."

Not that they hadn't tried. Not that I hadn't felt loved.

I just wasn't Danny.

The oven beeped as it came to the right temperature.

Before I could unfold myself from the couch, Wilder stood with that fluid grace and went to the fridge, taking out the pizza and unwrapping it from the cellophane. Then with it in the oven and the timer set, he came back to the living room with two glasses of water.

"I said I was doing the pizza," I said.

"You can take it out when it's done." He threw his arm over the rest, reclining against it like before, but this time, he kicked an ankle up on his knee, actually relaxing. "So you made it to Europe. Then what?"

I'd lived. I'd thrived. "I traveled. I had planned to spend the summer touring around. I honestly didn't have much of an agenda other than to see as many places as possible until my money ran out."

My parents had thought it was ridiculous that I'd spend every dime on a vacation. That all those long hours and hard-earned paychecks would be gone over the course of three months. But they'd never understood that it hadn't been a vacation.

That trip hadn't been about escaping reality. It had been about finding my path.

"I started in Paris," I said. "One morning, I was sitting in this little café drinking coffee and took a selfie. It was just my friends following me at that point, but as I kept posting and documenting my travels, my account took off. I don't know how. Luck, I guess."

Every time I'd post about my clothes, I'd gain followers. Every time I got a tattoo, I'd set a record number of likes. There had been ups and downs along the way, but with every journey, my following had grown and grown.

"It was just a hobby at first. I ran out of money, just like I'd expected. I was in London at that point, and I decided rather than come home, I'd get a job. Stay in Europe for two more months while I tried to get a visa. But after two months in London, I still wasn't ready to leave. So I went to Edinburgh and stayed there for two months."

"Two months in Edinburgh."

I nodded. "It wasn't until the trip after that to Dublin that I named my adventures. That I kept the time limit of two months on my various stays. But I've been doing it ever since."

"How long were you in Europe?"

"Four years."

Danny really hadn't told him anything? Good to know I'd been entirely absent from my brother's mind.

"Four years." Wilder stared at the windows like he was trying to let it all sink in. "Two months at a time."

"Basically. Give or take a week here and there. I came home for short trips." Though my visits had been few and far between in those years. Probably because every time I'd come home, my family had recognized me less and less. "Otherwise, I explored. I loved Italy so much that I stayed for nearly a year."

Rome to Naples to Florence to Palermo to Venice to Milan. Maybe someday I'd go back and do it all over again.

"And this influencing stuff was your job?" he asked.

"Not at first. I took on a few housesitting gigs that paid me in free rent while I waited for my visa. Then I waitressed mostly. The social media stuff didn't start to pay until about four years ago when I'd built up enough of a following that I could start earning on branded content."

The oven's timer dinged, and before he could move, I shot off the couch, wobbling a bit until I found my footing. The whiskey had gone straight to my head. My limbs felt loose and warm. But I hurried to the kitchen anyway, opening and closing drawers as I searched for pot holders. Before I could find them, a large body appeared at my side.

Wilder opened a drawer I'd already checked and pulled out oven mitts.

"I looked right at those, didn't I?"

"Sit down." He jerked his chin to the living room. "I'll take care of this."

"But—"

"Sit down, Iris."

A shiver rolled down my spine at the gravelly, firm tone. It had an edge I'd never heard from him before. Rough. Unmovable. Sinful.

God, it was hot when he gave orders. Why was it hot? I'd never had a thing for bossy men. Maybe because I'd been so determined to stay in control of my own life, and a domineering male was the last thing I'd needed. But I would totally let Wilder order me around for the next two months if he spoke like that.

Desire coiled in my lower belly, my insides liquifying. My vibrator was still stowed in a suitcase. Tonight, I'd be taking it out.

"Fine." I walked back to the couch, taking another drink of whiskey. Then I chugged the water in the hopes it would keep tomorrow's hangover mild.

Wilder worked quickly to take out the pizza and slice it into triangles. Then he brought over two plates, handing one to me before taking his seat.

"We could sit at the table," I said.

"I don't want to sit at the table."

Why? Because at the table we'd have to face each other?

His gaze stayed locked on the windows as he set his plate on his thighs.

That awkward silence reared its ugly head as our pizza slices cooled. I expected Wilder to inhale his dinner, then make some excuse to disappear.

But while he *did* inhale his food, he stayed as I ate mine at a normal pace. Even after finishing his third slice, he stayed on the couch. "When did you get your first tattoo?"

"Paris." I smiled and held out my arms.

From the exterior of my wrists to the juncture of my elbows were two different wings. On my right arm, the feathers were long and dainty. On my left, they were shorter and stronger, the veins more defined. The pieces were mostly black but a light orange and yellow gave them color.

"What do they mean?" he asked.

"Nothing." I shrugged. "I know everyone expects each of my tattoos to have some profound meaning. But I liked the artwork. Enough to see it on my skin every day for the rest of my life."

Wilder nodded, his gaze raking over the other tattoos on my arms. The plethora of flowers. A butterfly. A dainty skull and a line of shooting stars.

"It's cliché to say I found myself in Europe. But it's true. I bleached my hair because I'd always wanted to try blond. I found my own sense of style. I grew up. I grew into . . . me."

I liked *me*.

"Shocked the hell out of my parents and Danny when I came home for Christmas the year I'd left. I was only home for a few days, but had I stayed longer, I think they would have staged an intervention. But I was tired of trying to fit into their mold."

"So you made your own."

"Yeah. I did."

He stared at me as intently as he'd been staring at the windows. Almost like if he looked long enough, he'd figure me out.

I gave him props for trying. My family certainly hadn't bothered.

It was unnerving having those dark, unreadable eyes on mine, so I focused on my pizza, finishing the last few bites.

"What sort of brands do you work with?" he asked.

"Mostly fashion and beauty. I have a manager who lines up deals and negotiates contracts. I'm lucky these days that I get to post about brands that I loved before I started all this. In the beginning, I didn't have the luxury of being quite as picky as I can be now."

There were still days when I'd pinch myself to make sure this was real.

"I know it's temporary. Social media is a fickle, fickle world. My style isn't for everyone, but I'm lucky that a lot of people like it. So I'm capitalizing while I can. I have no illusions this will be a long-term career. Someday, my looks will change and the appeal will fade. At the moment, I'm a trend. And I'm okay with that. When it's time to move on, I'll move on."

Wilder's face was waiting when I looked up. It was as intense, as unreadable, as it had been before.

But his arm wasn't on the couch's side any longer. He wasn't huddled as far away from me as possible. He'd shifted, just slightly, until we were closer together than we were apart.

His eyes dropped to the hollow of my throat. To the flowers tattooed across my shoulder that bloomed just above my heart.

"Do you have any?" I asked.

His gaze lifted and he swallowed hard. "What?"

"Tattoos. Do you have any?"

"No."

"Do you ever want to get one?" I asked, inching closer. It

wasn't even a choice. He just drew me in toward that center line in the sofa.

But at my movement, his attention shifted. He turned to the windows, giving a slight headshake. Then he was gone, a blur as he swept his plate off the coffee table along with his tumbler.

He tossed the rest of his whiskey back as he walked to the kitchen. Then when both his plate and glass were in the dishwasher, he strode toward the hallway that led to his bedroom.

I sighed, picking up the whiskey bottle. Well, he'd lasted longer than I'd expected. "Goodnight, Wilder Abbott."

He spoke so quietly I almost missed him murmur, "Goodnight, Iris Monroe."

CHAPTER SEVEN

WILDER

"GOOD MORNING." Iris's voice startled me from where I stood beside the coffee pot.

I'd never met a person who could move so quietly. Or maybe I was just too used to teenagers who only knew how to be loud.

"Morning." I glanced over my shoulder as I spoke, then did a double take.

Her hair was pulled up into a messy knot that was askew on the top of her head. Her face was clean and without her makeup, the sprinkling of freckles across the bridge of her nose stood out.

She was dressed in a T-shirt that dwarfed her slight frame. There was enough material there to make an average-sized man a tent, and the hem hit her midthigh. Then there were those legs. That shirt covered more than the shorts I'd seen her wear, but holy fuck, it was hot. By far the sexiest thing I'd ever seen her wear.

Had she worn that to bed last night? The mental image

was so clear, of her in that T-shirt in the guest bedroom, my cock swelled and my mouth went dry.

Damn it. I faced the counter again, breathing through my nose as I summoned all my control to keep my body in check.

Iris had been at my place for a week, and it wasn't getting easier. It was supposed to get easier. When was it going to get easier?

"Coffee?" I asked through gritted teeth.

"I'll get some later."

"You're up early."

She huffed. "Don't sound so annoyed."

"I'm not annoyed."

I was annoyed.

Every day this week, Iris had been asleep when I'd gotten up and left for work. It had given me a reprieve and the quiet I preferred in the morning.

I pulled a travel mug from the cupboard, and when the brewer finished, I poured my coffee from one cup to the other. With the lid affixed, I nodded to Iris and walked to the door, not letting my gaze travel down those perfect legs again.

"Have a good day," she called.

I raised my mug in the air and grabbed my backpack, slinging it over a shoulder as I escaped outside. Thank fuck, I'd already packed my lunch.

The morning air was chilly and crisp, the smell of dew and wet grass clinging to the air. I breathed it in, letting it calm my racing heart.

Fuck, this had to stop. When was it going to stop? She was Danny's sister. Off-limits. But no matter how many times I reminded myself of that fact, it didn't seem to make my body want her any less.

My mood was as sour as it had been all week. Iris had decided to stay. At least, that was what I assumed, considering she hadn't packed up yet. We hadn't actually had a conversation about it. But every night when I returned home, she was there to greet me with a smile.

It wasn't as irksome to have company as it had been a week ago. Except it was Friday. I was facing a weekend with Iris, and unless she suddenly found my house entirely unappealing, we'd be stuck together.

Was there anything I needed in Bozeman? It was two hours away and at the moment, escaping to a different county seemed like a really fucking good idea.

Maybe I'd take a long hike on Saturday. A trip to the store Sunday. Maybe tonight I'd grab a burger from Jane's downtown. We were nearly out of food and I didn't feel like braving the grocery store. One foot in the produce section and I'd picture Iris.

Why couldn't I stop thinking about her? Why, of all the women in the world, was it her that turned me inside out?

My phone rang, the chime echoing through my truck's cab. Danny's name appeared on the console.

"Fuck." Could he read my thoughts from Utah?

This rabid desire for his sister screamed so goddamn loud in my head that it wouldn't surprise me if he could hear it from hundreds of miles away. Or maybe Iris had called him and tattled, telling him I'd been a grumpy son of a bitch.

In my defense, hiding this constant state of arousal would make any man a grump.

"Hey," I answered.

"Hey. On your way to work?"

"Yeah." The whirl of tires came from the background. "You too?"

"Yep. I'm over this week. My students are testing my limits."

Meanwhile, Iris was testing mine simply by being . . . Iris. "What's up?" I asked.

"Just checking in. See how it's going with Iris. Hopefully she's not making your life hell."

Oh, she was. But it was entirely innocent. The torture I was enduring was my own damn fault. "It's all good."

"I'm glad. Thanks again for doing this. I know it's a lot to ask."

He'd said as much when he'd called in this favor. And after a week, I was sure that either I had totally misunderstood everything about Iris's job. Or Danny had it all wrong. "She seems to be doing well. Sounds like her influencer gig is pretty successful."

"Come on, Wilder. It's a hobby."

"It seems like it's more than that."

He scoffed. "She can't post pictures of herself online forever and keep bouncing between homes two months at a time."

Why not? Why was he so negative about her job? Maybe he was right. Maybe this wasn't sustainable long-term. But it wasn't like Iris had delusions of doing this until she retired. She'd told me on Monday that it was temporary. She had her eyes wide open and had set realistic expectations. Had she and Danny never talked about that?

Guess not.

"Eventually she's going to need to find a real career," he

said. "Get an education."

"College isn't for everyone."

As a teacher, he should know that more than anyone. We saw the kids who were bound for an advanced degree. And we saw the kids who were on a different path. Some would go to a trade school. Some went straight into the workforce. One of the seniors was engaged to her boyfriend. He was a year older and as soon as she graduated, they were getting married. My guess was that before I retired from Calamity High, I'd have their kids in my class.

The world needed people in every station, influencers included.

"She's my sister, Wilder."

"I'm aware," I muttered. Painfully, achingly aware.

"I just want the best for her. I'm not asking you to become her therapist, but if the topic of her next destination comes up, maybe you could just encourage her to consider a town with a university."

I wasn't going to encourage her to do a damn thing. First, it would be pointless. Iris was a woman who made up her own mind. Second, she was an adult. If she wanted to go to college, then she'd go.

Our conversation from Monday struck a new chord as I replayed what Danny was asking. Iris had spoken so openly the other night. How she'd felt like the outsider in her home. How she hadn't fit into the same mold as Danny. How comfortable she'd become in her own beautiful skin.

The way she'd spoken about her family hadn't been bad, but it hadn't been flattering either. She'd felt trapped by their expectations, so she'd left for Europe without warning.

God, if I'd been her father I would have been so fucking

pissed. Danny too. Yet he'd never told me about that.

"You told me she went to Europe but you never mentioned that she left after high school without telling anyone," I said.

"No." He sighed. "That was . . . she scared the hell out of my parents. I've never seen Mom and Dad so worried. I almost got on a plane to haul her home, but I was afraid she'd just leave again."

"Makes sense, but why didn't you mention it?"

"You had enough to deal with."

Amie. That would have been two years after she'd died. Two years after I'd moved to Calamity.

Yeah, I'd been dealing with a lot. "You still could have told me."

"Sorry. Sounds like Iris told you though."

"She did." She'd painted a picture as vivid as her tattoos about a young woman who'd built a life on her own terms.

Fuck, but she was brave. Did Danny see that? *No.* He was too concerned about her lack of a college degree.

I pulled up to the high school, easing through the mostly empty parking lot to the section reserved for staff. "I don't think you need to worry about Iris. Seems like she's doing great."

"She's a master at illusion. You know that social media world. It's all fake."

True. But there had been nothing fake about her tears on Monday night.

"Look, if it makes you uncomfortable, don't worry about it," he said. "We're trying to convince her to come home for a bit after Montana. I'll try to talk to her then. If I can get her here and keep her here."

Doubtful. Maybe he'd have better luck if his wife weren't so fucking judgmental about Iris's tattoos. I liked Mary. But I liked her less after spending the week with Iris.

"Well, just my opinion, but I don't think you need to worry."

"She's my sister. I'll always worry."

Guilt crept through my veins. He trusted me to be a good influence. To be a friend. To stand in his stead. Instead, I was like a randy teenager, unable to stop thinking of anything but sex.

I swallowed hard. "I'll talk to her."

"Appreciate it. More than you know."

The silence in the truck was deafening as he ended the call.

This had to stop. I had to make it stop.

How? This craving I had for her felt so natural. So over-powering. So . . . right. Not wanting Iris would be like asking a cloud to hold in the rain.

I scrubbed a hand over my beard, then shut off the truck, gathering my things to head inside. An hour later, the halls were abuzz and filled with excited kids ready for a weekend.

Normally, that energy was contagious. This time of year, I was more than ready for summer break. But a pit of dread was forming in my gut, growing deeper and deeper with every passing day.

Iris would only be in Montana through June. Would I survive it?

By the time my last class of the day started, I was drained. Excited kids meant rowdy kids. No one wanted to be here, me included. Not that I wanted to go home either.

"Hey, Mr. Abbott?" Sadie raised her hand as the bell for class to begin rang.

"Hey, Sadie."

"I've been elected as class spokesperson."

"Oh lord." I cast my head to the ceiling. "Why do I have a feeling I'm going to hate this? And how did you get elected? Did you guys have a vote in the hallway before class?"

"We picked her because she's your favorite," Liam chimed in.

"She is a favorite," I said. "Want to take any guesses at who's my least?"

He puffed up his chest in pride. "Aww. Thanks, Mr. A."

Contrary to popular belief, I did not dislike Liam. Sure, he pushed my buttons and required more attention than most, probably because he wasn't getting it at home, but he wasn't my least favorite.

That honor went to Ryan. The shithead currently on his phone when I'd told them all to put their devices away as they'd walked through the door.

"Okay." I blew out a long breath, leaning my elbows on my desk as I stared at Sadie. "Your demands, Madam Spokesperson?"

The corner of her mouth turned up as her cheeks flushed. "We'd like a study period to catch up on outstanding work so we don't have to do it over the weekend."

"But there are five of you who don't have outstanding work," I challenged. "What are you going to do?"

She shrugged. "Hang out?"

Hang out.

I would probably regret it. They'd all end up wild and

loud. But I nodded. "Fine. Those of you with outstanding work, get it done and hand it in. When you're finished, you get to 'hang out.'"

"Yes!" Liam's arms shot in the air as the rest of the classroom cheered.

Ryan hopped off his stool, went to Sadie and framed her face in his hands to kiss her.

Her eyes bulged as she smacked his arm.

"Sit down, Ryan," I said. "Before I change my mind."

Sadie's face flamed red when he let her go. She scowled at his back as he walked to his seat. Another obnoxious boy with his chest puffed up.

Ryan was the cockiest student I'd ever had in my tenure. I was already looking forward to forgetting him after graduation.

The chatter died down as students took out books and notepads. Sadie and the girl beside her were two of the kids who didn't have any outstanding work, so they huddled over a phone, whispering at whatever they watched.

Halfway through the class, the quiet had vanished. Most had turned in their work, though some must have decided to leave it as homework. Clusters divided the room, and at the center of each, a phone.

I'd thought about getting Instagram this week, to check out Iris's page if for nothing else. But I'd decided that would only add fuel to this fire. I needed less time with her, not more. These kids would probably fight each other to the death, *Game of Thrones* style, if threatened with the idea of losing their devices permanently. It only reinforced my desire to stay firmly under the rock where I'd been living.

Sadie's table had five girls all squeezed together, their attention rapt.

I rolled my eyes and went back to grading the quizzes from my sophomores. My red pen scratched on the paper as I made an X on wrong answers but it froze midair when a familiar voice caught my ear.

"Get dressed with me for a Friday of exploring."

Iris. Her voice and laugh cut through the noise.

My attention whipped to Sadie's table. They were watching one of Iris's videos.

"She's so pretty. And I love her tattoos," Sadie said.

Me too, kid.

"Same." Another girl nodded. "I kind of want to get one after graduation. My parents would freak out if they knew."

A third girl sighed. "I wish I could wear stuff like Iris. Her style is so unique. I just don't think I could pull it off. Or afford all of the designer gear."

A vintage, custom Bronco. Designer apparel, according to my students. Iris was doing just fine. Hell, she probably made more than Danny or me, because teachers were paid next to nothing.

Ryan hopped off his stool and joined Sadie's group, looking over her shoulder at the phone. "Who's that? She's hot. Smoking body too."

I fucking hated that kid.

"For real?" Sadie looked up at him, her mouth open, then she snapped it closed and jabbed her elbow in his ribs. "Go away."

"Ooof." He winced. "Jesus, babe. What was that for?"

"Maybe because you're drooling over Iris Monroe when

your girlfriend, me, is sitting *right here*." Sadie rolled her eyes. "Nice, Ry."

"Just because I think she's hot doesn't mean you're not." He frowned and slunk back to his own table.

Sadie sat straighter, keeping her attention on her phone. "She's spending two months in Montana. Where do you think she is?"

My house. I grinned. If only they knew.

"Have you seen this one?" Sadie asked, pulling up a different video.

Iris had a Calamity fan club. Good for her.

Danny didn't realize just how popular she was, did he? He was too busy obsessing over the choices she made with her own life.

I returned to my quizzes, finishing up the stack a few minutes before the bell rang.

"Have a good weekend," I told the kids as they rushed for the hallway. "Stay out of trouble."

"Bye, Mr. Abbott," Sadie said, the last to leave. "Thanks again for helping me with my car on Monday."

"No problem. Have a great weekend."

"You too." She smiled, then breezed through the door.

I wasted no time cleaning up the classroom and putting it to rights. There was a strange swirling of emotions in my chest. Part of me wanted to stay here, avoid the house. The other wanted to get home. Learn more about Iris. Tell her I had some kids who followed her.

It was the desire to tell her about this Calamity fan club that sent me hurrying home. Except when I got there, the driveway was empty. Iris's Bronco was gone. And when I walked through the door, the house was still and silent.

"Iris," I called.

Nothing.

I had the house to myself. It should have been a relief. Wasn't this what I wanted? So why didn't it feel . . . normal?

Ignoring the odd, niggling feeling, I took my backpack to the sink, putting my lunch container in the dishwasher. The countertops were bare and tidy, no note from Iris explaining she'd left.

She hadn't moved out, had she? There was no sign of her in the living room or kitchen. Were her suitcases still in the guest bedroom?

I scrubbed a hand over my face, wishing I wasn't so uneasy about this woman. But in just a week, she'd turned my world upside down.

The urge to know was so overpowering, it sent me to the hallway leading to her bedroom. The scent of her vanilla and citrus perfume clung to the air. As I passed the laundry room, a flash of neon green caught my eye. Three bras hung on a rack to dry.

She hadn't left. Not yet. The air rushed from my lungs.

"Fucking hell." I dragged a hand through my hair. What was she doing to me?

One of her bras was lace. Black. Sheer. Would her nipples peek through the fabric? Were they little? Rosy? How would they fit in my mouth?

My cock sprang to life, instantly throbbing.

Shit. I spun from the laundry room so fast it made me dizzy. Then I marched for my bedroom, stripping out of today's jeans and white button-down shirt.

How was it possible to want her in my house and hate it all at the same time?

That woman had just ruined my laundry room. I'd never be able to go in there and not picture that black bra.

Dressed in a pair of shorts and my tennis shoes, I jogged out of the house and headed for my running trail. Maybe if I pushed my body to the brink, it would stop craving Iris.

The dirt loop I'd worn down from years of running wound through the open meadows on my property and the surrounding trees. My shoes thudded on the ground as I pushed my body hard, sprinting up the inclines until I was dripping with sweat. My lungs were on fire and the metallic tinge of blood caught in my throat.

My running trail was a mile long. I lapped it eight times before I finally felt like it was safe to venture home. That I had regained control of my body. When I rounded the front of the house, Iris's Bronco was still missing from the driveway.

Good. I needed a few hours of peace and quiet.

After guzzling a glass of water, I went to my bedroom, toeing off my shoes and stripping away my shorts before retreating to the shower. The lukewarm water sluiced over my skin, the soap washing away the sweat.

When I was clean, I let the spray run over my face. And my hand drifted to my cock. After that run, I shouldn't have had an ounce of energy left. But the moment I gripped my shaft, it sprang to life. The image of Iris in nothing but that lace bra made me rock hard.

What did she sound like when she came? Would she mewl? Scream?

I stroked and pumped, working myself harder. Faster. My legs began to tremble, my muscles tensing. My toes curled into the slippery floor, and I used my other arm to brace myself against the tiled wall.

Damn it, I needed more. Jerking off in the shower wasn't enough. I wanted Iris beneath me, squirming as I pounded into her tight body. I wanted her red-painted lips wrapped around my length. I wanted to feel her suck me until I spilled down her throat. Then I wanted to fuck her senseless until this urge was gone. Until I could put her out of my mind and stop thinking about those legs wrapped around my hips.

"Fuck." I pumped my erection with brutal speed, groaning her name. "Iris."

Faster. Harder. More. God, I needed more.

I needed her in my hands. I needed to feel her skin against mine. I needed to devour that mouth.

The mental image of her shifted as I kept stroking. The sheer bra. The black leggings. That oversized T-shirt this morning. Fresh. Perfect.

The sensation in the base of my spine hit first, then my orgasm ripped through my body. Hot spurts of come erupted from my cock, mixing with the water and swirling down the drain. "Fuck, Iris."

Iris. Iris. Iris. Her name was a chant. A prayer.

My heart was pounding when I finally let go of my arousal, my dick softening.

I cracked my eyes open and shoved off the shower wall. By the time she left in two months, I'd probably have calluses on my hand and a dick rubbed raw.

It had taken the edge off, but it wasn't enough. It was never enough.

Too bad it was all I was going to get.

CHAPTER EIGHT

IRIS

calamity jane's #thelifeofirismonroe

I WAS WALKING past the hallway that led toward Wilder's room when I heard my name.

"Iris." His pained groan made me change directions. Was he hurt?

His door was cracked, so I pushed it wider, peeking inside. "Wilder?"

The room was empty, but his bathroom door was open. Steam billowed out but it wasn't thick enough to hide the sight of him in the shower.

Holy. Shit.

Wilder's large frame was in profile. He had one hand braced on the tile above his head. And the other was wrapped around his cock.

My breath caught, and I froze. Warmth crept into my cheeks as I stared, refusing to blink as I took in the magnificence that was a naked, wet Wilder Abbott.

He stroked fast, his hips pistoning into his grip. The water slicked down his muscled back and shoulders and chest. His eyes were squeezed shut and his mouth was open, a droplet hanging from that perfect pout.

What was I doing? This was clearly private. I should sneak back to my room. Pretend I wasn't seeing this. But my feet didn't budge. My toes didn't even wiggle. I was firmly rooted in place, my eyes glued to that shower as he jacked himself faster.

He was lost in the ecstasy and heat. A throb pounded in my core, its beat matching my racing pulse. God, I wanted him. Now more than ever. I wanted to strip off my clothes, leave them piled beside his on the floor and walk into that shower to feel his long, thick cock inside me.

Wait. He'd said my name, hadn't he? I was sure I'd heard my name. Was he thinking about *me* in that shower?

"Fuck, Iris."

Oh my God. OH. MY. GOD.

He was thinking about *me* while he was in that shower.

My jaw hit the floor as he came on a moan, his release mixing with the water. His entire body trembled, those muscles locking tight. It was erotic and stunning. And he'd said my name.

He'd said my name.

What did this mean?

Wilder's arm came off the tiled wall as his other dropped his flesh. Then he opened his eyes, shaking the water from his face.

I came unglued, jerking away so fast I nearly tripped and fell on my ass. Then I spun around and ran on my tiptoes until I was outside.

My heart hammered against my sternum as I walked to the Bronco. The driver's seat was still warm as I slid behind the wheel. A bead of sweat tickled the hair at my temple.

"Oh my God," I whispered to the windshield.

I pinched my leg to make sure I was awake and this wasn't a dream. "Ow."

He'd called my name when he'd come. He wanted me. I stared at the house, shaken like a snow globe. Every moment of the past week replayed in my mind, from the day I'd arrived to the last two minutes.

Was that why he'd been so moody? Because he was as attracted to me as I was to him? Was that why he avoided eye contact and kept his distance?

Maybe he was just the brooding type. Or maybe . . .

Maybe he didn't want to want me.

Did he feel guilty because of his wife? Had he been with a woman since her death? What about Danny?

"Ugh." I dropped my head to the rest, letting out a huff. Why did this have to be so complicated? Why, when I finally found a man who made my pulse race, did it have to be Wilder?

Now what? How was I supposed to go inside and function? How was I supposed to pretend I hadn't just spied on him naked?

"Oh, hell." How had I ended up here?

Danny. It was all Danny's fault. I never should have listened to him. I should have found my own rental in Montana and planned this trip like all the others before.

There was no way I'd ever be able to look at Wilder the same way. All I'd see was him in the shower, head bent as he worked his cock.

Damn it, he was hot. So freaking hot I could hardly breathe.

The throb between my legs was brutal. My skin felt too hot and my pebbled nipples rubbed against my bra. I squirmed, needing some friction to relieve the ache, but even the slightest movement made it worse.

"Gah!" I smacked my hand on the steering wheel, then shoved out of the car. I couldn't hide out here forever. So I trudged inside, my cross-body bag still slung over my torso, walking through the door just as Wilder emerged from the hallway.

His hair was damp. He'd dressed in a pair of jeans and a simple black T-shirt, and his feet were bare. Damn him. Why did he have to be so hot?

My cheeks flamed as I pictured him without the clothes. *Son of a bitch.* Tonight would be brutal.

"Hey." He jerked up his chin.

"Hi." I waved and closed the door, taking a minute to pull my shit together.

Brother's best friend. Brother's best friend.

Grieving widower. Grieving widower.

It didn't help. I was still turned on. To. The. Max.

"I'm going to Calamity Jane's," I blurted, not trusting myself to leave the door. If I got too close, I might touch him. And if I touched him, I might not stop.

Leaving for the local bar seemed like the best idea I'd had all day.

"Okay." Wilder nodded. "I'll drive."

Um ... *WHAT?* "You're coming?"

"We're out of food. Jane's has good burgers."

"I figured you'd want an evening to yourself."

He did his one-shoulder shrug. "Why not?"

Why not? Why not? Because I needed to get away from Wilder, not spend an evening together at the bar. But I didn't dare tell him no. This was the most relaxed I'd seen him all week. Probably because he'd just had an orgasm. Lucky bastard.

"Great!" I chirped.

"Just give me one minute to grab shoes," he said, striding for his room.

No no no. This wasn't happening. I'd be squirming and miserable all night. And there was no time for me to sneak away to my room and pull my vibrator from the nightstand.

A whimper escaped my lips. I heaved a sigh, then turned and yanked the door open, stomping outside. The cool air did nothing to quell the fire beneath my skin. I paced the flagstone patio, shaking out my arms in the hopes that this sexual energy would trickle from my fingertips.

It didn't. I was still pacing when Wilder came outside, closing the door behind him.

He'd pulled on a baseball hat. The Calamity Cowboys logo was embroidered on its face.

"Seriously?" I muttered under my breath.

As if he hadn't already been sexy enough. That hat only seemed to accentuate the width of his shoulders. The strong flex of his jaw beneath that dark beard. His jeans sat low, clinging to his narrow hips. His T-shirt wasn't tight, but the sleeves still strained against his biceps.

My own style might be unique and nameless, but when it came to men, I'd never been drawn to fancy suits or designer trends. Faded jeans, simple tees and a baseball hat, that was my jam.

I practically melted into a puddle on his patio.

"What?" he asked.

"Nothing." I shook my head. God, I needed a drink. Or two. "Ready?"

He nodded and passed me for his truck. The scent of his soap, masculine and clean, hit my nose and I swallowed a groan.

Was it too late to change my mind?

The slam of his truck door snapped me out of my stupor, and I hurried to climb into the passenger seat.

It smelled even worse inside—if worse meant incredible and intoxicating. I was going to have to breathe out of my mouth so his delicious scent didn't go straight to my head, but if I left my mouth open, I'd start drooling. There was no winning.

The ride down the mountain was excruciating. I did my best not to squirm as I crossed and uncrossed my legs, but the bumpy gravel road did nothing but make the ache in my center worse.

"What's wrong?" Wilder asked as we pulled onto the highway.

Other than the fact that I was coming out of my skin? "Nothing. I'm just really hungry," I lied.

"Have you eaten at Jane's?"

"Not yet. But I did eat brunch at the White Oak Café."

"That's a good spot."

I hummed my agreement, taking a few long breaths as the whirl of tires on pavement hid the sound of my ragged breathing. This would be fine. I'd be able to sit across from Wilder and not picture him naked. No problem.

I forced myself to breathe as I smoothed my hands along

the fabric of my gray trousers. They were flowy and loose, the high waist coming to the base of my rib cage. I'd paired them with a cropped, hot pink tube top, leaving a sliver of midriff showing.

Not exactly Montana dive bar apparel, but I rarely dressed to fit in. Though, normally, I would have changed into something more casual. If not for the urgent need to escape Wilder's house, I would have found a pair of jeans.

The diagonal parking spaces in front of Calamity Jane's were all taken, but Wilder found an empty space in front of the local art gallery. Reese Huxley Art.

The paintings in the display window were bright and vibrant. The artist used a combination of chunky strokes and soft lines that made the landscapes leap from the page. The window's centerpiece was of a buffalo. Beside it, an elk.

"That's a local artist's gallery," Wilder said, coming to join me on the sidewalk. "I had his daughter in my class her senior year. That was the first year I moved to Calamity."

"I love his style." Honest. Vivid. Unapologetically bold. The way I wanted people to think about me.

I tore myself from the gallery's window, heading down the sidewalk for the bar. It wasn't like I had a home for artwork, but maybe someday.

Wilder fell in step beside me as we walked along First. Blaring country music poured from Jane's open door, and I followed him inside, letting my eyes adjust to the dim light.

The bar's wooden ceilings were tall. The walls were painted a forest green, though you could barely make out the color because of all the tin and aluminum signs covering it up. The center of the room was crowded with tables. High-backed black vinyl booths hugged the walls. Behind the bar were mirrored shelves teeming with liquor bottles. And there was a stage in the corner. Beside it, a taxidermied bison bust.

Not that I was an expert, but if Wilder's cabin embodied a Montana countryside abode, Calamity Jane's was everything a Montana dive bar should be.

"How about there?" Wilder pointed to the only empty table in the bar—a booth against the far wall. "Or we can sit at the bar."

"The booth is fine. I'll meet you there." I dug my phone from my handbag, pulling up the camera to snap a few photos and a quick video.

People at tables stared. I ignored them. I'd learned to ignore a lot in the name of scoring social media content.

After taking another burst of photos, I joined Wilder at the booth. The moment I slid into the bench seat, a waitress appeared and set down cardboard coasters.

She was older, maybe in her fifties, with tanned, leathery skin and white-blond hair pinned into a knot. "Abbott."

"Jane. How's it going?"

Jane. As in Calamity Jane?

"Busy." She winked. "Lucy is singing tonight. You know how that goes. You're lucky to get a table. Word of advice. If you want food, order quick. The kitchen is already backed up."

"I'll have a Coors Light. And a cheeseburger with fries."

"You got it," Jane said, looking my direction. "And for you?"

Her gaze shifted toward my tattoos. With the tube top, they were all on display. I'd had my share of pointed looks today as I'd wandered around Calamity, but not a hint of judgment clouded Jane's kind brown eyes.

I liked this bar already.

"I'll have the same. Extra fries."

She nodded. "Back in a minute."

The moment she left, I glanced around, taking it all in. "Cool place. I assume Jane is *the* Jane."

"She is. She's sort of a legend in Calamity."

"Think she'll mind if I post about her bar on social media?"

"Nope."

I unlocked my phone and pulled up my preferred camera settings before stretching it across the table. "Would you mind taking a few of me?"

Wilder didn't say anything as he took a few shots, then handed the phone back. "I'm not a photographer."

I swiped through the photos, picking my favorite. "I disagree. These are perfect."

"That's you, Iris. Not me."

My heart tumbled. I kept my gaze locked on the screen as my cheeks heated. The shower image popped into my head for the hundredth time, and I crossed my legs together beneath the table, squeezing my thighs as that pulse boomed in my core.

"Here you go." Jane came to my rescue, setting down two beers.

"Thanks." As she disappeared into the crowd, I swiped the bottle and chugged. Half the beer was gone when I set it on my coaster.

Wilder's eyebrow was arched when I dared look across the table. "Thirsty?"

Oh, I was thirsty. So goddamn thirsty.

"Who's Lucy?" I asked, not wanting to talk about why I was going to guzzle beer tonight.

"Lucy Ross."

"The country singer?" My jaw dropped. "I *love* Lucy Ross."

Most would take one look at me and think I preferred alternative rock. But in my heart of hearts, I was a country-music girlie, and I'd been listening to Lucy Ross's music for ages.

"She lives here." Wilder nodded. "She goes by Lucy Evans. Her husband is the sheriff. But she sings at Jane's from time to time. Always draws in a big crowd."

"I'm guessing you don't come down to hear her sing often, do you?"

The corner of his mouth twitched. "Might have talked you out of it if I'd known."

"Too late now." I lifted my beer to my lips.

His gaze tracked the movement. Heat flashed in his eyes before he looked away. His jaw flexed.

I was *such* an idiot. That jaw flex had never been annoyance, had it? Or maybe not entirely annoyance. He'd been attracted to me this whole time. And he was fighting it. We both were.

All because he was my stupid brother's best friend. Damn.

I took another long gulp of beer, then turned my attention to my phone, picking one of the photos Wilder had snapped. I adjusted a few colors and did a quick resize before uploading it to Instagram, adding a *calamity jane's* caption and a hashtag.

"I gave my seniors a free period today. A group of girls

were messing around with their phones. Heard them watching a few of your videos. They were fawning over you."

"Really?" I smiled. "That's sweet."

For the most part, I'd avoided social media today. Instead, I'd spent the morning and afternoon wandering around town.

"What did you do today?" Wilder asked.

It was loud in the bar, but the booth offered some privacy and a buffer from the noise. If not, I might have thought the question came from a different person. He'd been so chatty tonight. Well, not chatty, but chatty in Wilder terms.

Apparently, an orgasm put him in the mood to talk.

"Explored," I said. "I wandered along First for a while, then drove around aimlessly, scoping out places to visit again."

I'd woken up refreshed this morning. For most of the week, I'd spent some extra time in bed, catching up on some much-needed sleep and returning overdue emails. Kim and I had hopped on a few phone calls to map out upcoming content and discussing brand offers. But today, after batching some videos and sending the raw files to Kim for editing, I'd wanted to get out of the house for a bit.

So I'd come into town for a coffee. With it in hand, I'd wandered up and down First, soaking it all in.

"What did you think?" Wilder asked.

"Calamity is charming. I really like it here."

Wilder nodded, his attention drifting toward the others milling around the room just as a chorus of cheers erupted at my back.

I twisted in my booth as a couple walked into the bar.

The guy was dressed similarly to Wilder in faded jeans, boots and a T-shirt. If not for the man currently sharing my booth, this guy would have been the most attractive man on First.

His hand was clasped firmly with a blond woman's with a bright smile.

WOW.

That was Lucy Ross. She was even more beautiful in person than she was on social media or television.

"Okay, this is amazing." I laughed as Lucy and her husband made their way toward the stage.

He kissed her, long and sweet, then moved to a stool beside the bar, the seat closest to the stage. While the bartender took his drink order, the man kept his eyes trained on Lucy, like she was his entire world.

Lucy winked at her husband, then stepped up on stage as the rest of the band joined her.

While they got situated, Jane delivered our burgers. I was grateful for the food. And for Lucy Ross. And my beer. It all gave me something to focus on other than Wilder.

When his basket was empty, the red-and-white-checkered paper crumpled into a ball, he twisted in his side of the booth to stare at the stage. Then he relaxed into the seat, one arm braced casually on the table.

As the band started and Lucy began to sing, the conversation in the bar vanished. God, she had a voice. I'd loved that voice since I was a kid, and any other night, I wouldn't have wanted to blink for fear of missing a second of her performance.

Except every time Wilder shifted, so did my gaze.

How was it that he had such a pull on my attention? It

wasn't just because of the shower incident either. It had been like this since I'd come to Montana.

Ignoring it was my only option. This was going to be a long, long two months.

I reclined in my seat, my posture matching Wilder's, so I could stare at the stage without getting a kink in my neck. And I did my best to concentrate on Lucy during the first set —this was probably my only chance to see her perform live.

"Thank you," she crooned into the microphone. "We're going to take a quick break, then be back in a bit."

The bar erupted into applause and whistles as she waved, then jumped off the stage to slide onto the stool beside her husband.

"You want to stay for the next set? Or head home?" Wilder asked.

Home. That was a dangerous word. His house was already feeling too much like a home.

But staying here was dangerous too. One more beer and the control over my tongue would falter. I didn't trust myself not to say something about the lovely stone tile in his shower. "We'd better go."

Wilder jerked up his chin, and one minute later, Jane appeared with our check.

"I'd like to buy dinner," I said, digging my wallet from my purse.

He didn't argue, just slid out of his seat as I tossed two twenties on the table. Then he lifted a hand, waving to Jane, before motioning for me to lead the way outside.

The evening light cast Calamity in soft hues of gray and tan and gold. And as we strolled to Wilder's truck, I tried to shake off the feeling that this felt a lot like a date.

"Thanks for dinner," he said.

Not a date. NOT. A. DATE. "Thanks for all the meals this week. I'll chip in for groceries."

He hummed, not a yes or no, and kept his gaze trained forward, his eyes hooded by that damn hat.

I stifled a groan, bracing for the onslaught of his scent when we climbed into his truck. As expected, it was as wonderful as it had been earlier, other than my hair, which held a hint of greasy burger and beer.

Wilder drove with his wrist on the wheel, relaxed and at ease. His perfect forearm on display. His fingers relaxed and loose.

He'd used that large hand to get himself off and he'd done it with my name on his soft lips. He wanted me. And I knew, without a shadow of a doubt, he wouldn't do a damn thing about it.

Disappointment swirled with desire, the combination making my head hurt. So when we pulled into his driveway, I was out my door the moment the truck was in park.

"I, um . . . I'm going to turn in early," I said, walking across the patio. "Goodnight, Wilder Abbott."

"Goodnight, Iris Monroe."

I used both his names because I loved the way he said both of mine.

When I was behind the safety of my closed bedroom door, I sagged against its face and breathed for what felt like the first time in hours. "Ugh."

That restless, buzzing energy returned with a vengeance. The coil in my lower belly squeezed tighter.

My vibrator was shouting my name from the nightstand drawer, but I busied myself with a facial in the bathroom. At this point, foolish as it was, I was staying put. I'd done another vacation rental search yesterday and a third of the houses that had been vacant were now booked. So my options were to leave Calamity or stick it out at Wilder's.

Just this morning I'd unpacked the last of my suitcases. But that had been before the shower incident. If Wilder was fantasizing about me and I was fantasizing about Wilder, was this just unnecessary punishment?

So I finished my facial. And repacked my suitcases.

By the time I was finished and changed into a T-shirt for bed, it was dark beyond my window. I flopped on the mattress and covered my face with a pillow. "Gah."

Five minutes. If I had just spent five extra minutes downtown earlier, I never would have seen Wilder naked. I never would have seen that glorious, perfect body. I wouldn't have a clue that he was attracted to me too.

And I would have missed the hottest moment of my life. Watching him come undone was the definition of erotic.

It was one thing for a guy to kiss you. To screw you. But to know that I was a secret fantasy was the best kind of foreplay.

My core throbbed, so I shoved the pillow off my face and stretched for the nightstand, taking out my small vibrator.

The hem of my shirt was lifted, the cotton dragging across my sensitive skin. I slipped down my panties as the familiar buzz of my vibrator filled the room.

Tonight wasn't about play. I pressed the toy to my clit and chased that sweet relief. I came on a low moan of Wilder's name that was half relief and half frustration. My orgasm was swift. Short. Shallow. It took the edge off, but when I sat up and righted my panties, the ache wasn't gone.

I didn't want a toy. I needed a man who'd fuck me into oblivion. A man who'd leave me satisfied and limp. It had been so, so long. I just . . . wanted to be touched. I wanted to be worshiped by soft lips and large, strong hands.

Those wants would have to wait.

I stood and walked to the door, listening for a moment to see if Wilder was watching TV or moving around. But it was silent, probably because he'd disappeared to his own bedroom.

Was he in the shower again? Or maybe, like me, he was on his bed. My pussy clenched, and after some water, I'd probably use the vibrator again.

The house was dark, the lights off, as I padded down the hallway. I rounded the corner for the kitchen and froze.

Wilder was standing beside the island, shirtless. His hands were on the counter's edge, his muscles bunched. The glow that filtered in from the outdoor lights kissed the contours of his arms and shoulders.

His chin was ducked, hiding his face. His chest was dusted with dark, coarse hair. His stomach was tight, the washboard abs flexing. There was a trail of that dark hair beneath his navel, disappearing beneath the waistband of the black sweats that hung low on his hips.

Oh, hell. He had the V. He wasn't just strong, this man was ripped.

My mouth went dry. I heard my vibrator shouting again.

Before I could slink away, he lifted his head. His eyes, those black, endless pools, locked with mine. They were full of desire and restraint.

The tension in the kitchen spiked. He gripped the countertop so fiercely his knuckles were white. Wilder looked like he was about to come out of his skin. He looked exactly the way I'd felt all night. Sexually frustrated and depraved. Why—

Wait. My heart lurched. *Oh my God.*

How long had he been out here? And what exactly had he heard me doing in my bedroom?

CHAPTER NINE

WILDER

"I THOUGHT YOU WERE IN BED," Iris said, her voice a whisper.

"Water," I gritted out, holding tight to the island.

"Oh. Me too." She inched closer.

Even in the dim light, I could see the flush of her cheeks as she worried her lower lip between her teeth. Had she done that when she'd come? Or had she only moaned my name?

Fuck. I groaned, clenching my jaw.

There was no mistaking what I'd heard. I'd been passing by her hallway when I'd heard a faint cry. If only I'd kept walking. Instead, I'd padded to her door and heard a whimper. A hitched breath. Then my name.

Exactly what I'd done in the shower.

Fuck, I wanted her. Knowing that she wanted me was like pouring gas on the fire flowing through my veins. My entire body was strung tight, every muscle straining so I wouldn't move. Like I was raging against invisible chains.

Iris and I stared at each other for a long moment, neither of us moving other than the rapid rise and fall of our chests.

I'd been so lost in my own head, I hadn't even noticed that she'd been attracted to me too. Maybe I was just out of practice. Maybe she was better at hiding it than I was. But the spotlight was on bright and the chemistry between us swirled in the air, like smoke that kept getting thicker and thicker.

"Wilder—"

"Don't." Goddamn it, I was barely holding on. I was struggling just hearing her breathe. But if she said my name one more time . . . "Go to bed, Iris."

She didn't move. Of course she wouldn't move. Did she get some sort of satisfaction torturing me?

"Iris." It was a warning. And a plea. If she took one more step into the kitchen, I'd break. I'd strip that tent of a T-shirt from her body and have her on this counter. "Please. Go to bed."

"Fine." She nodded, turning from the island. But before she walked away, she twisted back. "I saw you. Earlier. In the shower. You left your door open. I heard my name and thought you might be hurt. But . . ."

But I'd been fucking my fist with her name on my lips.

My heart stopped. *No.* Mortification crept through my veins. "I'm sor—"

"Do you want me?" There was a slight tremor in her voice, like she expected a rejection.

"Yes." There was no use lying. It hadn't done me any good all week to pretend I didn't crave her. That I didn't think of her constantly. That I wasn't totally at her mercy.

"I want you too."

Christ. "Don't." I held up a hand. "Don't say that."

"Don't be honest?"

I opened my mouth, but what the hell was I supposed to say? This was never supposed to happen. This was a conversation that shouldn't *be* happening.

Even if we did want to fuck each other until dawn.

"Wilder."

I groaned. "Damn it, Iris."

The corner of her mouth turned up.

"You need to go to bed."

"I don't want to."

I scrubbed a hand over my face. Bad decision. The moment I let one hand go from the island, I felt my resolve begin to crumble. "Last warning."

"I don't need warnings. I need . . ." She gulped. "I want you."

Snap. The tether on my restraint snapped like a rubber band stretched too far.

I shoved off the counter as her feet unglued from the floor. We collided beside the island, a tangle of frantic hands and arms.

A whimper escaped her lips as I sealed my mouth over hers. She opened for me instantly, and the moment my tongue slid against hers, I knew exactly where this night would end.

In my bed.

My arms banded around her, hauling her off her bare feet as I delved deeper. She tasted like mint and honey. Sweet and cool and warm.

Iris wrapped her legs around my hips, her center pressing against my erection.

I tore my lips from hers on a hiss, my hands dropping to cup her ass.

She pulled back, her clear blue eyes hooded and filled with lust. "Don't stop."

I panted, clenching my jaw in an effort to regain some semblance of control. "Slow down."

"No." She shifted, bending to drop her mouth to my throat. Her tongue darted out, wet and warm, tickling my pulse. "Go faster."

"Hell." I shouldn't have let her play, but my head lolled to the side, giving her better access.

Maybe I was imagining it, but I swore she was smiling against my skin. "You wanted me to go to bed. So take me. Please."

My legs moved without permission from my brain. My body was taking orders, her orders, and if she wanted a bed, then we'd find a damn bed.

With Iris in my arms, her mouth still on my throat, I strode down the hallway for my room. The lights were off. I'd lived here for so long that I didn't need them to come to the kitchen for a glass of water.

Moonbeams scattered through the windows, giving the space a silver shadow. I walked straight for the bed, falling on top of Iris as we collapsed on the mattress.

"Oh God." She arched into the weight of my body, opening her legs so I could fit into the cradle of her hips. Her hands threaded through my hair, tugging at the strands as I peppered her neck and jaw with kisses.

My hands roamed everywhere, sliding beneath the hem of her tee as it rode up her ribs. I skimmed the soft skin of her thighs. I flattened my palms over her stomach, feeling my way up to her breasts.

They fit perfectly in my hands, small but lush and pert. I cupped and kneaded her flesh, rolling her pebbled nipples between my fingers. My cock strained against my boxer briefs, harder than I'd been in ages.

"Yes," she murmured. "Give me more."

"Fuck, Iris." I tore at her clothes, shoving her T-shirt up her ribs as her hands drifted to the waistband of my sweatpants, pushing them off my hips.

I grappled with her black lace panties, bunching the sides in a fist as I dragged them down her legs. Then I reached for her shirt, whipping it over her head.

The sight of her naked on my bed was nearly my undoing. "Fuck." I wasn't going to last. Not a chance.

Her rosy nipples begged for my mouth. The tattoos needed to be traced with my tongue. Her bare mound was perfect and that glistening pink center was magic. I squeezed my eyes shut, forcing air into my lungs.

Were we really doing this? Were we really crossing that line? What about tomorrow? Iris and I couldn't pretend this hadn't happened. We couldn't go back. Hell, we'd already gone too far.

She pushed up to a seat, reaching for me. The moment her hand cupped the back of my neck, pulling me forward to her lips, the doubts rattling in my brain quieted. They faded into the background, worries for tomorrow.

Our mouths stayed fused, our tongues tangling. My hands dove into her long hair, threading it between my fingers. It was softer than I could have imagined, like spun silk.

Iris trailed her hands over my back, leaving no inch untouched as she worked her way lower and lower. Her nails dug into my skin as she gripped my ass, forcing me closer. Then she rocked her core against my arousal, leaving just enough space to reach one hand between us.

She dove into my boxers, and the second she wrapped her fist around my shaft, I tore my mouth away.

"Fuck."

Iris nipped at my earlobe as she stroked. "Does my hand feel better than yours?"

"Yes," I hissed.

She gripped me tighter, stroking until I was shaking.

"Stop." I jerked away, hustling off the bed to stand at its side.

Her eyes widened, like she was afraid I'd stop. But I shoved my sweats the rest of the way off my legs and stepped out of my boxers too.

Iris's gaze locked on my cock. Her mouth parted.

God, I wanted to feel those lips around me. I wanted to spill down her throat. But not yet. Not tonight. If this was a one-time mistake, then I wanted to come inside her body.

I walked to the nightstand, taking a condom from the drawer to roll it on. Then I planted a knee in the bed, climbing on top of her. She parted her legs but not wide enough, so I pushed at her knees until she was spread wide.

"Look at you." I could spend hours with her beneath me. "You're so fucking perfect."

"Come inside." She trailed her nails up my forearm. "I want you to fuck me."

She kept her gaze locked with mine as I lined up at her

entrance. I hesitated, willing my body to last, then with a slow press of my hips, slid into her tight, wet heat.

"Wilder." Her moan filled the room as she stretched around me.

"Say it again." My name on her lips was a sound I never wanted to forget.

"Wilder," she repeated, arching her hips so I'd go even deeper.

I balled my hands into fists, summoning every shred of control I had over my body. "Fuck, you feel good."

"So good." She raised her hands, pressing them flat against my wooden headboard. Bracing herself.

Damn, this woman. I eased out and thrust inside again.

She gasped. "Oh, God."

"This will be fast," I warned.

She nodded as I lifted one of her legs higher, nearly pressing her knee into her shoulder. The change sent me nearly to the root.

I rocked us together, over and over again, until her limbs started to tremble. Her breasts bounced as I pistoned faster. The sounds of our ragged breaths and bodies colliding filled the room.

She moaned. I cursed. We fit together like she'd been made for me.

The rush of ecstasy was impossible to fight off. The base of my spine began to tingle long before I was ready, but she was too tight. Too wet. And my stamina was just too weak. But not a chance I'd come until she shattered, so I reached between us, finding her clit with my middle finger. Two swift circles, that was all it took for her legs to start trembling.

"Wilder," Iris cried as I pounded inside her hard. Fast.

Without restraint. She detonated, her body pulsing around my length. That squeeze, the throb and heat, sent me over the edge.

I roared as my orgasm hit, the raw, ragged sound blending with Iris's moans. The world faded to nothing. My vision was stolen by white stars. There was only Iris.

Surrendering to her was rapture and misery.

Coming down from the release was like floating back to reality. It came in bits. The rustle of fabric as she sagged into the pillows. The air cooling the sweat licking my skin. The sound of my own thundering heart.

My body was too wrung out to stay upright, so I collapsed on top of her, breathing hard as my pulse continued to race.

Iris wrapped her arms and legs around me, our bodies still connected.

With a quick twist, I rolled to my back so she wouldn't have to hold my weight. My arms stretched at the sides, my limbs boneless. My cock was softening inside her and I needed to take care of the condom, but damn if I had any energy to move.

She was asleep by the time I finally slid out from beneath her and pulled away. I eased her to a pillow, letting her hair spread across the cotton, as I escaped to the bathroom.

I didn't turn on the light. I wasn't ready to face myself in the mirror.

No, that would wait until the morning. After I'd spent the night sleeping on the couch.

Except when I stepped back into the bedroom, the sight of her hair spread across a pillow, and that perfect, beautiful face asleep, was like a magnet. I took a step toward Iris, not the door.

And like the fool I was, instead of leaving her alone, I crawled back into bed, doing my best not to disturb her.

But when my weight shifted the mattress, she stirred. Her eyes flitted open as I settled on my back. Without an invitation, she slid closer, draping herself over my chest. She was out again before I'd even closed my eyes.

Did I move her away? No. I let her use my chest as a pillow.

I wasn't sure where to put my hands. It had been a long, long time since I'd held a woman. Not since Amie.

The guilt was like a sledgehammer, beating against my chest.

I swallowed hard and worked to keep my breathing even. Did everything in my power to shut off my mind and just rest. But sleep was impossible. The guilt plagued me for hours, and when I finally couldn't take it any longer, I shifted Iris to the side and eased out of bed.

Dressed in my sweatpants and a T-shirt from my closet, I wandered to the living room, standing in front of the windows for a while, watching as the trees swayed in the breeze beneath the moonlight.

The view at night from this spot was equally as breathtaking as it was during the day.

Amie would have hated both. It would have been too quiet. Too isolated. The drive to town would have been too far.

Amie wouldn't have enjoyed sex like I'd just had with Iris either. She never would have told me to fuck her. Never.

She preferred the term "making love." It had always been sweet. Gentle. Slow.

The ache in my chest made it hard to breathe.

"Fuck." I dragged a hand through my hair. What the hell had I been thinking?

Sex with Iris had been more than I'd ever expected. And hell, it had barely taken the edge off. The insatiable craving I had for her still tore through my veins.

I wanted her. Again and again. But I couldn't. No more.

This had to stop.

A pair of delicate hands slid up my back, and I flinched.

"Sorry," Iris whispered as her hands dove beneath my T-shirt. She wrapped her arms around me, her palms flattening against my pecs. "You regret it."

"No," I answered, turning to face her and forcing her hands to drop. "No regrets."

Guilt, yes. But no regret, even though it had been reckless.

She'd pulled on her massive T-shirt. Her gaze followed mine, dropping to the faded Nirvana emblem.

"Thought you were into country."

She shrugged. "It was an old boyfriend's. I stole it to wear to bed."

That was another man's shirt?

Before she could say another word, I ripped it off her torso, balling it up and tossing it in a corner. Tomorrow it would go in the trash. Then I reached behind my neck, yanking my own T-shirt off to drag over her body.

She rolled her eyes as she put her arms through the sleeves.

"Come on." I grabbed her wrist, tugging her along as I walked to her room. "Time for bed."

"Time for bed?" She scoffed as I stopped outside her open door. "You go all possessive on me, trading my favorite T-shirt for one of yours. But then you put me to bed like a child because this scares the hell out of you."

"That's not—"

"That's exactly what you're doing." She fisted her hands on her hips. "Tell me I'm wrong."

She wasn't. Not even a bit. "I can't do this." I tossed up a hand, and like it had earlier, my control shredded. "Damn it, Iris. I want you more than I can explain. It's fucking maddening. But you're too young. You're Danny's sister. You're . . ."

Everything I wanted. Everything I didn't deserve.

Her face softened as her hands splayed on my naked chest. "You want me."

I tilted my head to the ceiling and groaned. "I want you."

She took my hand, pulling it to her body. Then she slipped it under my shirt, pressing my fingers to her bare center.

Soaking wet.

"Damn it, Iris."

She rose up on her toes, taking her free hand to clasp my neck and pull me closer. "You want me. So have me. Don't overthink this, not tonight. We can worry about everything tomorrow."

God, that sounded like a good idea. My fingers slipped through her wetness.

"Please," she murmured.

In a flash, I had her pinned against the wall. "What are you doing to me?"

"The same thing you're doing to me." She pressed her lips to the corner of my mouth. "Take me, Wilder."

Following her orders seemed like the only option. So I carried her back to my bedroom, this time exhausting us both so that when she collapsed on top of me, I crashed too.

CHAPTER TEN

IRIS

weekend vibes #twomonthsinmontana

DAWN AT WILDER'S house was something from a fairy tale. The sunlight was soft and gentle as it danced through the windows. Birds chirped outside, their song a cheerful greeting to a new day. There was no traffic. No blaring horns or wailing sirens. There were no noisy neighbors in next-door apartments to shatter the silence.

It was the epitome of peace.

And Wilder's plush bed was nothing short of a dream. I snuggled deeper into my pillow, breathing in the scent lingering on the sheets. Masculine spice. Wood and leather and that hint of anise. I didn't need to crack my eyes to know that his side of the mattress was empty.

He was probably somewhere in the house, brooding over last night. Not that I blamed him. He had plenty to think about. So did I.

I opened my eyes, staring at his abandoned pillow.

Last night, he'd promised no regrets. Had he changed his tune this morning?

There was only one way to find out. I flipped the covers off my body and swung my legs over the edge of the bed, standing to stretch.

My muscles were sore, like I'd just worked out for the first time in months. Considering how long it had been since I'd had sex, the tenderness between my legs was not surprising.

Maybe Wilder regretted last night, but I didn't. It had been incredible. There'd been so much passion, so much desire, that my inhibitions had vanished.

For the first time in a long time, sex had just been . . . fun. Freeing.

Never in my life had I been so bold with a man. Never had I made such demands. My cheeks flushed just thinking about it. Demanding that he fuck me.

Was that how his wife had acted? Had he pictured her in my place?

My stomach churned, so I shoved those thoughts away and made my way to the bathroom on wobbly legs. The T-shirt he'd pulled over my head last night was somewhere in the hallway. He'd stripped it from me before we'd made it back to his room. Rather than emerge naked, I rifled through his closet, pulling a Calamity Cowboys tee from a drawer.

Just like I'd expected, it was enormous. It hit me midthigh and covered my ass. The arms fell to my elbows. Not a chance Wilder was getting this T-shirt back.

I found my panties beside the gray quilt that had fallen on the floor last night. For any other man, I would have left the bed unmade. But those rumpled white sheets would probably only increase Wilder's guilt, so I quickly tidied the room, hiding every trace that he'd fucked me senseless in here last night. Then I padded down the hallway, my shoulders pinned and my heart ready for a swift rejection.

Wilder stood in exactly the same place I'd found him last night, in front of the windows with his gaze locked on the glass. Was he even looking at the mountains? Did he see the fluffy white clouds in the sky or the sunbeams kissing the evergreen treetops?

He was dressed in tennis shoes, shorts and a T-shirt. My Nirvana tee was nowhere in sight.

The corner of my mouth turned up at that obvious jealousy. At the way he'd growled last night.

What was the word he'd used? *Maddening.* He wanted me more than he could explain and it was maddening.

Yes, that was the right word. Maddening.

I cleared my throat on my way to the coffee pot. "Morning."

"Morning."

I poured myself a mug and took it to stand beside him.

Wilder wasn't drinking coffee. There was no cup on the counter or tables. Was he just waiting to have some later? Or was that coffee he'd brewed for me?

"Want some?" I asked, blowing on the steaming liquid.

"Later." He walked to the front door, leaving without another word.

Guess we'd have to talk *later* too.

Well, he hadn't exactly rejected me. But he hadn't *not* rejected me either.

I shook my head and wandered closer to the windows, expecting to hear the sound of his truck roar to life. But he passed both our vehicles, walking to the small shop built twenty yards from the house and disappearing inside.

A workshop maybe? A garage? Did Wilder have any hobbies? He was a science teacher. Maybe that was his secret laboratory where he worked to find the cure for cancer. Or maybe he was a woodworker. Or, given his clothes this morning, that was his gym.

Having spent most of the night asleep on that strong, muscled body, there was no way that man didn't exercise regularly.

I sipped my coffee, giving him the space he so clearly desired. Though I was considering it a win that he hadn't escaped to that shop hours ago. That he'd waited for me to wake up. That he'd made me coffee.

That was something, right? Or maybe I was reading too much into everything Wilder Abbott.

Heaving a sigh, I turned away from the windows and headed to my room for my phone. With it in hand, I snuggled into a corner of the couch to scroll through Instagram.

Kim had posted already this morning. She'd edited a photo I'd sent her last week and added a *weekend vibes* caption.

The picture was of me on Wilder's front porch. I was sitting on the ground, a coffee mug in my lap with my legs stretched out across the concrete slab. The tattoos on my thighs and shins were on full display along with the hem of my ripped jean shorts. And my toes were bare, my nails freshly painted blue.

The focus of the photo was more the sprawling field beyond Wilder's house than on me. The mountains in the distance looked small but they stood proudly blue, nearly the same color of my nails.

Posts without my face never performed as well, but I preferred their artistry and aesthetic.

As I checked a few of the recent notifications and read through my emails, I finished two cups of coffee. Wilder still hadn't returned from the gym by the time I poured my third.

The shower was calling, but I didn't want to wash off his scent from my skin, not yet. Not when if I closed my eyes, I could still feel his touch. Breakfast held no appeal thanks to the knot in my stomach.

Last night had been incredible. Consuming. Sex had never felt like that before. From that first, brutal kiss, he'd set me ablaze. I should be singing and dancing and smiling ear to ear. Except I felt like . . . the other woman.

I wasn't enough.

I wasn't his wife.

Amie.

It was strange to pity a woman and be jealous of her at the same time.

I stood from the couch and wandered to the front door, peering out the inset window toward the shop. Was the reason he'd snuck out of bed last night because of Amie? Because of his guilt for sleeping with me?

It was rare that I was scared to ask a question, but that one terrified me. Knowing I wasn't the right woman in his bed was one thing. Hearing him confirm it was another.

So what now? Did I hide out here and pretend like last night hadn't happened? That was what Wilder was going to do, wasn't it? He'd disappeared to his shop to hide from me.

And when he came back, he'd probably return to giving me averted gazes, jaw clenches and single-shoulder shrugs.

I'd be his houseguest again. Nothing more.

No. No way. That wasn't going to work for me. Too much had changed.

With my coffee mug in hand, I walked out the door before I could lose my nerve. The patio and flagstones were cold on my bare feet. The grass was dry and prickled my soles with every step, but I tiptoed to the shop anyway. Blaring music greeted me before I reached the door.

Turning the knob slowly, I peeked inside. The shop was the size of a garage, but rather than park his truck inside, he'd turned it into a gym. The scent of rubber and metal hit my nose. Wilder's stereo was on so loud the sound waves vibrated my chest. The clank of crashing weights barely carried over the rock music.

Wilder was against the far wall, his head bowed and his hands braced on his knees. Beside him on the black floor mats was a kettlebell.

Sweat soaked his T-shirt, causing it to stick to his skin and highlight the muscle definition in his back.

Wilder stood tall again, oblivious to me watching. He lifted the kettlebell with both hands, pivoting to face a mirror on the opposite wall. Then he swung the weight between his legs, bringing it up in a smooth arc so his arms were straight and the bell was level with his heart. Then down it went again, between his knees.

He did fifteen reps, each with a breath I could see but not hear over the music. Then he dropped the weight and raked a hand through his damp hair.

Did he even know how sexy he was? Did he have a clue

how infatuated I was with him already? I couldn't tear my eyes away as I sipped my coffee.

He did one last set of fifteen reps, and only then, when he went to return the weight to its storage rack, did he notice me in the doorway.

His gaze flicked to my T-shirt. *His* T-shirt. He'd been so set on ignoring me this morning, he hadn't taken in what I was wearing.

His jaw clenched. He turned his eyes to the nearest wall.

"Back to that again," I murmured.

"What?"

"Nothing." I waved it off and walked to where his phone was sitting on a table beside a speaker. I didn't turn it off, but I did turn it down. "Nice gym."

He stared at me, his chest rising and falling rapidly. Either he was out of breath from the workout or angry I'd interrupted his time ignoring me. Probably both.

I took a slow lap around the space, inspecting the weights, stair climber and treadmill. Everything was clean and well spaced. Organized. But it was all so cold. There weren't posters on the wall to hint at Wilder's personality. The only personal touch was his music. And if I opened up his phone to find some generic workout playlist from Spotify, that wouldn't surprise me either.

Who was this man? What did he like? What did he hate?

I'd spent a week living in his house and had no idea what he did in his free time. There were no framed photos of him fishing or hiking or . . . living.

Maybe yesterday, I would have been able to ignore it. Maybe if I hadn't let him inside my body, I could have kept the curiosity at bay. But too much had changed.

Whether he liked it or not, I couldn't go back. I wouldn't forget.

"Why did you become a science teacher?" I asked, bending to set my now-empty coffee mug on the floor before taking a seat on a black, padded bench.

Wilder hadn't moved as I'd lapped the gym. He'd stood statue still, his hands fisted on his narrow hips, and stared at the wall.

But the moment I spoke, he sighed and dropped his head. Sweat gave his face a shiny hue and soaked the hair at his temples. "Already with the questions."

"I gave you an hour." I smirked. "Are you this grumpy with everyone in the morning? Or just the women you sleep with?"

He tensed. "Iris."

"I'm not going to pretend it didn't happen," I said. "So either you can tell me why you became a science teacher, or we can talk about having sex last night. Your call."

Wilder swallowed hard, remaining quiet. As the silence stretched, I was sure his next move would be for the door. That he'd run away from me again. But he faced me, finally meeting my gaze. "I like science and math. I like that they have rules. It's logical. And I like teaching."

"What about it do you like? The kids?"

"Yeah, I like the kids. I like helping them work out a problem in their heads. Figure their way through it. Teaching high school, there are always the kids who are a pain in the ass. But for the most part, I like that age, when they say more interesting things than not."

The knot in my stomach loosened. "See? Was that so hard?"

128

His expression flattened, but his shoulders relaxed, falling away from his ears.

"Now it's your turn," I said.

"My turn for what?"

"To ask me a question. That's how this works. It's called *comm-un-i-ca-tion*." I enunciated each syllable as I waved a hand between us. "I go. Then you go. I go. Then you go. Now it's your turn."

"Are you always this sassy? Or is that just for the men you sleep with?"

I giggled. "Well played, Wilder Abbott."

He walked to an open spot on the floor, sitting to stretch out his hamstrings. "What's your favorite city?"

"I refuse to pick."

"Least favorite?"

"Mount Pleasant. Though that's not really a city." My hometown, two hours south of Salt Lake City, was the farthest thing from a large metropolis. It was closer to the size of Calamity.

"I didn't realize you hated it there," he said.

"Hate isn't the right word. I just don't have any desire to live there again. Probably because I lived there most of my life. That's part of the reason I've been hopping around, living in places two months at a time. It's long enough not to feel like a tourist. But not so long that I wouldn't want to visit again."

Wilder nodded, shifting on the mat as he stretched. "Why did you pick Montana?"

"It sounded right. That probably makes no sense, but each time I've moved, I've done it on feel. Montana seemed like the next step. I wanted to get away from the city. Get some rest. There was no way I'd go home to Utah, but I needed a change of pace. And Danny has told me about Calamity for years. Figured it was time to check it out. So far, it's everything I'd hoped for and then some."

Calamity reminded me of the best parts about Mount Pleasant. It was quaint with an old-fashioned feeling, almost like stepping back in time ten years. It was friendly. Unhurried. It had been so refreshing yesterday to wander downtown and not feel rushed.

There was a lot to love about a big city. There was something beautiful about being one of many. Of being lost in a crowd. But those crowds had grown too lonely lately. Too loud. Too much.

"Deep down, I'm a small-town girl. The cities have been fun, but it was time for a change." My roots were beginning to show. For the first time in years, I was going to let them. "And I know I sound like a broken record, but I love your house. I *needed* your house. Something quiet. A place to recharge. It's liberating to be out here with no one around. No neighbor to see that I'm not wearing panties."

"Iris." Wilder groaned. "Christ."

I laughed and stood from the bench, crossing the open space. His legs were spread wide, so I stopped between them.

"I thought we were 'communicating.' " His gaze flicked to the hem of his shirt.

He looked so damn good, sweaty and strong. Before this living arrangement was over, before either of us came to our senses, I wanted him just one more time. "Do you really want to keep talking?"

"No, I don't." His hand reached for the shirt, lifting it

enough for him to see my black lace panties. To see that I'd lied. Wilder's gaze narrowed, then he fisted the shirt, tugging it hard enough that I dropped to my knees.

His mouth sealed over mine and I opened for him instantly, savoring that smooth slide of his tongue. He devoured my mouth, licking and sucking. He held my face to his, slanting me at exactly the right angle so he could plunder.

Damn, but this man could kiss.

My hands dove into his hair, tugging at the strands, urging him to kiss me harder. Faster. Then I crawled onto his lap, rocking my center against his growing arousal.

He hissed and tore his mouth away. "Fuck."

"Yes." Please. I wasn't ready to call this quits just yet.

"Condom." He inhaled sharply through his nose. His molars ground together so hard I could hear them scrape. "They're inside."

I refused to think about why he'd had condoms in his nightstand last night. I couldn't have been the only woman since his wife. Or maybe he'd bought those for me. At this point, I didn't care. I just wanted him inside me. "I'm on birth control. And it's been a long time."

Wilder stilled, his breath ragged, as he leaned back to look at me. "You sure?"

I nodded, reaching between us for the hem of his own shirt.

He let me drag the damp cotton off his body, but the moment it was gone, he took control, slamming his mouth onto mine. He kissed me until I was breathless, until I was squirming on his lap, desperate for him to satisfy the ache in my core.

"Wilder," I moaned as he moved his lips across my jaw, lowering his mouth to suck on my pulse. The scrape of his beard against my sensitive skin only made the throb in my center beat harder.

His hands splayed across my hips, his fingertips kneading into my slight curves. Then his hold tightened, and in a quick lift, he had me off his lap and kneeling on the mat as he jackknifed up and moved behind me.

"What—"

He took my jaw in one of his large hands, turning my face forward. My gaze locked on the mirrored wall and my breath hitched. He was going to fuck me right here in front of the mirrors so that we could both watch.

I whimpered.

His fingertips tickled my outer thighs before dipping beneath the T-shirt. But he didn't rip it off. He just trailed his hands along my thighs until he came to the waistband of my panties. Wilder shoved them to my knees before backing away.

While I shimmied them off my calves, he shoved down his shorts, kicking them aside with his shoes. Once he was naked, he placed a hand on the center of my spine and pushed me forward until I was on all fours.

"Fuck, Iris. Feel what you do to me." He pressed the head of his cock against my slit, dragging it through the entrance, coating his shaft in my wetness. "Damn it, I want you."

He hated to admit it, didn't he? He hated that I had crawled beneath his skin.

Well, too fucking bad.

I pressed my core against his arousal.

He let out a groan and took me by the hips. Then he lined up at my entrance and, in one fast thrust, impaled me on his cock.

"*Wilder*," I cried out, so loud it carried over the music still playing. My eyes squeezed shut as I adjusted to his size, my body stretching around his. "Move. More."

He pulled out to thrust even deeper, holding me to him until I dared to open my eyes. Until I dared a look in the mirror.

His face was masked in pleasure. Everything I'd missed last night in the dark was on full display. Lust. Relief. Submission.

Not to me, but himself. He didn't have the strength to fight this pull.

Neither did I.

He eased out slowly before bringing us together again. I'd expected a quick fuck but he was deliberate as he moved, like he wanted to draw this out.

My body had other ideas. A new song began in the background and before it was over, my limbs were trembling, my body on the cusp of a release.

"Oh God." I bit my lip, wishing I could make this last. But the feel of him bare inside me was exquisite.

Wilder wrapped an arm around me, hauling me off my hands so that my back was pressed against his chest, my bottom supported by his bulky thighs.

The change in angle made his thrusts shallow but he didn't stop moving. The T-shirt on my body rode up higher. I stared at us together in the mirror while Wilder dropped his mouth to my neck, kissing and sucking as a hand snaked around my front and settled against my clit.

A few circles with one of those long, talented fingers and I was gasping for air. "Oh God."

He worked me higher and higher, never stopping as I moved with him, chasing my own release. "Come, Iris. Let go."

I hadn't even realized I'd been fighting it. But I closed my eyes, let the pleasure wash over my body and came apart. White stars broke across my vision as I shattered. Pulse after pulse, my body quaked and jerked, moving on its own accord as the orgasm rocked through every muscle, every bone.

Wilder's mouth latched on to my neck, sucking hard enough to leave a mark, before his lips found my ear. "Your pussy was made for my cock, Iris. Feel how deep I'm buried."

"Yes," I cried out, his words drawing out my orgasm.

Then he came apart too, pouring inside me on a groan.

His finger never stopped. Wilder kept toying with me, drawing out my orgasm and his own, until finally I collapsed against his chest, my body spent and languid.

When I dared to crack my eyes open, I found Wilder's waiting in the reflection. A flush had crept into my cheeks. It bloomed at the intensity of his dark, unreadable gaze.

Before I could attempt to make sense of that look, he shifted, lifting me off his lap to break our connection. Then he stood and swiped up his shorts, dragging them up his legs.

I pushed to my feet too, righting my T-shirt over my ass.

His come trickled down my thigh, but I didn't bother with my panties. When we got inside, I'd take a shower, so I swiped them up from the floor and headed for the door.

This time, I was going to leave first.

"Wait."

I turned at Wilder's command.

"Where are your shoes?"

"Oh, I didn't wear any."

"Of course you didn't," he muttered. A frown marred that handsome face as he held up a finger.

Wilder snagged his T-shirt, not bothering to pull it on. Then he stepped into his shoes before crossing the gym to retrieve his phone and shut off the speaker.

The absence of the music was jarring. It made space in my mind for the doubts and questions to rush forward.

Did he regret this time too? Would he ask me to leave later? *Should* I leave?

Wilder met me at the door, and I shuffled out of his way, assuming he'd open it for me. Instead, he picked me up with a quick sweep beneath my knees. Then he carried me outside and to the house so my feet wouldn't be poked by the grass or gravel.

"I don't want to talk about it," he said as we walked.

"It meaning sex."

He nodded.

"All right." I tightened my grip around his neck. "Does that mean we'll continue having sex?"

"I just said I don't want to talk about it."

I ducked my chin to hide a smile. "Can I assume that means yes?"

He stayed quiet.

But he did answer my question. Because instead of carrying me to my shower. He carried me to his.

CHAPTER ELEVEN

WILDER

DANNY CALLING.

The ring filled the truck's cab as his name appeared on the center console. "Shit."

I punched the decline button so fast it jerked the steering wheel. But I couldn't talk to him, not yet. Not with this much guilt crawling beneath my skin.

Danny had called more in the past two weeks since Iris had come to Montana than he had in the past year. He no doubt wanted to check up on her and our living situation, but I didn't trust myself to talk to him right now. Not when I might blurt the truth.

How's Iris?

She's fantastic. I fucked her before I left for work this morning and left her asleep in my bed just like I have every day this week.

And as soon as I made it home, I'd fuck her again before dinner.

How would I ever face Danny? Even if he never learned

the truth, there was no way I'd be able to look at him in the eye again after what I'd done.

After what I continued to do, night after night.

Iris and I were greedy. Insatiable. She was my new pastime and had consumed me wholly.

We'd have sex the moment I walked through the door. Then I wouldn't let her out of my sight. She'd watch me cook, always offering to help and scrunching up her nose each time I refused. Since the weather was so nice lately, we'd take a walk around the property after our meal. Last night, I'd fucked her against a tree.

When we'd get back to the house, she'd snuggle in on the couch and mess around on her phone while I read a book or watched a baseball game.

Or attempted to read a book or watch a baseball game. Usually she thwarted my plans with her unending curiosity.

Never in my life had I met a person who asked so many questions. And I was a high school teacher.

But I'd answer those questions, biding my time, until darkness fell beyond the windows. And then I'd whisk her away to my bed where we'd spend hours exploring each other's bodies until we collapsed.

I'd slept like a damn rock all week, even with Iris out cold on my chest.

This had to stop. Damn it, I *needed* it to stop. But asking me to stay away from Iris would be like asking the sun not to shine.

This obsession with Iris made no fucking sense. We had nothing in common. She was too young. Too vibrant and energetic.

Iris talked incessantly. While I was cooking. While I was

reading. While I was breathing. It surprised me that she didn't talk in her sleep.

She'd forced me to tell her about my students, which were my favorite and least favorite. She'd wanted to learn about baseball, so I'd had to tell her the rules one night as the game had played on the TV.

Last night, I'd gotten so sick of answering questions I'd finally decided to ask some of my own. She'd told me about the various places she'd lived and the path of her travels.

Iris was, by far, the most adventurous free spirit I'd ever met. She was a butterfly, flitting from place to place at the whim of a breeze.

She was unlike any woman I'd ever met.

Especially Amie.

But I wasn't letting myself dive into the comparison of my lover and my wife. That would wait until after Iris was gone from Calamity.

The mental countdown had already started. There were only six weeks left of her two-month stay. Dread and anticipation swirled like oil and water.

Iris's Bronco was gone when I pulled up to the house. Disappointment surged but I shoved it aside and headed inside, pretending it was just another Friday afternoon. Before Iris, I'd spend my Fridays relaxing. Decompressing. Now, every thirty seconds, I glanced outside, hoping to see her car drive up the lane.

Where the hell was she anyway? I'd rushed through my afternoon routine to get here fast. Hadn't we established a routine?

I rinsed my lunch containers and put them in the dishwasher, then quickly changed clothes and headed for the gym. My workout was unfocused and short. How was I ever supposed to work out again when all I did was picture Iris on all fours in front of the mirror? And I didn't turn on the music, wanting to hear when she got back.

But by the time I finally called it quits an hour later, she still wasn't here. So I opted for a shower, hoping she'd be back soon enough to join me. Only I washed alone.

Dressed in a clean pair of jeans and a T-shirt, I snagged a beer from the fridge, once more checking the time. I made sure I hadn't missed a call from her either. *Nope.*

Had she gone to the store or something? Maybe the car wash? Her Bronco was always clean.

With my beer in hand, I headed for the porch with the novel I'd started a couple weeks ago. Except reading was futile. Every sound drew my attention. A bird squawked and I'd glance toward the road, searching. I read the same paragraph five times before I finally tossed the paperback aside.

"Damn it, Iris. Where are you?" I checked the time on my phone for the hundredth time. Six o'clock.

Had she gone to Jane's again? Was she downtown? Should I make dinner or wait?

"Fuck," I cursed to no one.

She'd call me if she got a flat tire, right? Could she have gotten in an accident? That thought made my blood run cold. Before thinking twice, I hit her name on my phone, listening to it ring.

"Hey," she answered.

The air rushed from my lungs.

"Where the fuck are you?" I barked.

Iris answered by hanging up.

"What the—"

The crunch of gravel and the hum of an engine echoed off the trees. Then came a flash of white through the forest before her Bronco rounded the last corner and appeared, rolling along the drive until she parked beside my truck.

My heart raced, the pulse a dull drum in my ears.

She stepped out of her car and plucked the sunglasses from her face, glaring at me with those clear blue eyes.

I stayed quiet, dragging my gaze up and down her body. She was fine. Two legs. Two arms. That beautiful head sitting squarely above her shoulders.

She was wearing a short-sleeved black dress that draped to her ankles. Two slits ran up each side of the skirt, revealing her toned thighs. The front had a deep V that stretched nearly to her navel. On both wrists were stacks of bracelets, some gold and silver. And dangling over her heart, that compass rose necklace.

Beautiful. She was so fucking beautiful.

And here. She was here. Unharmed.

The panic subsided. The worst-case scenarios that had crept from the dark corners of my mind retreated to their hiding places as I filled my lungs and drew in the fresh mountain air.

"When I say 'Hey,' you say 'Hi.' Not 'Where the fuck are you.' " She arched a perfect eyebrow. "Let's practice. Hey."

That sass. Did she realize it only made me want her more? "Hi."

"Better." She opened the back door of her car, pulling out a box of pizza. Then she marched for the house.

I met her at the door, holding it open for her as she stormed inside.

She kept that scowl on her face, avoiding eye contact, as

140

she moved around the kitchen, taking out plates and napkins and silverware before flipping open the lid to the Pizza Palace box.

"Iris."

"I don't like being cursed at when I answer the phone," she snapped.

"Look at me." I stood on the other side of the island, hands braced on the counter until she finally met my eyes. "I was worried when you weren't here."

"I was just in town. I didn't realize you were taking attendance, Mr. Abbott. I don't like reporting to anyone."

No, she wouldn't, would she? She'd created a life where she was her own authority. Where she was free to come and go however she pleased.

Iris needed that freedom, didn't she? As much as I needed a tether between us.

"I need . . ." I had no right to ask her for this, but for my own sanity, I was going to do it anyway. "Will you report to me? Please?"

She opened her mouth, like a *no* was on the tip of her tongue. But before she let it loose, she studied my face.

Did she realize why I was asking? Could she see the explanation I didn't want to give?

"Just . . . tell me where you are. Where you go. What time you think you'll be somewhere. I don't care what you do, just tell me so I know where you are."

Her shoulders fell as her expression softened. "Okay, babe."

I swallowed hard and tore my eyes away, needing to regroup. Needing to put the walls back in place. "Babe?"

"It slipped out." She shrugged. "But I don't hate it."

"No one has ever called me babe."

"Really?" She cocked her head to the side, dishing out a slice of pepperoni pizza to our plates. "What was your wife's pet name for you?"

There it was. The topic we'd both been avoiding.

There was no way to dodge this subject forever. No way to keep tiptoeing around the ghost who floated over my shoulder. But that still didn't make it easier.

Iris's eyes lifted to mine. They were full of compassion. Of sympathy.

It had taken a lot for her to ask that question, hadn't it? She seemed so at ease. So nonchalant as she spoke. But there was no hiding the way her posture stiffened. Her expression grew wary, like she was expecting me to toss her out the door.

"Sugar," I answered. "Amie used to call me sugar."

Iris nodded and plucked a piece of pepperoni from her slice, popping it into her mouth. "Did you like it?"

"Not especially," I admitted. No one, not a soul in this world, knew I didn't like that endearment. It was easier that way, keeping the truth locked inside.

"What was she like?"

My fingers began to twitch. An uneasy stir swirled in my gut. That familiar, too-hard thump began in my chest.

There was a reason I'd moved to Calamity, to a place where no one here asked about Amie. Most in town didn't even know I'd been married. Because if no one asked, I didn't have to tell.

Until Iris.

"Sorry." She held up a hand. "I'm prying. Forget I asked."

There was hurt in her voice. It was probably like having a friend hold out a hand to help you up from the ground, but instead of taking it, you kicked them away.

Maybe I was so used to kicking people away that I wasn't sure how to stop.

"Go ahead and eat. I'm going to change." She moved away from the island, about to disappear to her room, but I moved in a flash, snagging her elbow to stop her from leaving.

"Iris."

"It's okay, Wilder. I understand why you don't want to talk about her."

"It has nothing to do with you."

"I know." She gave me a sad smile, reaching up to cup my cheek. Her thumb stroked my beard, then she dropped her arm, once more trying to escape. But I kept my hold on her firm, tugging her back with enough force that I had to catch her at the hips.

With a quick lift and spin, I hoisted her on top of the island, stepping close so that she had to open her legs to accommodate my hips. Then I dropped my forehead to hers. "Hey."

She closed her eyes. "Hi."

My hand traveled up her arm, my fingertips skating along her skin. Then I buried both hands in her hair, pushing her head back so I could have open access to her throat.

I dropped my mouth to her jaw, kissing along the sleek line from her ear to her chin. My tongue darted out to lick her skin before I moved to the long column of her neck, sucking on her pulse as I dragged in her sweet vanilla scent.

"Why can't I stop touching you?" I asked.

She hummed. "Why do you think you need to stop?"

I wouldn't. As long as she was here, I'd worship her body.

With a hand on her heart, I eased her backward until she was lying on the countertop. Then I hiked up the skirt of her dress, bunching it at her waist as I peppered kisses along the insides of her thighs.

She moaned, drawing up her knees as I inched toward her center.

My fingers tugged at her panties, dragging them away until she was bared to me. And then I feasted on that sweet pussy, alternating licks through her slit with flicks of my tongue over that perfect little bundle of nerves.

"Wilder." Her back arched off the counter as her hips began to rock.

Fuck, but she was delicious. I devoured her, flattening my tongue against her center as a string of sexy sounds filled the kitchen.

She came on a cry, her body pulsing and quaking while I sucked on her clit, drawing out her orgasm until she was limp and panting on the island.

I kissed along her belly, knowing she was ticklish.

She laughed and rolled, swatting me away. Then she took my hand as I helped her to a seat and righted her skirt.

"Good?"

"Yes." She reached for a piece of pizza, handing it over. Then she took her own, eating it as she sat on the counter and I stood by her side.

Two bites. That was all I was able to manage before the questions started.

"Who teaches sex ed at the high school?"

"Not me."

"Do you dissect animals for your class?" She waited until I nodded. "Which ones?"

"You really want to talk about that while we're eating?"

"I'm not squeamish. Are you?"

The questions came rapid fire as I ate three pieces of pizza and cleaned up the kitchen. Normally Iris was curious, but tonight, her inquisitiveness took on a whole new level. Almost like if she asked enough safe questions, it would erase the one I hadn't answered earlier. It would shove it so far away we could forget she'd asked about Amie in the first place.

Either she did that for my sake. Or her own.

CHAPTER TWELVE

IRIS

calamity

WILDER WAS SITTING on the couch, reading a book, when I emerged from my room. He glanced up as I stopped in front of him, holding out two handbags.

"Lime? Or pink?"

He closed his book. "Is it supposed to match?"

"Both match."

He blinked.

I glanced down at my yellow mini skirt and black lace camisole. "Okay, so they don't match. But both go. Which one goes better?"

"Is this a trick question?"

"Just pick one."

"Lime."

"Excellent." I bent down to kiss his cheek. Then I retreated to my room to put the pink handbag away, grab my shoes and pull on my favorite leather jacket. "I'm heading into town for coffee."

From the couch, he cast a pointed glance at the coffee pot on the kitchen counter. "Something wrong with the coffee here?"

"No. But I need to do some work today."

His gaze shifted to the empty dining room table. "And you can't work here?"

"You and I both know that if I stay, I won't do any work." Beyond the work it took during sex.

And as much as I wanted to spend the day in bed with Wilder, I had a feeling that he might need some space.

Or maybe I was projecting my own feelings.

We'd gone from awkward encounters and stilted conversations to all-consuming nights and rabid desire. My head was spinning and a few hours alone might do us both some good. It might help me make sense of last night.

Wilder had answered every one of my easy questions while we'd shared that pizza. But the hard question, the question about Amie, had lingered. It had prodded the back of my mind, refusing to be dismissed, until dinner was over and Wilder had carried me to his room, where all talking had ceased.

But the sex could only serve as a distraction for so long. This morning, I'd had to restrain myself from peeking into one of Amie's boxes in the closet.

What had she been like? What about her did Wilder love so much?

My curiosity was getting the better of me, and my attempt to mollify it with nonsense questions was barely working.

I wanted to know anything and everything about this man who'd so completely snared my attention. And maybe if I kept learning, kept persisting, he'd get used to my questions. He'd realize talking to me was easy and that his secrets were safe. That *I* was safe.

But not today. This morning, we could both use a break from the questions.

"When will—" He stopped himself short and shook his head.

When will you be back?

"I'll be back by lunch."

"Thanks." His frame relaxed and he picked up his book, opening it to the page where he'd left off.

I wasn't used to telling anyone where I was going or when I was coming back. My life for the past seven years had served my whims and moods.

The idea of having to check in with someone chafed. It felt too much like living with my parents. Dad had always kept a tight leash on my activities, and Mom had hovered so closely I could still feel her chin on my shoulder at times.

Except when Wilder had asked me to report in last night, I'd agreed. For him, I could change habits for a couple of months.

I didn't remember much about Wilder from years past. He'd just been that friend of Danny's. But I did remember when Amie had died. Killed by a drunk driver.

Danny had come over to Mom and Dad's to break the news. It was the first time I'd ever seen my big brother cry.

We hadn't been little kids together. He was a teenager by the time I'd started kindergarten so I'd never seen him cry over a scraped knee or lost baseball game. But that day, the pain in my brother's voice had been so sharp it had left a mark. He'd cried, not just for Wilder, but himself. Amie had been Danny's friend too.

Sure, I could ask Danny all there was about Amie. But I didn't want his perspective. I wanted Wilder's.

And even though I still had six weeks left, I probably wasn't going to get it.

Not that I wouldn't keep trying. Later.

"Want me to pick up something to eat for lunch from the White Oak?" I asked as I slipped on my chunky Prada loafers.

"Sure."

I walked to the couch and bent over his head, kissing the corner of his mouth. "Bye, babe."

The endearment slipped out as easily this morning as it had yesterday. I waited for him to cringe or scowl or clench his jaw. But he just went back to the book he'd been reading.

It was probably dangerous to call him babe. To pretend that this was anything other than sex. But I didn't need to worry about Wilder getting attached. Not when his heart belonged to his wife.

So as long as I could walk away at the end of my two months, what was the harm in sinking into this all the way while I was here? The only thing at risk was my heart.

With a wave, I left the house, climbed in my car and drove to town. First Street was quiet as I eased into an empty parking space. That was the reason I'd come down early. I'd wanted to take a few photos without people filling the shots.

No matter what city I lived in, I liked to experience as many aspects as possible.

My favorite time in Amsterdam was in the morning,

when the canals were still and the water reflected the early light of dawn. I loved afternoons in London, when tourists were out in full force exploring and snapping photos. Barcelona evenings were beautiful.

I wasn't sure which time of day I'd love Calamity most. So far, I loved it morning, noon and night.

So with my phone in hand, I set out along the sidewalks, taking a few photos as I strolled toward the coffee shop.

The town was located in a mountain valley in southwest Montana. Indigo mountains with snowy caps peeked above the rooflines of the downtown buildings.

Kim had done some research on Calamity this past week, mostly for content ideas in case my creative well went dry. According to her Google search, Calamity was home to approximately two thousand residents. She liked to give me suggestions on places to visit or restaurants to try—her list this time around was short and included every restaurant within a fifty-mile radius. And while I did want to try the café and a few other spots, if I spent the next six weeks eating meals solely in Wilder's house, I'd leave happy.

The Bronco was parked in front of Thatcher Law. The office's windows were dark, the firm closed for the weekend. The shops weren't open yet but most had someone inside preparing for Saturday patrons.

Nearly every store along First had a Western element. The buildings alternated between square, barnwood façades or red brick and mortar walls.

Checking both ways for traffic first, I jogged into the middle of the street, taking a photo of one particular wall I'd noticed yesterday. *Candy Shoppe* was legible in extremely faded white paint against the rough surface.

How long ago had those letters been painted? Fifty years? One hundred? I made a mental note to do my own research into Calamity's history this week. Not for social media content. Just for my own knowledge.

Since there wasn't any traffic, I quickly took a few more photos, one aimed all the way down the street to the unique barn-shaped grocery store. Then I jogged back to the sidewalk, continuing my stroll.

I passed by The Refinery, a fitness studio with plate-glass windows. A yoga class was in session. I walked a few more blocks, taking note of more before circling back to the coffee shop.

The scents of espresso and cinnamon greeted me inside the door. The shop hummed with idle chatter. It wasn't a large building, and all but one of the tables had been taken. I went to the counter, ordered a latte from the barista, then stole that last remaining table, taking off my coat and getting comfortable.

While I let my coffee cool, I checked notifications and comments. Kim managed most of the daily activity, but I liked to check in at least once or twice to keep my finger on the pulse of what was working—and what wasn't.

No one in the recent comments had called me a trashy whore—*HOORAY*—so I closed down Instagram before a troll could put a damper on my day. Then I opened up the photos I'd taken this morning, editing and cropping them to size. I posted three of my favorites in a carousel with the simple caption *calamity*.

Task complete, I shifted in my chair to drink my coffee and stare out the shop's windows. This really was a charming town. No wonder Wilder had made it his home.

Did he have friends? In the two weeks I'd been here, the only places he'd gone, to my knowledge, were the school, the grocery store and home. He'd gone to Jane's but that had been my idea. What kind of a social life did he have?

Jane had known him the night we'd gone to the bar. And he'd nodded and waved at a few other people, but no one had come over to talk. Was that because I'd been with him? Or had Wilder secluded himself so thoroughly that Montana was effectively his private, deserted island?

I wasn't any different. I had no room to judge or criticize.

I'd traveled all over the world for years and my best friend was Kim. But did it count when your best friend was also your employee? When you only saw each other on the occasional video conference?

If Wilder's life was solitary, mine was too. Surrounded by people, followed by millions, and I was sitting at a coffee shop alone.

Strange. It hadn't bothered me until this moment. I'd been too busy traipsing around the world to realize I'd traipsed so far that I'd left everyone else behind.

"Oh my God." Someone gasped. "You're Iris Monroe."

A young girl stood beside my table, her mouth agape. Her long blond hair was curled into waves, and she wore a Calamity Cowboys crewneck, the design on the front the same as the T-shirt I'd stolen from Wilder.

Was this one of his students? One of the girls he'd told me about who followed my account?

"Hi." I set my coffee down and waved. "Yes, I'm Iris."

Since I'd started influencing, I'd only been recognized once in New York. In the city, I was just one in the masses. In Calamity, I'd stick out like a neon sign.

"I'm Sadie." Her cheeks flushed. "And I'm a huge fan."

"Thank you."

"Can I buy you a coffee or something? That's probably weird, right? Sorry. I just . . . I'm really a huge fan." Sadie fidgeted with the hem of her sweatshirt, tucking it under, then out. She shifted her weight from foot to foot, like she was debating whether or not to bolt for the door.

She was adorable and shy. Exactly like I'd been at that age.

I liked her immediately.

"I'm good on coffee," I said, raising my half-full cup before gesturing toward the empty chair across from mine. "But you're welcome to sit down. I'd love company."

Her eyes widened. "Seriously?"

"Seriously." I couldn't wait to get home and tell Wilder about this.

Wait. Was this okay? I wasn't Wilder's girlfriend, but I was sleeping in his bed. Was it allowed for me to talk to his students? Maybe the invite to chat had been a bit hasty. Except it was too late to rewind.

Sadie pulled out the chair, sliding into the seat. Her hands clasped together on the table before she pulled them back to her lap. On the table. Off the table.

"I'm guessing you're from Calamity," I said. Maybe if we talked for a bit, her nerves would settle.

"Yeah." She nodded, her gaze lifting.

Her eyes were tinged pink, and puffy circles sat beneath them. There was a wetness on her lashes I'd initially mistaken for caked-on mascara. She'd been crying this morning.

My heart squeezed. Maybe I could cheer her up.

153

"I'm living here for a couple of months," I said.

"Two months in Montana."

She hadn't been joking. She really was a fan. "Yes. And so far, I love Calamity. But I want to go to the places that just the locals know about. Got any recommendations?"

Sadie sat a little straighter, her brown eyes sparkling. Then she spent the next hour telling me all about her hometown. She was so proud of Calamity. Listening to her talk was like seeing this place with fresh eyes.

Sadie was sweet and funny. She had a dry sense of humor and even though she was still in high school, she had a maturity that made her seem much older than eighteen.

"Have you eaten at the White Oak yet?" she asked.

"Yes, it was amazing. I'm planning on getting lunch there today. I had a sandwich last time. Anything in particular I should try?"

"It's all good. And I've had literally everything on the menu. My boyfriend and I used to go there a lot on dates." Her smile faltered. "Well . . . ex-boyfriend. We just broke up last night."

Ahh. The source of the tears. "I'm sorry."

"It was my idea." She lifted a shoulder. Just one, like Wilder did. "But it still sucks."

"Yeah. Breakups are the worst."

This was what I had in store for me when I left Montana, wasn't it? A heavy heart and sad eyes. Not that Wilder and I would break up. We'd have to be together to break up. But in another six weeks, when I left that handsome man and his lovely house, it was going to hurt.

"I don't want to be like a creepy stalker or something. And you can totally say no." Sadie held up a hand. "But I

154

sort of started an Instagram account to just . . . I don't know. Post about my life and stuff. I love your pictures and style. I'm trying to be smart about how I set up everything, like a business or whatever. Just in case it turns into something real someday. I don't suppose you do any mentoring, do you?"

"Oh." I sat a little straighter. Whenever we did a Q&A on Instagram, there'd be comments about becoming an influencer. Those were usually the questions we'd skip, mostly because the answers were complicated and "It depends" was such a brush-off, even if it was the truth.

But to mentor someone in person? My interest was piqued. Except, what about Wilder? Would he care if I met with his student? The prudent answer would be a maybe.

Except the hope in Sadie's eyes, the vulnerability in her voice and that bit of desperation, made it impossible for me to say maybe.

"Sure. I'd be happy to answer your questions."

"Really? Oh my goodness, thank you so much. Maybe we could meet again, um, tomorrow?"

Oh boy. I hoped Wilder would be okay with this. "I'll be here."

CHAPTER THIRTEEN

IRIS

some call me impractical

THE COFFEE SHOP was apparently the place to be on a Sunday morning. Since Sadie and I had arrived and snagged a table in the corner, it seemed like nearly every person in the county had come through its front door.

One of my favorite pastimes was people watching, and this shop delivered. It was going to be my new Sunday morning ritual.

In the past hour, Sadie had asked me question after question about becoming an influencer. And as we'd talked, as I'd shared in her palpable excitement, I'd fallen a bit in love with this girl.

Her curiosity reminded me of my own. She was genuine and kind. Every time someone would wander over to our table to tell her hello, she'd stand up and either shake their hand or give them a hug. She had a quick wit I suspected was lost on most of her high school classmates.

No wonder she was Wilder's favorite student.

I'd told him about meeting her at the shop yesterday and asked if he had concerns with me mentoring her. He'd thought there wouldn't be much harm in a couple of meetings at the coffee shop, especially since she didn't need to know I was sleeping with her science teacher.

Phew. It would have sucked to cancel on Sadie. She'd come armed with a spiral-bound notebook and a list of topics to discuss.

"I love the photo you posted today," she said. "But those are not the same shoes."

"Nope." I laughed, glancing down at my Golden Goose crystal-embellished sneakers. They were on the conservative end of the spectrum compared to the shoes I'd been wearing in today's post.

The picture Kim had posted today was of me on the dirt road to Wilder's house. My back was to the camera and my shoes, a pair of Louboutin Mary Jane platform pumps, were the focal point. The red soles were a stark contrast to the blues, golds and greens of the landscape. They were entirely impractical for the rugged scenery, exactly as Kim had captioned.

"Only about a third of the pictures and videos I take are posted on the same day," I told Sadie. "Most of my content is scheduled and coordinated by my social media manager. I definitely recommend scheduling posts so you can get ahead."

"Ah. That makes sense." She nodded. "If becoming an influencer doesn't work out, then social media manager sounds like my backup dream job."

"There are a ton of opportunities out there with influencers. I'd be happy to connect you with my business manager so you can use her as a reference. She's always got a line on people who are hiring."

Sadie's jaw dropped. "For real?"

"For real."

"That would be amazing." She pressed a hand to her heart. "Thank you."

"Welcome." She'd have to self-motivate and hustle, but I had a feeling that wouldn't be a problem. "What are your plans after you graduate? Besides your social media stuff?"

She groaned. "I don't know yet. Everyone has their next year figured out except me."

"There's no law that says you have to decide right away."

"Yeah." She blew out a long breath. "It's a lot of pressure."

The coffee shop's door opened before I could respond, two teenage guys walking inside.

Sadie stiffened.

Both boys were grinning. One of them scanned the room and the moment his gaze landed on Sadie, he smacked the other kid in the arm and pointed to our table.

The other boy stopped walking. His smile was replaced with a scowl as his gaze landed on Sadie. His expression hardened. His hands fisted at his sides. He just glared at her. Then slowly, he raised a hand. And held up his middle finger.

"What the hell?" I sneered. "Who is that little prick?"

Sadie shifted in her chair, pivoting so that her back was to the boys and the door. She kept her shoulders straight and her chin raised, but her cheeks flushed. "That would be

Ryan. My ex-boyfriend. He's being a dick and is sooo embarrassing."

"Ignore him," I said, braced for drama.

But thankfully, the boys turned and walked out of the coffee shop.

"Boys are the worst." She sighed, checking over her shoulder as the door swished closed. "He came over last night with all my stuff in a box. He even brought me back all the gifts I've given him."

I winced. "Ouch."

"What do I need with football gloves?" She rolled her eyes. "He's just being petty because his ego got bruised."

"Sorry." I put my hand over hers.

She shrugged and sipped her coffee.

Most of the men I'd dated weren't the egotistical or petty type. That, and they knew better than to expect anything longer than two months. There'd been a few guys who'd wanted to try for something long-distance, but once I'd realized they'd caught feelings, I'd broken it off.

It had been all too easy to walk away from the men in my past. To move on to the next city, the next adventure, and forget. No guy had left a lasting impression. I hadn't missed a single one of them.

Wilder would be different, and not just because he was connected to Danny. There was no forgetting a man like Wilder Abbott. I would miss him terribly. Maybe he'd do something to annoy me in the next six weeks. For my heart's sake, I almost hoped so.

"Why did you and Ryan break up?" I asked Sadie.

"He's hot. Obviously." She flung a hand out to where he'd been standing.

Yes, Ryan was good looking. Young, but handsome, with a broad frame that he'd fill out in time. His dark hair and bright eyes probably meant he could have any girl at Calamity High School.

And Sadie had dumped him.

Burn.

"He just wasn't nice to me sometimes."

"Wait." I sat a little straighter. "He didn't hurt you, did he?"

"Oh, no." She shook her head wildly, waving her hands. "Not that kind of mean. The kind of mean where he flips me off in a coffee shop full of people. Or talks about how hot other girls are in front of me. Or brags to his friends that we have sex. Like, duh . . . we're dating. Of course we're having sex. But did he have to broadcast it?"

Yep, Ryan was a little shit. Exactly what Wilder had told me yesterday. He liked Sadie. Loathed Ryan. He grinned when I'd told him that the pair had broken up.

"He thinks he's better than everyone. That I should be falling at his feet."

I saluted her with my coffee mug. "Excellent decision to dump his ass."

"Thanks." She gave me a sad smile. "It just sucks right now. I thought about waiting until after school was out but . . . I couldn't. The other day, after school, we went to his house to . . . you know."

Have sex. "Yes."

"After, he took me to my car at school but it wouldn't start. I called him like fifteen times to come back and help me, but he didn't answer. I found out later that he didn't want to answer because he was going to a friend's house to

160

play video games. And since he'd already gotten what he wanted from me, why answer? I want a guy who doesn't ignore me."

"And that's what you deserve."

"That's what my mom said too." Sadie leaned a little closer, making sure no one around us could overhear. "Besides, I actually like someone else."

"Ooh, good for you."

"I've never told anyone that before. Not even my friends."

I crossed my heart. "Your secret is safe with me. Who's this new guy?"

"Someone from school. I won't do anything about it, not until after graduation. Ryan would freak, everyone would freak, and I don't have it in me to deal. But I really, really like him. And I think he might like me? It's complicated."

"You should just go for it."

"Nah. I'll just wait until Ry leaves for college."

"No college for you?"

She shrugged. "My parents are pushing hard for me to go to Montana State. They told me if I didn't decide on a college by graduation, they'd decide for me."

"Oof." That was entirely too familiar.

"I just don't know if college is for me."

There'd been a few moments today, like this one, when looking at Sadie was like looking into a mirror.

At her age, I'd been drowning in the expectations of others. Fighting to find my own footing. Staring into the future, realizing the dreams everyone else had for me weren't my own.

"When I was your age, my parents put a lot of pressure

on me to go to college," I said. "I think I would have liked it. I'm sure I would have made friends and had a nice time. But I wouldn't have *loved* it, you know? I would have been doing it for them, not me."

Sadie nodded. "That's how I feel. My parents told me that if I go to college, they'll help me pay for my car and rent and stuff. But if I don't go, then I'm on my own."

A threat. A threat I'd received myself. Before it put a wedge in their relationship with their daughter, I hoped that Sadie's parents, unlike my own, would realize that skipping college wouldn't make Sadie a failure.

"You'll figure it out."

"Yeah." Her fingertip traced a circle around the rim of her coffee mug. "Enough about me. Do you have a boyfriend?"

"Not a boyfriend. But there is someone. He's a good guy, and a friend of my brother's. But his wife died and he's not looking for anything serious. So we're mostly casual. Relationships are tricky when you move around as often as I do."

"Maybe you could stick around longer?" She perked up. "Calamity isn't as exciting as a city, but the summers here are fun."

"Maybe."

Her eyes narrowed. "Does that maybe mean no?"

"I think so." I laughed. "I've loved it here so far, but I think two months is all I can manage."

Without risking my whole heart with Wilder.

"Dang." Her shoulders sagged. "Where will you go after Montana? Home? Where is home, by the way?"

"My family lives in a small town in Utah. But I haven't

thought of it as home for a long time. I guess . . . I don't have a home."

The statement gave me pause.

I didn't have a home.

That wasn't something I'd admitted before. To anyone. To myself. "I think the closest thing I have to a home is my Bronco."

My mail went to a post office box in California, where Kim lived. If there was anything important, she'd forward it to wherever I was staying at the time. Everything else was digital.

It didn't bother me to bounce from place to place.

But it was strange to realize it through a conversation with Sadie, that I didn't have a home.

The early years after high school, Mount Pleasant had been home. But seven years later, too much had changed. It wasn't like I couldn't afford a house or condo. I just hadn't bothered, because living two months at a time only required vacation rentals.

"I love the Bronco, by the way," she said. "It's probably the coolest thing ever to drive."

"It's pretty great."

"My favorite place to visit is Hawaii. Maybe you could go there next?"

"Maybe. I could rent a condo or something on the beach."

Hawaii. Did I want to go to Hawaii?

I waited for it to click. For that feeling I normally had when I picked my next location. The surety. The excitement.

But nothing came. Not a prickle of eagerness. If anything, a pit of dread formed in my gut.

Why was I even worrying about this right now? I wasn't ready to pick my next place. I wasn't done with Calamity yet.

So I changed the subject to fashion, letting her ask more questions about how I got in with designer brands. We talked for a while longer until our coffees were gone. Then I waved goodbye, making plans to meet on Wednesday after school to have a Zoom and introduce her to my business manager. And as she walked to her car, I headed for the Bronco, driving back to Wilder's place.

Inside, he was on the couch reading his book. Yesterday, he'd been at the beginning. Now he was nearly finished.

"How do you feel about Hawaii?" I asked as I walked through the door.

"Huh?" He looked up from the page, blinking twice like he hadn't even heard me come inside.

Well, if that wasn't the most adorable thing. He was totally lost to whatever story he was reading.

"Never mind." I giggled and crossed the room, bending to kiss him. Then I pointed to the windows. "I'll let you keep reading. I'm going to take a few pictures outside."

"Okay." His attention dropped to the page.

Why was a man reading so attractive?

I left him on the couch and headed for my room, snagging my portable tripod. Then I slipped outside, setting up beside the house.

The log exterior was the perfect, dark backdrop for today's outfit of cream trousers and a satin corset top. I'd tied a baby blue sash around the brim of my straw hat. The blue was the same shade as the cardigan I wore on my shoulders, the arms loose so my tattoos would show.

I set up the shot, moving back and forth, trying to get the camera angle just right. But with every review of the photos, I hated them all. My poses looked forced and unnatural. The tripod's feet kept shifting on the grass.

"Ugh." I swiped through the last batch, frowning at the screen as I deleted everything I'd taken.

"Want some help?"

I jumped, smacking a hand over my heart as I spun. Wilder was leaning against the corner of the house. "Warn a girl, would you?"

"Sorry." He chuckled as he shoved off the house and walked over.

"I thought you were reading. How long were you watching?"

"When you came in, I only had five pages left."

So a while. No one ever watched me work. Well, other than strangers. A sudden shyness made my cheeks flame. It was one thing to take photos of myself, to pose and make faces alone. But entirely another with an audience.

"Give me your phone." He held out his hand.

"You don't have to help."

"Why not?"

"I've never had anyone take my pictures before who wasn't Kim." And even then, it had been awkward. I wasn't sure how to act when someone else was behind the camera.

Though that night at Jane's, when I'd asked him to take a photo, it hadn't been awkward. In fact, it had been easy to smile that night. And the photo had turned out to be a personal favorite.

"Who's Kim?" he asked.

"My assistant."

"Ah." He snatched the phone from my hand before I could stop him, then swiped up, holding it to my face to unlock. "Think of me as Kim."

"Wilder."

"Scoot." He swatted my ass, then moved away, lining up the camera.

I huffed and walked to the spot.

"Smile."

I smiled.

"A real smile, Iris."

"This is weird."

"Then stop being weird." He pinched his fingers on the screen, like he was zooming in. "Stick out your tongue."

I stuck out my tongue.

"Good girl."

"Oh my God." I closed my eyes, shaking my head as I laughed. "Promise to say that to me later tonight in bed, okay?"

"Promise." He grinned. "Turn to the side a little. No, the other way."

I obeyed, letting him direct me around as he took pictures for ten minutes. "Can we be done?"

"What else were you going to do out here?"

"Take a video."

He swiped across the screen. "Okay, go."

"Not a video of me."

"Why not?"

"Because. We're done." I took a step toward him.

He took a step back, the phone still raised.

"Give it back." I raced for him, laughing as he held the phone up high.

I jumped for it three times, but it was useless. He was too tall.

"Kiss me and you can have it," he said.

"Blackmail? Really?" I poked him in the ribs at a ticklish spot I'd found one night while I'd been licking my way up and down his body. It forced his arms to drop, and I stole my phone back. "Thief."

His mouth found the side of my neck just as I turned off the video.

"You were gone a while." His arms wrapped around me as he pulled my back into his chest.

"Don't pretend like you missed me. You were totally engrossed in your book."

"I had to read. You left me with nothing else to do."

"Aww. Poor Wilder."

He nibbled on my ear. "How was coffee?"

"Good." I twisted and looped my arms around his neck. "Sadie is a sweetheart. Very studious."

He hummed his agreement, kissing along my jaw.

I melted against him, pulling myself closer. Then his mouth was on mine and the world disappeared. It was hours later when we emerged from his room, both of us with damp hair from a shower.

"I'll make dinner," he said as he walked to the kitchen.

"I'm going to put some clothes on."

"Why?"

I rolled my eyes. "I'm not eating dinner in this towel."

"You look perfect in that towel."

My heart tumbled. God, this man. That statement was

167

laced with sexual promise but there was something else beneath the words. An affection he couldn't mask.

Maybe he heard it too because he dropped his gaze and moved to the fridge, focusing on the task of cooking.

I slipped away to my room and traded my towel for an oversized Columbia T-shirt that I'd stolen from a guy in New York. Then I sat on the edge of the bed and swiped through the photos Wilder had taken.

They were good. Perfect, actually. Far better than those I'd attempted to take alone. Somehow he'd captured the best moments when I was laughing or smiling at him, not worried about the camera.

My favorite would have been the frame of me sticking my tongue out at him. Except then I watched the video.

It was wobbly and candid, mostly of me trying to chase him down. But at the very end, when I'd reclaimed the phone and turned it to shut the video off, there was a quick glimpse of his broad shoulders and those forearms I loved so much. In the background, his gravelly chuckle sounded.

I replayed it three times before I finally stood from the bed and joined him in the kitchen.

Wilder stood at the stove, pushing chicken strips with onions and peppers around a frying pan.

"Fajitas?" I asked.

He nodded, glancing at me from over his shoulder. Then he did a double take, his gaze narrowing on my torso.

"What? I told you I was getting dressed."

He turned the gas down on the stove and set his spatula aside, then closed the distance between us in two long strides. One second I was wearing a T-shirt. The next, he'd ripped it over my head and was marching it to the garbage can.

"Hey." I huffed. "What did my shirt ever do to you?"

"Where'd you get this shirt?" He held it above the trash, giving me a chance to save it. But the only way that would happen is if I lied.

"Um . . . no comment."

"That's what I thought." He stepped on the can's foot lever, the top popping open. Then into the garbage went my shirt.

"I liked that one." I glanced down at my naked breasts. "Should have kept the towel on."

"You know where my closet is." He moved back to the stove.

"Are you giving me permission to raid your T-shirt drawer?"

"You're the one who wanted to ditch the towel and get dressed."

That meant yes. So with a smile, I went to his closet and found a different T-shirt.

A shirt he also ripped off my body after we'd eaten dinner.

A shirt I tucked away in my suitcase the next morning.

CHAPTER FOURTEEN

WILDER

THE CHIME of Danny's text filled my empty classroom. I ignored it, just like I'd ignored every text and call of his since Iris and I had started sleeping together. As far as friends went, I was the worst of the worst. The guilt burned, but I ignored that too and shoved the last of my ham sandwich in my mouth.

A knock came at the classroom door, and expecting a student, I did a double take when Iris walked into the room.

"Hey." She smiled.

"Hi." It came out muffled from the food, so I chewed faster and swallowed the bite, chasing it down with a gulp of water. "Hi."

"Sorry to interrupt." She spun in a slow circle as she took in the room. Then she went to one of the tables, running her hand over its smooth surface before climbing onto a stool. "How's your day going, Mr. Abbott?"

Damn it, that shouldn't have been sexy. That was where the kids sat. My biggest fear was having a student develop a crush on me. When I was in this building, romance was the furthest thing from my mind. But having Iris there, her perfect ass perched on a seat with that sultry smile and my name on her lips, made my cock twitch.

"Good," I said, wiping the corner of my mouth with a napkin. Then I leaned my elbows on my desk, taking in her outfit.

She never failed to surprise me with her ensembles. Every day she wore something new and unique. Today, she had on a pair of floral-patterned black tights and leather shorts, her tattoos peeking through the sheer fabric. She'd paired the shorts with a cropped graphic tee, a few inches of midriff showing. Her shoes were the rainbow platform sneakers I hadn't seen since her first day in Calamity.

Twin stacks of bracelets climbed all the way up both of her wrists. Nearly each finger was adorned with a ring. And that compass rose necklace caressed the space over her heart. She'd painted her lips a bright, sinful red too.

It was an outfit that would have gotten a student sent home to change. I couldn't wait to rip it off her later. And smear that lipstick.

"What's up?" I asked.

"I had a whim."

"Okay," I drawled, bracing for something that would undoubtedly shove me out of my comfort zone.

"Don't look so terrified." She rolled her eyes. "It won't hurt. Well, it won't hurt you."

"Excuse me?" What the hell was she doing that would hurt?

"I had an idea for a new tattoo." She patted her thigh. "There aren't any studios in Calamity so I'll road-trip to Bozeman. I talked to an artist and he's working on some sketches so we can get started tonight."

"Tonight?" No way I'd heard that right.

"Yeah. I'm going to get a hotel since it will probably be late by the time he's done."

She was driving to Bozeman to have a man ink her thigh. Tonight. Alone. On a whim.

I opened my mouth, about to tell her *fuck no*, but snapped it shut as my hands balled into fists.

Iris wasn't mine to control. I had no right to tell her this bothered me. That I hated the idea of her on the road. That I didn't like her sleeping in a hotel or spending the night away from my bed. So I just stayed quiet, letting the annoyance fester inside.

"I'm thinking of a mountain and trees. Montana has inspired me." She took out her phone and unlocked the screen, then hopped off her stool and came to my desk, holding it out.

There was a photo of a tattoo on the screen with a black outline and watercolor shading.

"I want this style but using a picture I took from Calamity."

"Great." Not fucking great.

Her smile faltered at my tone. "What?"

"Nothing." I waved her away, balling up my napkin and tossing it in the trash beside my desk. Then I stood and went to the whiteboard at my back, taking the eraser to the notes I'd written during my last class.

I erased with fury, wanting this tightness in my chest to vanish. This was why it was easier if you didn't have anyone in your life. If I was alone, I didn't have to worry about a woman's impulses or tattoos.

"Wilder," she said.

"Yeah." I didn't glance over my shoulder.

"What's wrong?"

"Nothing," I lied again.

Wasn't it about time I got used to the idea of her leaving? This could be a good test, right? It might not be the end of her two months in Montana, but that was coming, sooner rather than later. So she could go get her tattoo.

Why the sudden rush to do this now? We had a limited number of nights left. Couldn't this tattoo be done later?

"You're mad," she said.

Yep.

"Why? Isn't this what you wanted? For me to check in with you before I go somewhere?"

Yes. It was exactly what I'd asked for.

I put the eraser away, wishing I could articulate this frustration. To Iris. To myself. It should not have bothered me this much. But here I was, about to explode. "It's fine."

"You don't seem fine."

"I'm fine," I clipped.

"Okay, then I guess—"

Another knock at the door interrupted Iris.

"Hey, Abbott. Want a—" Larke Thatcher walked into the room with a plate of cookies. "Oh, sorry. I thought you were eating lunch alone."

"It's fine," I said. Everything was fucking fine.

"A student brought in these cookies. Want one?"

"What student?" I asked. "Actually. Never mind. No."

I didn't want a cookie. I wanted both of these women to

leave the room because having Larke in here with Iris was too much.

Larke narrowed her gaze. "Grumpy today. That's a new look for you," she deadpanned.

I scowled.

Iris pulled her lips in to hide a smile.

Larke looked between the two of us, waiting for me to give an actual introduction. She'd lived in Calamity her entire life and knew everyone who graced the school's halls.

"Larke, this is Iris," I said. "She's my best friend's little sister."

Iris tensed. It was so subtle that I doubted Larke caught it. But I did. "Yep. That's me. The best friend's sister."

"Nice to meet you." Larke extended her free hand. "Are you new to Calamity?"

"No, just visiting. I'm crashing with Wilder for a short while."

"Ah." Larke held out the plate. "Cookie? And don't worry, they're safe. The girl who made them is planning on culinary school. She knows my pregnancy cravings are always for sweets, so she's been bringing in treats. She's not the type to spit in a teacher's food."

Iris took a cookie. "Good to know. Thank you."

"You're welcome." She took another cookie and set it on the edge of my desk. "Eat a cookie, Abbott. Maybe it will fix your mood."

"Not likely," I muttered.

"Okay." Larke shook her head, clearly exasperated. Her chestnut hair, the exact shade of Amie's, swished across her shoulders.

I swept the cookie from my desk, about to toss it in the

trash, but instead I took a bite. "Happy now?"

Larke dismissed me with a flick of her wrist, then gave Iris a genuine smile. "Nice to meet you. Enjoy Calamity."

"Thanks." Iris nodded, waiting until Larke had left for her classroom. Then her smile dropped as she faced me, hands planted on her hips. "Are you rude to all of your coworkers? Or are you just taking out your frustration with me on her?"

My jaw clenched as I kept my mouth firmly shut.

There was no reason for me to dislike Larke Thatcher. She was a nice woman and a good teacher. But the resemblance to Amie wasn't easy to handle. And it was fucking uncanny.

In my head, I knew they were different people. Larke was snarky where Amie had been emotional. But when I looked at Larke, I still saw glimpses of Amie, and the guilt that came rushing with that recognition was crippling.

This wasn't a Larke problem. It was all on me.

And I didn't have a damn clue how to fix it. I'd been trying for years.

The best solution I'd found was to avoid Larke. It had been a hell of a lot easier to do that when she'd taught in elementary school. But last year, she'd moved to the high school to teach English. And because the universe liked to fuck with me, they'd placed her in the classroom across the hall from mine.

"Back to the silent treatment, huh?" Iris scoffed.

What else was there to say? "Watch for deer on the road to Bozeman."

Her mouth parted, then she snapped it closed and marched out the door.

I waited until her footsteps disappeared, then raked a hand through my hair. "Fuck."

The bell rang and seconds later, kids flooded the hallways, coming in from their own lunch break.

I inhaled the rest of Larke's cookie, chewing with ferocity before my next period's students streamed into the room. Then me and my shitty mood taught science until the day was over.

The kids didn't seem to care that I was short and irritable. Either they were oblivious or they'd become used to my moods.

Was I this surly so often that they expected it? Did everyone at Calamity High just dismiss me as that grumpy science teacher?

I wasn't always cranky, was I?

My recent moods seemed tied to one beautiful free spirit currently on her way to Bozeman. Alone. Leaving *me* alone.

Just the way I liked it. Except as I drove home, every mile grated on me more and more, knowing I'd get to the house and Iris's Bronco wouldn't be in the driveway.

It was the sex. That was the problem. It had to be the sex.

I'd gone so long without it that now, having it regularly had made me an addict. The idea of going back to my fist in the shower made my mood plummet to a new low.

The house was silent when I walked through the front door. Silent and still. My house. My routine. It wasn't lonely, it was just . . . normal.

It wasn't lonely.

"I'm not lonely."

My quiet, still house all but laughed at me.

"Fuck this." I strode to my bedroom, stripping off my shirt as I walked. I pulled so hard one of the buttons popped off. I gritted my teeth and balled it up, throwing it into the hamper. Then I traded my jeans for a pair of shorts.

If I wasn't having sex, I'd burn off this energy in my gym.

I pulled on my tennis shoes and walked down the hall, coming around the corner just as the front door opened.

Iris flew inside and dropped both her handbag and a backpack on the floor.

My heart skipped. It fucking skipped.

She hadn't left and it was because of me. I knew it without a doubt.

I was a motherfucking asshole. But the relief was bone crushing.

"Is this a fetish?" she asked at the same time I said, "I thought you were going to Bozeman."

"I did," she snapped. "Now I'm back. I had my appointment with the tattoo guy. I drove over there, met with him for a whole two minutes, then came back here to yell at you."

"Hold on. You what?" Gone was the relief. In its place, a new fiery rage. "That drive is two hours, one way. How fast were you driving?"

"Don't you dare." She held up a finger. "I get to yell. Me. Not you. And I asked you a question. Is this a fetish?"

"What?" My mind was reeling.

"A fetish. Is that what this is?" She flung a hand out between us. "You get to fuck your best friend's *little sister.*"

"What the fuck, Iris?" What the hell was she talking about? No, it wasn't a fetish. The way she said it made my skin crawl.

"That's how you introduced me to Larke."

Despite how much I didn't want to think about it, she was Danny's sister. "So you think I introduced you that way because I have a fetish. What did you expect me to say?"

"Anything else." She threw up her hands. "How about a friend?"

It was the crack in her voice that shot straight to my heart. That I'd hurt her because I'd immediately jumped to her as Danny's sister. Not as someone in my life.

"Iris." I sighed. "I don't . . ." How did I tell her this? How did I explain without talking about Amie?

Impossible. Either I told her the truth. Or she'd leave. And at the moment, with her anger infusing my house, she wouldn't come back.

I wasn't ready to lose her. Not yet.

"I don't talk to Larke much. We're not friends."

"So?"

"So . . ." I swallowed the thickness in my throat. "I have a hard time with Larke."

"But she seems nice. Why don't you like her?" Iris crossed her arms over her chest.

Of course she'd ask why. There was never an end to her questions.

Though if I was standing in her rainbow platform sneakers, I'd want to know why too.

"She looks like Amie," I blurted. "Now let's get back to you driving to Bozeman and back. How goddamn fast—"

"Wait." Iris held up a hand. "She looks like Amie?"

I nodded, turning my gaze to the closest wall. There'd be no way for Iris to know about Amie. They'd never met. And I didn't have any pictures in the house. Those were all in a box in the closet.

"I don't understand," she said. "They look alike? How much alike?"

"Enough that I avoid Larke. Amie had brown eyes, like Larke's. Same color hair. And they both smile a lot."

"Wilder." Her voice was gentle now, all traces of the anger gone.

"What?" Could we just be done with this?

"Will you look at me?"

I met her gaze. It was soft. Gentle. Understanding. I didn't want soft and gentle and understanding. If Iris knew the truth, she wouldn't be pitying me right now. She'd call me a sorry son of a bitch.

That look was too much. Too crippling. And I wanted it gone. Immediately.

Sex was a safe topic. The only safe topic at the moment.

"I don't have a fucking fetish because you're related to Danny. Is that understood?"

"Understood." She nodded.

"I'm fucking you because I love the way you scream when you come. I'm fucking you because you're so tight. And you let me do whatever the hell I want when we're together."

"Okay." She took a tentative step closer but was still wearing that soft expression.

"I'm pissed that you decided to go to Bozeman on a whim. I can't get enough of you and clearly, you have no problem walking away. When you could have told me about it and waited so I could go with you this weekend."

A smile tugged at the corner of her mouth.

"Do not smile at me." I pointed at her nose.

She smiled. "I should have invited you. But I didn't think

you'd want to come along."

"Why?"

"You don't exactly seem to crave public outings." She lifted a shoulder. "And it's not that I don't think of you. But I've been serving my whims for a long time. I come and go as I please. That's why I'm here, after all."

I huffed. "Yeah."

"I don't want you to worry about me. That's why I came to the school in the first place, to tell you I was going to Bozeman."

Normally, she would have just left.

Well, shit. She was trying. And I'd gotten pissed at her instead.

"Want to go to Bozeman with me on Saturday so I can get a new tattoo?" she asked.

"Yes." No hesitation.

Iris closed the gap, her hands coming to my bare chest. "Were you going to the shop?"

"Yes."

"Are you set on working out or . . ."

I crushed my mouth on her red lips, smearing that stain just like I'd wanted to earlier.

The moment my tongue tangled with hers, the tension left my body. The tightness eased from my chest, and the world faded to a blur.

I picked Iris up and carried her to my room.

Her legs wrapped around my waist, her arms resting on top of my shoulders. She poured all of the emotion from today into that kiss, giving as good as she took until we were both breathless. Until my shorts were littered on the floor along with her clothes.

I laid her on the mattress, and the second her back was on the bed, I lined up at her entrance and slid home. "Fuck, but you feel good."

And I needed this. Her.

I hadn't needed a woman in a long, long time.

It scared the hell out of me.

"Wilder," she purred.

The fear was propelled to the back of my mind as I kept my focus on Iris. As I worked us together, thrust after thrust, as she writhed and begged for release.

A single press of my finger to her clit was all it took. When she came, it was on a cry that echoed through the house followed by my own roar as I poured inside her body.

We collapsed on the mattress, a tangled mess of sweaty limbs and ragged breaths. Instead of getting a cloth to clean her up, I dipped my finger into her slit and rubbed my come against the tender flesh of her thighs.

She laughed into the crook of my neck, squirming against me. "That tickles."

"Tell me about this tattoo," I said.

"I already did."

"Tell me again. I wasn't listening earlier."

"Of course you weren't." She rolled her eyes and climbed out of bed, snagging her shorts to pull a piece of paper from the pocket. Then she joined me against the headboard, unfolding the page so I could see the artist's sketch.

It was beautiful. Feminine, but bold. It was Iris.

And two days later, we drove to Bozeman. I sat with her in a tattoo parlor, holding her hand while she got the piece inked on her skin.

CHAPTER FIFTEEN

IRIS

montana ink

"DO you ever sit on this side of the couch?"

Wilder didn't tear his eyes from his book. "No."

"What about when I'm not here?"

"No."

I hummed and went back to my phone, scrolling through my Instagram feed. My feet were tucked under Wilder's thigh.

He had an ankle kicked up over a knee, his feet bare and the hem of his jeans rolled up so he wouldn't walk on them. After coming home from school, he'd changed out of his button-down and into a plain T-shirt. Its sleeves strained around his biceps.

We'd fallen into this routine over the past week. Ever since we'd come back from Bozeman, our nights had been the same.

He'd come home from teaching and we'd have sex, somewhere other than in his bedroom. Sometimes it was here on the couch. Other times it was on the dining room table. Tonight, we'd gone at it against a wall just inside the door.

I'd practically tackled him when he'd walked inside.

Then Wilder would make dinner, always insisting on cooking no matter how many times I tried to insert myself and help. On Tuesday, I'd annoyed him so much that he'd picked me up and set me on a stool.

We'd eat dinner together, and when we were finished, we'd retreat to his couch, where I'd mess around on my phone while he read a book.

Every night was basically the same. I hadn't had this much consistency since living with my parents in high school.

I kept waiting for that restless feeling to hit. For me to get the itch to do something, go somewhere. But there wasn't a place I'd rather be than sitting with Wilder on this couch as he read his book.

Oddly enough, it had become a part of our foreplay, waiting for what was to come. That anticipation infused every moment, every heartbeat.

Maybe that was why this didn't bore me to tears. By the time he'd close his book each evening, I'd be vibrating and desperate for his touch.

Was this how other people felt about sex? God, I had been missing out. No other lover in my past had been as attentive as Wilder. He worshiped my body with an edge of dominance that got me off every single time.

In the mornings, he'd wake me with his hands between my legs. Sex would be slow and lazy, drawn out until the very last moment, when he'd rush through his shower and hurry to work. Then there was the frantic, hard fucks when we'd spent too many hours apart. And at night, it was like rolling the dice.

Would he be gentle and slow tonight? Or would he take me from behind, hard and rough?

A shiver rolled over my shoulders, and I pulled my bottom lip between my teeth to hide a smile as I looked over the edge of my phone to his profile.

He was so serious. His eyebrows formed a hard ridge. His mouth was set in an equally firm line. The bridge of his nose was perfectly straight, a feature I'd never noticed on another man. But I was drowning in Wilder's features.

Was his beard my favorite? Or those dark, stunning eyes?

"Iris."

"What?" I feigned innocence as I ducked my chin. It was the third time he'd busted me for staring tonight.

Clearly he wasn't ready to move on to the next portion of our evening, so I returned to my phone, reading a few comments from today's post.

montana ink

The photo was of me at the tattoo studio in a chair, propped on one side while the artist worked.

Wilder had taken the shot, close enough to show the detail of the design, but he'd also managed to capture my face. I was smiling despite the pain.

Kim had made a comment on our phone call today that my photos lately had been next level. So I'd admitted it was because I'd met Wilder and he'd become my own personal photographer.

Maybe she could tell he was different than the other men

I'd dated, because she'd squealed when I was done telling her about him.

Maybe it had been foolish to tell her. It would have been easier if he'd stayed a secret. That way, when I left Montana, I wouldn't have to answer questions about him. But I'd needed someone to know about Wilder.

It made him real. It made what we had real.

I missed him already. I had over a month left in Calamity, but I was already dreading the day I'd drive away.

The sound of a page flipping was the only noise. I wiggled my toes further under his leg, wanting to burrow even closer.

"Do you ever read e-books?"

"Sometimes," he murmured.

"Do you prefer paperbacks?"

"Yes." His gaze never left the page.

I pulled up my camera on my phone and took a photo on the sly. He'd probably make me delete it if he knew, but this was a picture I'd visit time and time again. When I was lonely. When I missed him.

At least I'd have some sort of evidence of our time together beyond the T-shirts I'd been snatching from his drawer.

Putting my phone aside, I leaned into the back of the couch, not caring if he caught me staring again. His eyes crinkled at the sides as he turned the next page, like the story was getting serious.

I loved so much that he was a teacher. Wilder could pass as a lumberjack or an underwear model or a professional athlete. But I loved that he'd chosen science and high school. I loved that he seemed so oblivious to his sex appeal. I loved that his closet was color coded and the books in his office were alphabetized by the author's last name.

Would he always live out here alone? Would he ever remarry?

My heart broke a little bit each time I wondered if there'd be another woman in his bed years from now. I wished, not for the first time, that I was ten years older. That I had met him first, before Danny.

Before Amie.

God, how he must have loved her. To struggle to even look at Larke because she resembled his wife. What kind of love was that?

My parents loved each other. I'd grown up in a house full of love. But I had a feeling it was different. That the way Wilder loved Amie was the soulmate kind of love.

My jealousy of a ghost never did get easier to swallow.

What had Amie Abbott been like? I wanted to know so badly I could hardly stand it. What was so special about her that she'd ruined Wilder for any other woman?

He turned another page. "What's wrong?"

"Nothing," I lied.

"You're tense."

Yes, I was. He could read that from his end of the couch. But there wasn't a chance I'd tell him the real reason I had a knot in my gut. It would just be pointless.

No matter how many questions I asked, Wilder wouldn't answer any involving Amie.

"How long have you had a beard?"

"Twelve years? Thirteen maybe."

So he'd grown it after he'd gotten married. Had Amie liked it? How could she not have liked it? I could barely remember what he'd looked like without it all those years ago.

"I wouldn't have recognized you," I told him. "If we had just passed each other on the street, I wouldn't have recognized you."

Those coffee-black eyes swung my direction. *Finally.* He put his book aside and stretched an arm across the back of the couch. "I saw you at the grocery store."

"When?"

"The day you showed up in Calamity."

"What?" I drew my feet back, sitting up straighter.

"I didn't recognize you. Just saw this beautiful woman and her colorful tattoos and thought . . . damn. Couldn't tear my eyes away."

When he said things like that, so raw and honest, it was hard to breathe.

Wilder had never judged me for my style or tattoos. He'd never once looked at me sideways. And that had gone all the way back to when we'd been two strangers, passing each other in the grocery store aisles.

What would have happened if we really had been strangers? Would he have approached me? Maybe invited me out for a drink? Or would he have kept on walking, always tied to Amie, regardless of whether he thought I was beautiful or not?

"Why did you owe Danny a favor?"

He sighed, taking one of my ankles to drag a foot over his lap. Then he went to work on the arch, massaging and kneading with those large, capable hands.

"You're trying to distract me."

"Is it working?"

"Nope." I giggled. "But don't you dare stop."

The corner of his mouth turned up.

"The favor."

"The favor," he muttered. "Danny and I always had fun in college. Especially those early years. We partied a lot."

"I can't picture him partying." Not once had I seen my brother drunk. He'd have the occasional glass of wine at holiday family functions, but I wasn't sure he even kept alcohol in his house.

"I was the instigator," Wilder said. "Danny usually came along for the ride. And he was usually the one to keep me from doing something stupid."

"Like what?"

He shrugged. "I once thought it was a good idea to walk home from the bar in zero-degree weather because I was drunk. He talked me into a cab. Stuff like that. It was never anything major, he was just the voice of reason."

My brother was a good big brother to anyone who'd let him assume the role. "So he looked out for you."

"Yeah. There were times when the roles were reversed. He got it in his head once to smoke a pack of cigarettes one night while we were out drinking. I knew he'd end up miserable the next day, so when he wasn't looking, I crushed the container."

"I can't picture Danny smoking."

"He had two. Never seen a guy turn green so quickly."

"Smoking. Drinking. It must have been something bad if you owed him a favor for this long."

Wilder groaned. "Do we have to talk about this?"

"Yes." I used my free foot to press against his hip, urging him on. "You said you'd tell me."

"I was hoping you'd forget."

"Have I ever forgotten?"

He chuckled, leaning his head back on the couch to stare up at the ceiling. "No. You're relentless."

"You like it."

He turned his head, his eyes softening.

He liked it. "Our sophomore year, we went on a road trip to Vegas for spring break."

I didn't remember that, but Danny hadn't been living at home, and at the time, the details of his life had been mostly a mystery to me.

"We stayed at a cheap hotel. Used fake IDs to drink and get into clubs. Gambled. It was just for a couple of nights. Then we were going home. But the last night, I tied one on. Danny and I were walking around the strip and there was this woman. I knew she was a prostitute."

I gasped, my eyes widening. *Oh God.* "You didn't."

"No." He shook his head. "But I'd never met a hooker before, and I got this dumb-fuck idea to talk to her. Nothing else. Just talk. Why, I'm not sure. I was a drunk idiot. So I went over to talk to her, even though Danny told me not to."

That seemed so strange coming from the man who always put up a fight about conversation. Maybe that was my problem. I hadn't seen Wilder drunk. Maybe if he was hammered, he'd tell me everything I wanted to know.

"What did you talk to her about?"

"Hell if I can remember. I wasn't even coherent. But whatever I said she took it as a proposition. One minute I was on my feet, the next she had me shoved against a parked car and two other cops came rushing over. She was undercover."

My jaw dropped. "No."

"Yep." He nodded. "I was heading to jail. But then Danny intervened. He explained that we were just messing around. That I had no intention of hiring her for sex. I was a wreck at that point, but somehow, he convinced them to let me go. The next day on the drive home, in between puking my guts out, I promised him a favor. Anything. I owed him huge."

And I was the huge favor.

If it was their sophomore year, I would have been ten. They would have been twenty. "Wait. You've owed Danny a favor for fifteen years?"

He nodded. "Yeah."

"Huh." I let it sink in. "A fifteen-year favor and Danny used it so I'd stay with you."

Either he really cared about me. Or he really cared about Wilder. That, or maybe he had no faith in my abilities to act as an adult. At this point, it hurt my brain trying to discern my brother's motives.

"I honestly don't know how to feel about that," I said.

"He cares about you."

"He worries about me."

"Is that such a bad thing?" Wilder asked. "To have people worry about you?"

"No." Maybe.

When it came to my family, worry usually came with chains. It wasn't endearing the way Wilder seemed to worry. His was genuine, sourced from fear. The worry from my family felt different. Like it was sourced from expectation or disapproval.

But I had a feeling Wilder would go to Danny's defense,

so I steered the conversation elsewhere. "Did you guys take any other spring break trips?"

"No. That was the only one."

"How come?"

A shadow might as well have covered his face given the way his expression clouded. Wilder didn't answer. He didn't need to answer.

"You met Amie."

That was why he hadn't taken trips with Danny. He'd had a girlfriend to travel with. A woman who'd come into his life and stolen his heart.

Wilder's jaw clenched at her name. His hands left my foot still draped across his lap, like he didn't want to touch me while her name echoed in the room.

Ouch.

"You can talk about her with me," I said. "I don't mind."

He stood from the couch, my leg falling to the floor as he stalked toward the windows. "I don't want to talk about her."

With anyone. Not just with me.

There was at least some comfort in the fact I wasn't alone. I was on the outside of his walls, along with everybody else.

"Okay." I stood from the couch and moved behind him, snaking my arms around his waist.

He tensed for a few heartbeats, then his frame relaxed.

We stood together for a few moments, my cheek pressed against his spine. Then he took my hand, pulling me to his bedroom, where the next portion of our evening commenced. Where he didn't have to worry about me asking questions.

Because his bed was the only safe space in his house.

Was that why we had sex so often? Because if he was fucking me, I wasn't asking him uncomfortable questions?

Probably. I'd let that sting tomorrow.

Tonight, I shoved it aside and got lost in Wilder's body. Until he exhausted me so thoroughly all I could do was fall asleep on his chest.

His heartbeat had become the soundtrack to my dreams. Even though it would never truly be mine. Not when it would always belong to Amie.

CHAPTER SIXTEEN

WILDER

IT WAS JUNE.

School ended in June. Iris was leaving in June.

Fucking June.

"Slut."

My head whipped toward the hallway.

Slut? No way I'd heard that right.

"Fuck you, Ryan!"

Now *that* I'd heard without question. A shriek that sent me to my feet.

It was loud enough to carry over the noise of kids slamming locker doors and chattering as they packed their things for the day. But most of the noise had stopped by the time I made it to the hallway. Kids stood wide-eyed staring at Sadie and Ryan.

"Don't call me a slut." She shoved at his shoulders as tears welled in her eyes.

So I had heard it right.

Ryan bent down, getting in her face. "You fucking cheated on me."

"No, I didn't! I just said I liked someone else and that's why I don't want to get back together with you."

"Who is this other guy, huh?" Ryan's voice was nearly a shout. "Is it one of my friends?"

"It's none of your business," she spat.

"Who?"

"Hey," I barked, loud enough to snare everyone's attention.

Larke came rushing out of her classroom, no doubt having heard the argument too.

"Everyone but Ryan and Sadie, get going." I crossed my arms over my chest and jerked my chin toward the doors. "Anyone here after thirty seconds has detention for a week."

Kids burst into action, stuffing books and jackets in backpacks before running for the exit.

When the last student filed out, Larke went to stand by Sadie's side, putting an arm around her shoulders.

Sadie ducked her chin until her blond hair curtained her face, but it wasn't enough to hide the tears and quiet sobs.

"My classroom." I snapped my fingers at a fuming Ryan. "Now."

With a huff, he marched my way.

Larke gave me wide eyes as she steered Sadie that direction too.

I took a long breath, casting my gaze to the ceiling. Fuck, but I hated this kind of drama. Summer break couldn't come fast enough.

Sadie was furiously wiping her cheeks dry when I joined everyone in the room.

Larke and I shared another look, and in it, a silent conversation.

Did she want to mediate this one? Or was I taking the lead?

She shrugged. My call.

Fine. I'd be the heavy.

"He thinks I cheated on him," Sadie blurted. "But I didn't."

Ryan's nostrils flared, but before he could speak, I held up a hand.

"I didn't ask what happened. You two need to sort this out on your own time. Cursing at each other in the school's hallway is not the place."

Sadie's mouth turned down at the corners. More tears.

God, I hated tears.

"You two broke up, right?" I braced my hands on my hips.

Iris had met with Sadie a couple of times to answer questions about being an influencer, and she hadn't mentioned any reconciliation between the teens.

"Yeah," Sadie sniffled.

"Then what does it matter?" I asked Ryan. "Sounds like she's moved on. You should too. Let it go."

He dropped his scowl to the floor. The shithead wouldn't listen.

"And watch your language in these hallways," Larke told Sadie. It didn't have as much bite as my scolding for Ryan, but at least they'd both gotten reprimanded.

"You each have detention," I said. "I know today is the last day for seniors, but I expect to see you Monday afternoon. If you skip, you can forget your diplomas."

Ryan's jaw clenched along with his fists.

"Sadie, get your stuff and head home."

She nodded, giving Ryan a lethal glare as she passed him for the door.

We all stood around in silence, listening as she opened her locker and collected her things. Then once the locker door slammed and the exterior door swung shut, I sighed.

"Ryan, word of advice that you're probably not going to listen to, but I'm going to give it anyway."

He didn't look up from the floor.

"Someday, you're going to regret the things you say to a woman in the heat of the moment. Be cautious with your words. They'll end up hurting you more than they'll ever hurt her."

I felt Larke's stare but didn't take my eyes from Ryan.

He thought about it for a long moment, then he jutted up his chin. "Can I go?"

Yeah, he wasn't going to take that advice to heart. In one ear, out the other.

"Go." I waved him toward the door.

Larke blew out a long breath once Ryan was gone. "I'm so glad it's Friday."

"Same." I walked to the hallway just as Ryan blew through the nearest exit.

Larke fell in step beside me as we walked to the door. Hopefully, Sadie had already headed home, but just in case, I wanted to make sure her argument with Ryan didn't get relocated to the parking lot.

The afternoon sun was bright. Laughter and voices filled the air as kids made their way to school busses or their parents' vehicles. The middle schoolers and some elementary kids came running over to the bus loop from their school.

"Still miss fifth grade?" I asked Larke.

"Every day." She laughed, her hand splaying across her pregnant belly. "Though high school is growing on me."

A younger student waved at her, then came rushing over to give her a hug. Probably one of her former fifth graders.

While Larke asked the girl about school and weekend plans, I scanned the parking lot for signs of Sadie. I didn't see her but I found Ryan storming to his car and ripping the door open. Then he slid into the driver's seat and roared out of the parking lot.

Would it break my heart if he got pulled over by the sheriff's department? Definitely not. They often stationed a cruiser on the next block to keep the high school kids from speeding.

A minute later, when the wail of a siren filled the air, I grinned.

"Well, that was an eventful end of the week," Larke said as the girl she'd been talking to jogged away to catch her bus. "I'm so ready for summer."

"Me too."

"Any plans?"

I shook my head. "Not really. Same as usual. My parents come to visit from Utah every June. Otherwise, I usually have plenty of work to do around the house and yard. I'll go fishing and hiking. Maybe take a road trip somewhere. We'll see."

Larke gave me a sideways glance.

"What?"

"I think that might be the most you've ever spoken to me before. At least, about yourself."

I scoffed, though she was right. This might be the most I'd ever voluntarily spoken to Larke, period. But something was different today. The tightness in my chest when she was around was still present but . . . less. Why?

Was it because I'd told Iris about Larke and Amie's resemblance? Was it because Larke was pregnant and it had changed her features slightly, softening them over the past few months?

Huh. I rubbed my jaw, not sure what to think about this.

"Well, have a good weekend, Abbott."

"You too," I muttered as she walked away.

I lingered outside for a while longer, watching as the kids left and the busses pulled away. Then I headed inside to finish up. I'd just zipped up my backpack when my phone vibrated in my pocket.

COME DOWNTOWN

I chuckled. Iris liked to text in capital letters.

Not even a please?

Her reply was instant. *PLEASE*

Where?

FIND ME

I left the school in more of a hurry than normal, excitement fueling my steps. It was busy downtown, the beginning of the summer tourist rush. There were more out-of-state cars than Montana vehicles parked along First.

The only free space was at the far end of the street, so with my keys and phone stowed in a jeans pocket, I set out along the sidewalks, weaving past people window-shopping and exploring.

It only took three blocks until I found Iris. Her back was to me, her blond hair covered in a straw hat. The scarf she'd tied around the brim today was black with small, pale-pink flowers. The scarf coordinated with her magenta satin dress. Not to match, but to *go*.

The dress's slinky straps crisscrossed over her shoulder blades, and the hem of the skirt hit her high on her thighs, showcasing that new tattoo she'd gotten in Bozeman.

The dress could have passed for lingerie. Hell, maybe it was. I didn't give a shit. She looked incredible and there was something addictive about knowing I'd be the man to take it off her later tonight, and that dress would be puddled on my bedroom floor.

Damn, but I craved her. More and more each day. What was I going to do when she left?

Guess I'd find out in a month.

Iris had her phone raised, arms high in the air as she tried to take a photo aimed toward the end of the street.

I came up behind her and snatched the phone from her grip.

She whirled, the shock on her face instantly shifting to a smile when she saw it was me. "You found me."

"I found you." I jerked my chin ahead. "Go stand over there."

"Why?"

I waved her phone.

She skipped ahead about twenty feet, then dazzled me with a blinding smile. She had on round sunglasses, hiding those brilliant blue eyes. Another piece of her ensemble I'd remove later, just like her platform heels.

After taking a handful of photos, I gave her back her phone, then the two of us started walking.

"Where are we going?" I asked.

"Nowhere. Anywhere. We're just wandering."

My knuckles brushed against her arm but she didn't try to hold my hand. I hadn't held hands with a woman in, well . . . a long time. Maybe Iris could sense I didn't like it. Maybe she didn't like it either.

But the longer we walked, the more I relaxed.

"When is the last time you just walked up and down First?" she asked.

"Years." When I came downtown, it was for a purpose. Either to grab dinner at the White Oak or a drink at Jane's. Even those instances were rare.

"That's why I put a limit on where I stay. So I can appreciate each place. When you live somewhere for years on end, it's too easy to take it for granted. Stop appreciating it."

Sure, maybe some people did take their hometown for granted. Maybe she saw that with her own family in Mount Pleasant. But that didn't have to be the only outcome when you chose a place to grow roots. "I don't take Calamity for granted."

She looked up to me. "You just said you never come down here to walk around."

"That doesn't mean I don't appreciate my town. But I don't need to explore. This place is already a part of me. I don't take that for granted."

Iris nodded but stayed quiet. Did she believe me? Or was she so used to bouncing from place to place, reveling in the newness of a town, that she'd already dismissed the idea of settling in and becoming part of a community?

"Hey, Mr. Abbott." Liam came running our direction. He was with a few of his other buddies, seniors out celebrating their last official day of high school.

"Liam."

He held up his hand for a fist bump. "Gonna miss me?"

Actually, I might. "Definitely not."

He guffawed, about to join his friends as they passed by us, but then he noticed Iris. His eyes bugged out as they traveled down her dress.

She just laughed. "Hello."

"H-hi." He blushed the same shade of hot pink as her dress.

"Have a good weekend, Liam. Stay out of trouble." I put my hand on the small of Iris's back, urging her on and away from my students.

We walked another block, then Iris took out her phone, snapping more photos as I nodded to the few familiar faces we passed.

"Where are you going next?" It was a question that had been plaguing me all week.

Maybe if I asked about it, if I talked about her leaving enough, it wouldn't bother me so much when she was gone. It would be my constant reminder that this was temporary. I couldn't get accustomed to her in my house, my life.

"I don't know." She put her phone away. It was hard to tell how she was feeling with her eyes covered, but there was a change of tone in her voice. A sadness.

Or maybe that was just me, hoping she'd miss Calamity.

"I've had this strange feeling lately," she said.

"What do you mean?"

"I don't know. It's hard to describe." She slowed her

pace. "I guess some days I feel lost and found, all at the same time. I don't know where home is and that bothers me. But I don't know if I need or want a home. I just feel like . . . I don't know. Does that make any sense?"

"Yeah." I brushed my knuckles against her arm.

She looked up and gave me a forced smile. "Have you ever been to Hawaii?"

"Once." My honeymoon.

"I haven't. Maybe what I need is a vacation on the beach to fix my mood. The last time I was at a beach was a year ago in Ibiza."

"Ibiza."

"Ibiza." She let out a dreamy sigh. "You know that green T-shirt I was wearing the other night with the Spanish flag?"

Another man's shirt. Some asshole from Ibiza.

My jaw clenched.

"Kidding." She giggled. "I'm only kidding. It's so much fun to torture you."

I laughed, something I'd done more since she'd come to Montana than I had collectively in years.

Iris shifted her sunglasses, her gaze locked on my mouth.

"What?"

"Your smile. I love to see it."

That was the way I felt about hers. "Your torture might make me smile, but the torture from my students today? Not so much."

"Uh-oh. What happened?"

As we walked, I told her about Sadie and Ryan's fight. A worry line creased her eyebrows.

Sadie had invited Iris to her graduation party next weekend, and after making sure I didn't have a problem with it,

Iris had accepted. Hopefully by then, the drama with Ryan would be old news.

"Dinner?" I asked as we walked past Jane's.

"Yes, please. Lunch was forever ago. I'm starved. But if I have a beer, you'll have to drive home."

"We'll leave my truck downtown tonight. Come get it in the morning."

We ducked into the bar, finding an open booth. We each devoured a burger with fries, watching as people milled in and out. And when we finally paid our tab and ventured outside, the sunset colored the horizon gold.

Maybe it was the beer I'd had with dinner, but as we walked to where she'd parked the Bronco, I took Iris's hand in mine, just to see how it fit.

Perfectly. Too perfectly.

The best it had ever been.

That realization made me drop her hand. But ten seconds without and my palm felt too empty. So I picked it up again.

And held it the whole way home.

CHAPTER SEVENTEEN

IRIS

that bold red lip #thelifeofirismonroe

THE LAST GRADUATION party I'd attended was my own.

Had it been this stuffy and boring? Probably.

I sipped a glass of lemonade from the chair I'd taken in the corner of Sadie's deck. Most of the guests were in the yard, standing in clusters, also drinking lemonades or iced teas. The conversation was muted and demure. Laughter was as sparse as the shade.

I shifted my chair deeper under the roof's overhang, out of the direct sunlight. But before this seat had come open, I'd spent an hour standing at the deck's railing. The tops of my shoulders felt much too hot. The sunscreen I'd slathered on before leaving Wilder's wasn't cutting it.

Sadie's dad walked out of their house carrying a massive umbrella. Cheers rang out as he took it toward the yard. It was the most excitement I'd seen since getting here.

There was a table on the other side of the deck with its own umbrella, but the chairs were occupied by grand-mothers and aunts—Sadie had done introductions when I'd arrived earlier. According to my phone, it was only in the seventies. Far from scorching temperatures. But there wasn't a cloud in the sky and the sun was relentless in its quest to give me a nasty burn.

Sadie walked out of the house, wearing a shaky smile. She spotted me and immediately came over, almost like she was hiding from everyone else. "Thanks for coming today."

"Of course." It was the fifth time she'd thanked me for being here.

"Be right back." She ducked inside again, emerging with a chair that must belong at the dining room table. She set it right against the house, like me, slinking into the shade. "Sorry this is sort of boring."

"Not at all," I lied, giving her a kind smile.

It was fucking awful.

Not a soul at this party other than Sadie had attempted any sort of conversation with me. Sure, when she'd done introductions, the other guests had said hello. But it had been impossible to miss the judgmental stares and whispered comments about my tattoos, my clothes or my makeup.

I'd thought today's outfit of a white tube top and gray trousers was fairly conservative. It was less revealing than most.

Yet the men here had all given me sideways glances, keeping a healthy distance from my chair. The women either avoided looking my direction entirely or had stared a bit too long and hard. It was like going home to visit my parents and tagging along to Mom and Dad's church.

Maybe I should have gone with pink lipstick instead of red. Was the bold shade the element that pushed my ensemble beyond a small-town graduation party's boundaries?

Whatever. My followers on Instagram and TikTok seemed to appreciate the red from the tutorial video I'd posted earlier. The people at this party could take their attitudes and fuck right off.

But for Sadie's sake, I kept my smile wide and posture relaxed. "How's it going? Get any good presents today?"

"Yours was the best. Thank you again. You didn't need to do that."

"A girl should always have designer perfume." A bottle of my favorite scent from Louis Vuitton had arrived yesterday, just in time for her party.

"Sadie." Her mother waved her over to the table.

"Sorry." She sighed. "Be right back."

As she hurried to the table, I took another sip of lemonade and tried not to make it obvious as I checked the time.

Wilder had been busy this past week with the final days of school for the freshmen, sophomores and juniors. Yesterday, they'd dismissed the school at noon, but he'd stayed late to help prep for graduation today. Then he'd disappeared this morning for the ceremony.

I'd worked while he was gone, filming the lipstick video and taking photos for Kim. Then I'd driven into town for Sadie.

Wilder had been invited to a string of parties, proof that he wasn't as grumpy with his students as he pretended to be.

Clearly, they loved him enough to invite him to their parties, Sadie included. But he hadn't made it here yet.

I'd planned to wait for him, but I wasn't sure I could take another hour of sour lemonade and equally bitter smiles. Since everyone here was ignoring me, I'd just ignore them right back. I opened my phone and started to scroll.

Most of the comments and messages Kim had already tackled. I loved her efficiency but today, I needed her to slack a bit. Since there wasn't much new activity, I opened up my photo album and tapped on the video I'd watched countless times. The video of Wilder and me outside his house when he'd taken photos of me and held my phone hostage. The volume wasn't on, but I didn't need it to hear the low rumble of his laugh. I watched it twice. Halfway through the third round, Sadie returned.

"I'm back. Sorry. Want more lemonade?" she asked.

"No, thanks. Are you having fun?"

She shrugged. "I guess. It will be more fun once my friends come over. But they all have their own parties first."

"Are you doing anything fun to celebrate tonight?"

"The school has an annual all-night party for the seniors after graduation. A bunch of us are going. The parents plan it, probably so we all don't go out drinking. It should be fun as long as Ryan doesn't act like a jerk."

Wilder had told me about his "slut" comment on the last day of school.

Definitely not liking Ryan much.

"What about the guy you like? Is he coming over today?" I asked.

"He said he would." Her cheeks flamed. "I hope so. I'll point him out. You're probably the only person here who—"

"Hey, Sadie." Her dad walked over, cutting her off. At his side was another man wearing a University of Montana polo. "Rich and I were just talking about the School of Business at U of M."

"I know the dean of students pretty well from my time in Missoula," Rich said. "Your dad said you're coming for a campus visit soon. I could set up a meeting."

"Um, sure." Sadie's smile was as forced as the ones I'd been sending out all day. "Thanks."

Her dad nodded, following Rich back to their spot in the yard. But that nod made my skin crawl. It was the same nod I'd gotten from my own father during my senior year. He'd taken my agreement to apply to colleges as my acceptance of the future he wanted me to chase. Of the path he wanted me to follow.

Sadie waited until they were gone, then slouched in her chair. She studied her hands in her lap, almost like she was afraid to look at me. Like she had to worry that *I'd* judge her.

"I have another gift for you," I said, reaching behind my neck to unclasp my compass rose necklace.

It was an impulse to take off the jewelry. My neck felt naked without it, but something in my heart said this was the time to let it go. That Sadie needed it more than me. "Here."

"Oh, no. This is too much. Plus the perfume."

"Take it." I took her hand, prying her fingers open, then dropped it into her palm. "I bought this in a little jewelry shop in Prague. It's always been a good reminder that I am finding my own way. That even though others might think I'm lost, I'm exactly where I am meant to be. Maybe for you, that's college. Maybe not. All that matters is you set your own course."

Her eyes flooded as she held the necklace, staring at it for a long moment. "I can't take this. It's too special."

"That's why you have to take it. We all need special gifts."

It just happened that for me, that necklace was a gift I'd bought myself. And each time I'd held it, it had given me courage. But I didn't need that bravery anymore. I wore the necklace because I loved it, not because I needed it.

"Someday, when you're ready, give it to someone else who needs it," I told her.

She didn't move. She just stared at her open hand.

I closed her fingers over the necklace. "Okay?"

"Okay," she whispered. Then with trembling fingers, she took the necklace and put it on.

"Pretty." And exactly where it should be.

Sadie reached for me, pulling me into a crushing hug. "Thank you."

"Welcome."

The doorbell rang, forcing us apart.

"Sadie, will you get that?" her mom called.

She nodded and swallowed hard, wiping under her eyes before darting inside.

I finished the last bit of my lemonade, about to stand and sneak away, when a towering form followed Sadie through the patio door.

"Mr. Abbott. Welcome." Sadie's mom practically leapt from her chair as she hurried to come over and shake Wilder's hand. "Can I get you some lemonade?"

"Sure." He dipped his chin, then scanned faces. Searching.

The minute he spotted me in the corner, his forehead furrowed.

But before he could come over, a group of guys from the lawn walked onto the deck stairs to shake his hand and say hello.

He was inundated with small talk. And as much as I wanted to watch him in full-blown Mr. Abbott mode, I was too hot and very ready to go home. So I slipped out of my chair and made my quiet getaway.

The driveway was crammed with cars. I squeezed through the narrow gaps to the street, looking both ways before walking to the Bronco parked on the opposite curb. There looked to be at least one other graduation party in this neighborhood farther down the block.

I had dug the keys from my handbag, about to unlock the Bronco's doors, when I heard my name.

"Iris." Wilder caught up to me, wrapping his hand around my elbow. "Where are you going?"

"Back to the house. I'm graduation partied out."

"You okay?"

"Yeah," I lied. No. Maybe. I just felt . . . blah.

That party had been so much like being at home. I had a strange, icky feeling. It was the first time I'd felt such blatant judgment since I'd been in Calamity. And I didn't want to stay so long that it put a damper on my love for this little town.

"Hey." He slid his hand up my arm, bringing it to my face.

"Hi." I leaned into his touch. "How were the other parties?"

"I'm graduation partied out too."

"You can't leave yet. Sadie's the sweetest, so you have to stay just a little while."

"I will." He sighed. "You seem off."

"Totally on. But I think I got a little sunburned. I just need to cool down."

His eyes narrowed.

Somehow, in just over a month, he'd gotten too good at reading me. I equally loved and hated that familiarity we had with each other. People who were just having casual sex shouldn't be good at seeing through the other's lies. They shouldn't make the other dinner every night and coffee every morning. They shouldn't spend every available minute together.

They shouldn't fall in love.

Not that Wilder loved me.

Not that I loved Wilder. Not quite. Not yet.

But damn, it was so close. It was inevitable. Like the spinning of the earth or the rising of the moon. Before I left Montana, I would be in love with Wilder Abbott.

And that fucking sucked.

His heart was already taken. I was selfish enough to want all or nothing. I wanted his whole heart, and the hard truth was I'd never have it.

"You go party." I smiled, hoping it reached my eyes. "I'm feeling like pizza tonight. I'm going to swing by the Pizza Palace."

" 'Kay." He traced his thumb along my cheek, not letting me go. Then he bent and sealed his lips over mine, undoubtedly smearing my lipstick across his mouth and mine.

His other arm banded around my back, hauling me closer until just my toes touched the pavement.

Wilder held me to him, our mouths pressed together. His tongue tickled my lower lip, but before he deepened the kiss, he loosened his hold and pulled away.

"Uh-oh." I reached for his lips, wiping at the lipstick. "Definitely not hiding that."

The corner of his mouth turned up before he brought his hand to his mouth, wiping it too. "Did I get it?"

I laughed. "Not even close."

He passed me for the Bronco, bending to inspect his mouth in the window's reflection. Then he stood tall and turned to me again, taking my face in his hands. Wilder kissed my forehead, then let me go. "See you soon."

We both turned to see Sadie standing at the mouth of the cramped driveway.

Her gaze darted between us, her eyes wide.

It wasn't like Wilder and I had been a secret around Calamity. Anyone who'd been at Jane's or downtown could have seen us together. But the shock on Sadie's face suddenly made me feel guilty. Like I should have told her I was staying with her teacher.

"Sadie—"

"Him?" She blinked and shook her head. "You're with Mr. Abbott?"

"Yes?" Sort of.

I wasn't sure what I'd expected but the look of sheer betrayal, of hurt, that crossed her face was definitely not it.

She shook her head again, her hands going to her hair. Then she turned on a heel and raced away, the skirt of her white sundress flowing behind her as she disappeared inside the house.

"What the hell was that about?" Wilder asked.

"I don't know."

Why would she be upset that I was with Wilder? Because I hadn't told her about him at our regular coffee meetups? No way. Sadie was so levelheaded. Something else had to be going on.

"I'll go talk to her." I took a step but stopped.

Standing nearly in the middle of the street, it hit me like a speeding bus.

Sadie liked someone else. That was why she'd broken it off with Ryan. She'd told me she wouldn't do anything until after graduation. That Ryan and everyone would freak. And on the deck earlier, she'd been in the middle of saying something to me. About how I would be the only person to . . . something.

To what? To understand?

"Oh my God." I slapped a hand to my heart as my stomach dropped. "No."

"Iris?" Wilder's hand came to my elbow.

"I'm such an idiot."

"What is going on?"

I looked up at him, at those beautiful, dark eyes and that insanely handsome face, and knew my hunch was right.

Wilder was perfect. And in all his years of teaching, I doubted that Sadie was the only student to have a crush on him.

CHAPTER EIGHTEEN

WILDER

THE DRIVE from Sadie's house to my own didn't erase my shitty mood. I parked beside the Bronco and climbed out, slamming the truck's door too hard before stomping inside behind Iris.

If she was upset about Sadie, it didn't show.

Meanwhile, my frustration was rattling my bones.

Sadie had a crush on me. That was Iris's theory. I'd denied it at first, refusing to believe it was true. But, maybe? This was my fucking nightmare. And this was so fucked up.

"Are you okay?" Iris asked as I kicked the door closed.

"Nope." No, this was definitely not okay.

What if Iris was wrong? She could be wrong.

She *had* to be wrong.

"Maybe I should have tried talking to her." Iris sighed.

"It's best that we just left."

When she'd offered to go back inside Sadie's house, I'd insisted that we leave. This was something that could destroy my career. Effective immediately, I had no reason to talk to Sadie Brown again. If she did have a crush on me, the last thing I needed was to be seen with her.

I tossed my keys aside and moved toward the couch, but I was too antsy to sit, so I paced in front of the windows and dragged a hand through my hair.

Sadie had a thing for me. *No. No way.* She'd been with Ryan for most of the year. Was this why he thought she'd cheated? Because she wanted me?

My stomach roiled.

"She's just a kid." That was the only way I'd ever seen her. A kid. A student. I was her teacher.

Iris went to the leather armchair and sat on its edge. "She's not that much younger than me."

"You're twenty-five. She's eighteen. That's a big difference."

"Seven years."

"Don't," I snapped. The idea that she'd compare herself to one of my students made my skin crawl. "It's not the same."

Iris held up her hands. "I'm just saying it's not all that shocking that a student has a crush on you."

Why wasn't she more shocked by this? Why didn't this seem to bother her? It was almost like . . . *she knew.*

What the hell? "Did you know about this?"

Iris blinked. "What?"

"Did you know about this?" I repeated. "About Sadie and if she had a, uh, you know." I couldn't say it. I couldn't even fathom a student having sensual feelings toward me, let alone speak it aloud.

Iris stared at me for a long moment, her mouth parted

and her eyes wide. There was the shock I'd been missing. With it came hurt and insult. *Shit.*

Before I could backpedal, her blue eyes narrowed and her nostrils flared. "I cannot believe you just asked me that."

"Well, you're the one who's spent all this time with her," I muttered.

The glare she sent me could flay a man. "I met with her three times. Three. You saw her every day. Why didn't *you* know about this?"

"Probably because I was busy teaching her, not socializing over coffee and telling her about my galivanting lifestyle."

If Iris had looked pissed before, her expression was murderous now.

Fuck my life. This was the time when I should shut up. When I should stop digging myself into a deeper hole. Hadn't I learned anything from Amie? Hadn't I learned to shut the hell up when arguing with a woman?

No. Clearly, I hadn't learned a goddamn thing.

"You do not get to take your frustration out on me." Iris shot to her feet, hands fisted at her sides. "You do not get to blame this on me. She's eighteen. She's got this whole future ahead of her and everyone is shoving her down one road while she wants to take another. And yeah, maybe that road she's on means she'll be *galivanting* around. That's her choice. It's her life. And she's trying to figure it all out."

Her chest heaved, her body practically vibrating with rage.

This time, I stayed quiet.

"Is it really so shocking that a student would have a crush

216

on you? You have a mirror, Wilder. Do you really think she's the first student who has had feelings for you?"

I cringed. Fuck, I didn't want to think about that. To reevaluate the kids I'd had in class and overanalyze our interactions.

It wasn't like I hadn't thought about this. But I kept my distance. Most of the time I was such a grumbling ass, the kids were the ones to steer clear. If I'd even had an inkling that Sadie had feelings, I would have done things differently. *Shit.*

"I get that you're uncomfortable," Iris said. "I get that this is surprising. But before you lash out at the only other person in this house, take a minute to think. She's young. She's at a pivotal time in her life. You're handsome. You're witty. And I'm guessing you're one of the only people who isn't pressing her to make a decision about what she'll do next."

Maybe. I didn't know. I didn't know Sadie well enough to gauge her personal problems. I wasn't the school's guidance counselor, and unless a student came to me asking for advice, I kept my opinions to myself.

I just taught science.

Though Sadie had asked me for advice. And I'd told her college wasn't for everyone. I'd told her she was smart and witty and kind.

Was that a mistake? Should I not compliment students anymore? *Fuck my life.*

"This is no one's fault, Wilder. Not mine. Not yours. Not Sadie's. She's entitled to feel how she feels. But you getting pissed off at me is complete bullshit." With that, she left me standing alone in my living room.

Iris slammed the door to her bedroom so hard it shook the walls.

"Son of a bitch," I groaned, tipping my head to the ceiling.

Nine years and I'd forgotten how it felt to fight with a woman. To lose a fight with a woman. Though Iris fought differently than Amie had fought.

Amie would have cried. Any time I'd made an asshole remark, she'd burst into tears.

Not Iris. There'd be no tears tonight.

Though she might castrate me in my sleep.

Trudging to the couch, I sat down and unbuttoned the cuffs of my shirt, rolling up the sleeves. Then I leaned my elbows to my knees and stared outside.

Sadie? Really?

I replayed the past year. The years before that. The apples she'd bring left over from her lunch. Her small talk about my weekend plans. Had that dead battery on her car this spring been a ruse?

Should I have noticed? Why hadn't I noticed?

A chill rolled down my spine. I was old enough to be Sadie's father.

At least the school year was over. My only reprieve was that come Monday morning, I'd have an empty classroom and wouldn't be forced to see Sadie. Though I was sure I'd never stare at her stool the same way again.

And I'd never take another apple from a student.

"Damn it." I pinched the bridge of my nose, letting the sting of Iris's tongue-lashing fade. Then I replayed her lecture, this time, hearing the words.

It wasn't her fault. It wasn't Sadie's. It wasn't mine.

But it was still fucked up.

"Hell," I muttered, then stood, walking to Iris's bedroom.

When I knocked, she said, "Go away."

I opened the door anyway.

She was sitting in the middle of her bed, legs criss-crossed. In the few minutes since she'd left me in the living room, she'd wiped off the rest of her red lipstick and changed out of the tube top and into an oversized T-shirt, this one blank and dusty pink.

For once, maybe it was a shirt she hadn't stolen from a man.

But just in case I was wrong, I'd rip it off her later too.

Her feet were bare and her flowy pants pooled at her calves. Her mouth was pursed and her eyebrows pulled together with a scowl.

She looked mad.

She looked like mine.

That realization rocked me on my feet. I leaned into the doorjamb, letting it take the weight of my shoulder.

Iris was mine.

Somehow, she'd worked her way into my life over the past month. The idea of letting her go was worse than any student crush. Worse than the idea of telling Danny I was falling for his sister.

Worse than knowing she'd likely leave even if I asked her to stay.

But if the past nine years had taught me anything, it was how to carry on. How to survive. Past the guilt. Past the regret. Past the heartache.

I'd survive when Iris was gone.

But that didn't mean I had to like it.

"Hungry?" I asked. Her plan to get pizza had been abandoned after the Sadie incident.

"Not really." She picked at a piece of invisible lint on her knee.

"It caught me off guard. Sorry."

She shrugged.

"Iris."

"Wilder."

I waited until she finally looked up and met my gaze. "I'm sorry."

Her anger deflated with her posture.

We stared at each other but didn't speak. Usually it was her job to fill the quiet moments. She asked the questions. She insisted on the communication.

Without her voice to fill the void, it was miserable. Lonely. A hint of what was to come when the month was over.

It was so unsettling that I tore my gaze from hers, the first to break, and glanced around the bedroom. There wasn't much reason for me to spend time in here.

It was a room I'd set up specifically for my parents. It had the necessities, a bed and two nightstands. But other than occasionally coming in to dust and vacuum, there wasn't a reason to be in here. And it was easier to avoid that closet if I just stayed away.

This was the one room where Iris and I hadn't had sex. We'd been together in every other room, on nearly every surface. Just earlier this week, I'd found her in the laundry room and rather than carry her to my bed, I'd hoisted her up on the dryer and plunged inside her tight body.

Part of me wanted to leave this bedroom immediately. To

jerk my chin and have her follow me out. But there was something in Iris's gaze, a challenge maybe, like she could read my thoughts and fears.

Was I so scared of the boxes stacked behind that closed closet door that I wouldn't even cross the threshold?

Maybe. Only one way to find out.

I shoved off the door and took a step. Then another.

Iris tracked them both, her gaze darting to my shoes before lifting to my face again. Then, once more proving she was in my head, she licked her bottom lip. It still had a faint trace of the red tint.

Fuck it.

I was on her in a heartbeat. My hands framed her face as I laid her down, her legs uncrossing and stretching long before wrapping around my back.

My cock swelled as I ground it into her center, earning a hiss. "Kiss me."

She lifted up off a pillow and placed a gentle kiss on the corner of my mouth. Then she did the same on the other corner, slowly working her way across my lips, side to side.

I braced on my elbows, hovering above her, as her fingers slid across my beard to my hair.

She gripped the strands and held me to her as she parted my lips with her tongue and slid inside. A low hum escaped her throat, the sound making me rock hard.

Even though I wanted to peel the clothes from her body, I let her play. She licked and nipped, soft and slow at first until that hold on my hair tightened and she forced my head to a slant so she could delve in deep.

Then her playtime was over. I dove into her mouth, devouring her as she held me close. Everything I should say got poured into that kiss. How much I craved her. How much I needed her. How much I wanted her to stay.

Iris arched her core against my arousal, earning a bite on her top lip. Her laugh filled the room with the sweetest sound. Almost as incredible as the sound she made when she came.

I broke away, leaning back to take her in.

Her cheeks were flushed. Her mouth rosy and wet. And those blue eyes were hooded, full of desire.

Weeks ago, I'd been in the kitchen when I'd heard her come. It had been muted and faint. Just a whimper and cry.

Either she'd used her finger. Or she had a toy.

An idea sparked.

Iris reached for my belt, but I swatted her hand away, instead loosening the clasp on her trousers. Then I climbed off the bed, taking the pants with me. Her panties came next, dragged down those toned, tattooed legs until they were tossed aside, unnecessary for the rest of the night. The shirt came off next—it would be optional once we were finished. If she wanted to walk around naked, I wouldn't stop her.

The compass rose necklace was gone, but I'd ask her about that later.

She stared up at me with those intoxicating eyes, watching my every move. When I stretched an arm for the closest nightstand, her breath hitched.

"You were thinking about me when you came." A statement, a reminder, as I felt around the drawer.

My fingers brushed a metal cylinder. Bingo. The toy was a small, bullet vibrator no bigger than my index finger. Its buzz was nearly as erotic as Iris's mewl when I turned it on.

"Have you used this lately?" I dragged it over her flesh, bringing it to a pebbled nipple.

"No." She arched into the contact, her eyes fluttering closed. "Not since we started."

"Good." With a knee, I nudged her thighs apart, bringing the toy over her heart and down the soft line of her belly.

Her breaths were shallow, her body tense with anticipation.

"How often did you use this before me?" I asked her.

Her eyes popped open.

"Tell me." I dragged the vibrator around her navel in a slow circle. "Every day?"

Iris nodded and pulled her bottom lip between her teeth, lifting her hips so I'd bring the bullet to her center.

"Show me," I ordered, my hand stilling.

She swallowed hard, then covered my hand with hers. With a gentle push, she brought the toy to her core, straight to her clit.

The vibration melted into my skin as she clutched my hand harder, adding pressure as she brought it up and down, circling that bundle of nerves until her mouth parted and a string of whimpers escaped.

Fuck, but she was gorgeous. As perfect as the sunrise. As dazzling as the stars. She hummed and moaned, her grip firm on mine as she eased off her clit to drag the toy through her wet slit.

"Come inside. Please," she begged.

So much of me wanted to watch her explode just like this. To have that memory for the years when she was gone. To picture her in some faraway hotel room, making herself come with this little vibrator. Hopefully with my name on those luscious lips.

But I wanted her to have a different memory. When she used this toy, I wanted my face in her mind. I wanted her to remember how it felt with my cock buried inside her while she massaged her clit.

So I pulled my hand away, taking the toy with me as I stripped out of my clothes.

She watched me, unblinking, as I returned to the bed and fitted myself between her legs. Then with the head of my cock at her entrance and the bullet on her clit, I thrust inside that wet heat.

Heaven.

"Wilder." She closed her eyes, a faint smile on her mouth. "Yes."

I pulled out and slammed forward so hard her breasts bounced. "You feel so fucking good."

"More." She met my thrusts with the roll of her hips. Her hands cupped her tits and her fingers twisted those pretty nipples.

The buzz of the vibrator mingled with our ragged breaths and the sound of our bodies colliding. It took next to no time for her inner walls to begin fluttering. Then her back arched and she gasped, just as her orgasm broke.

Her body jerked so hard she nearly came off the mattress, her pussy pulsing and clenching like a vise.

God, I'd never get enough of this. Never ever.

I closed my eyes, reveling in the heat coursing through my veins. The sheer pleasure building higher and higher.

Iris's limbs were still trembling, her orgasm drawn out by the toy, as I exploded, pouring inside her on a roar.

Every time it was better. Every. Fucking. Time.

How was that even possible? If we had years together, would it always be this good? Or was it good because we had two months?

We'd always be good. I knew that to the depths of my soul. We fit together. In perfect unison.

When I finally came down from my release, sweat coated my skin. The toy had fallen out of my grip and was resting on the bed, still vibrating.

Iris tossed an arm over her head, her chest heaving as she regained her breath. I pulled away and rolled, collapsing on the bed beside her to let the last of the white spots clear from my vision.

Then the vibrator's buzzing stopped. Iris tossed it aside.

"We're moving that toy to my room," I said.

A slow smile spread across her mouth. "Don't expect me to argue."

CHAPTER NINETEEN

IRIS

next stop? #thelifeofirismonroe

RESTLESS. I was restless.

I couldn't sit down for more than five minutes without getting up to do something. Anything. Get a glass of water. Look out the window. Lap the kitchen island, search for a crumb to sweep away.

Concentrating felt impossible. Social media couldn't hold my attention. Neither could the to-do list I'd been procrastinating.

I was restless.

Was I restless? Or was I just expecting to be restless, therefore I'd made myself restless?

"Ugh." I paced Wilder's living room.

Maybe this feeling was nothing but habit. I didn't know how to get off the hamster wheel. I'd been moving from place to place for so long that I'd forgotten how it felt to stop.

Could I stop? Did I want to stop?

Yes. An answer that scared the shit out of me. Because the place I wanted to stop was here. Calamity. How would Wilder feel about that?

He'd probably run for the hills.

After his early morning workout and sex in the shower, he'd gone to school for the day. The students were on break but the teachers were doing whatever it was that teachers did during those work weeks when there were no kids. When I'd asked Wilder about it, he'd just given me that one-shoulder shrug and said he'd be putting his classroom to rights and finishing up paperwork.

Normally, I would have asked for specifics. But I'd been in this strange mood since dawn, so I'd just smiled and hid my fidgeting fingers until he'd left the house. Then I'd let this restless energy out of its cage.

The monster was eating me alive.

I'd had such high hopes that I wouldn't feel like this in Calamity. That there'd be no itch to find my next destination. Things had been going so well. I'd settled into this slower pace in Calamity and into a routine with Wilder.

But then I'd woken up this morning and everything had just felt . . . wrong.

The jitters were impossible to quell. There was no focusing on anything but the jitters. And it had progressed to the point where I was coming out of my own skin.

Did I actually want to leave? Or was I just manifesting the expectations of others?

Kim had posted a photo today that was months old. It was a selfie of me wearing a quizzical look with a caption asking followers where I should go next. The comments had been flooding in for hours.

Morocco. Australia. Japan.

None sounded appealing, but people expected me to leave Montana. That was what I did. I lived in places two months at a time. My life was *go, go, go*.

Round and round. The wheel just kept on spinning.

I walked to the kitchen island and picked up my phone. Maybe my problem was I didn't have enough happening. Was this boredom?

Content for my latest brand deal was complete and approved. Kim would take care of scheduling the rest. We were negotiating another two deals but they were in their infancy. If they came to fruition, it would still be weeks before material was due.

There were always pictures to take for the feed, a video or two, but everything I captured at the moment felt shallow. Nothing was remotely as good as the pictures Wilder took.

Was I hungry? Maybe I was just hungry. I walked to the fridge and ripped open the door. But I wasn't hungry, so I slammed it shut. "Gah."

What was wrong with me?

Why couldn't I just relax and enjoy my time here? Read a book or something. Wilder had hundreds to choose from.

Should I call my family and check in? Definitely not.

Wilder had told me that Danny was still calling and texting a couple times a week. He was terrified, I was terrified, to talk to my brother.

So we were both ignoring Danny instead.

The chances of me winning Sister of the Year were slim.

I hadn't spoken to Danny in weeks. Wilder and I hadn't exactly come to an agreement, but there was an unspoken understanding between us.

This tryst or relationship or whatever the hell I was supposed to label us, was a secret we'd both keep from my family.

The guilt was there but it wasn't crippling. Danny had been texting Wilder, not me. And I hadn't heard from my parents either. These days, we usually only spoke whenever I was moving from one location to the next.

Just like everyone on my Instagram following, Mom, Dad and Danny were probably expecting a call soon, announcing my next destination.

If I stayed in Montana, would they come visit? In all of my travels, not once had my parents deigned to see where I was living. It had been easier not to feel bitter about that when my addresses had all been in Europe.

Utah wasn't exactly a stone's throw from Montana, but it was sure a hell of a lot closer than the United Kingdom.

I was bored. That was my problem. I didn't want to leave, I was just bored. Right?

My fingers flew across my phone's screen as I sent Wilder a text.

I'M BORED

Maybe he'd come back and solve this problem with his mouth. I paced for five more minutes, waiting for his reply. Nothing came.

I pulled up Sadie's name, my heart squeezing. Would she even want to hear from me? Guess there was only one way to find out.

COFFEE?

Another five minutes of pacing and neither of them had replied.

The walls were starting to get too close, too familiar, so I snagged my keys and wallet, then headed for the door.

It was busy downtown. Calamity was crawling with tourists. The line at the coffee shop was ten deep, and waiting to get a latte was excruciating since I had the patience of a gnat at the moment. But I waited since I had nothing else to do.

Were Danny and my parents right about my future? Was it time for me to get a real job? To go to college?

With my iced latte in hand, I walked up and down First for an hour. The movement helped. Sort of. By the time I returned to the Bronco, I didn't feel quite so uncomfortable, but I still had energy to do something else.

What? In another time, I'd hit the road and see where it took me. But Wilder would freak, and I didn't want him to worry.

Was that part of my problem? Was this imaginary leash beginning to choke?

No. In my heart of hearts, it didn't bother me that Wilder worried. That I changed habits so he wouldn't get anxious about my whereabouts.

That's just what you do when you love someone.

I loved him, didn't I?

"Freaking great," I groaned as I turned off the highway and onto his gravel lane.

I was in love with Wilder Abbott.

That wasn't supposed to happen. My poor, foolish heart wasn't strong enough to be broken. My stomach was in a nasty knot by the time I parked outside the house. The restless energy I'd shaken on the trip to town came back in force.

Maybe this had nothing to do with me leaving Montana.

And everything to do with the fact that I loved a man who didn't love me back.

It was almost like my body had realized it before my mind.

Dropping my head to the steering wheel, I sighed. "Well, this sucks."

I forced myself out of the Bronco and inside. And because I was still feeling antsy, I headed for the cleaning cabinet in the laundry room. The bed in my room was still rumpled from our escapades on Saturday, so I stripped the bedding and brought it to the washer. Then I deep cleaned the bathroom, leaving it gleaming.

Wilder's parents were coming to visit over the weekend. We hadn't talked about where I'd be sleeping. The couch? For all I knew, he'd gotten me a hotel room in town.

I wasn't going to hope that I'd be sharing his bed while he had guests. For this tryst to stay a secret, it would be best for me to play the part of his begrudgingly welcome houseguest.

Good thing I liked the couch.

With the bathroom clean, I moved to the bedroom to dust and vacuum. Then I opened the closet, finding a mess of my clothes on the floor and my three suitcases exploding.

It would be so much nicer to hang up my clothes, but not only were there zero hangers, the boxes took up most of the space.

Amie's boxes.

I stared at them, stacked and brown. They looked lonely. Forgotten. What was in them? Her clothes? Pictures? Keepsakes?

My fingers were fidgeting again.

Leave this closet, Iris. *GO.*

I sidestepped a suitcase, checking over my shoulder as I moved closer to the back wall.

What the hell was I doing? I pulled my lower lip between my teeth as I took another step closer.

The box in the top center of the stack wasn't taped like some of the others on the bottom. Instead, the flaps had been folded together.

DO. NOT. IRIS.

I picked up the box and set it on the floor. My fingers moved of their own accord, tugging one flap until the others popped open.

Wilder would evict me if he knew what I was doing. I'd be lucky to sleep on the couch.

I checked the door again and stood statue still, listening for any noise. Nothing. The house was dead quiet. So I leaned forward, peering past the flaps.

A familiar pair of dark eyes caught my attention. I crouched and reached inside, careful to lift out the photo.

Amie and Wilder's wedding photo.

Pain speared my heart. It robbed the air from my lungs. My balance faltered, and I landed with a thud on the closet's hardwood floor.

In the photo, they were standing at an altar in a church. The satin train of Amie's white, strapless gown spilled down a small set of stairs. Her arm was linked with Wilder's and in her hand was a bouquet of white roses.

She was gorgeous, breathtakingly so. Her chestnut hair was curled and pinned in an elaborate updo. She had the most symmetrical face I'd ever seen. It was flawless, with rosy cheeks, a cute nose and pretty smile.

And just like Wilder had told me, she looked so much like that other teacher—Larke—it was uncanny.

Wilder stood at Amie's side, broad and bold compared to her slender, willowy frame. He was dressed in a sharp black tuxedo. Without the rugged beard covering his chiseled jaw, he looked so much younger.

The smile on his face was brilliant. Blinding. It made the ache in my chest double.

Not once had I seen him smile like that.

Yes, I'd scored a few elusive smirks. Enough to make me believe I'd achieved my goal to see Wilder smile. But this picture only made me realize that I'd failed.

He'd been happy, hadn't he? Then she'd died and taken that happiness to her grave, leaving him alone with these memories hidden away.

Was that why this box hadn't been taped? So he could access it easily?

The edges of the picture were crisp, the corners sharp. It didn't look like a picture he'd touched a thousand times. Why wasn't it framed? Or had Wilder just been that careful with this one?

Below the wedding portrait, more loose photos were stacked haphazardly.

It had always bothered me that Wilder didn't have framed pictures in the house. Had he recently taken these down? Or had they lived in this box for years?

Careful not to scratch the surface or bend a corner, I set the wedding photo aside and took out the next. It was a picture of Amie dressed in a black graduation robe and square hat.

Wilder was in the background, also dressed in a gown, and talking to someone I couldn't make out.

It should have been easier to see since they weren't standing together. But they had been *together*. All of his memories from that time were with her. Graduation. Parties. Celebrations.

How many pictures had he taken since she'd died? Or was he clinging to the past, to the memories tucked away in these boring brown boxes?

I went through the pictures methodically, one by one, learning more about the man who'd captured my heart. And the woman who'd already claimed his.

If her clothes were anything to go by, she'd loved pastels. Soft and sweet. She'd worn glasses, and more often than not, her hair had been in a ponytail. She hadn't worn much makeup. She hadn't needed it with so much natural beauty.

Every other picture was of them together. Camping. Hiking. Attending a concert. Having drinks at a bar.

It was agony. But photo by photo, I made myself study them. Because this box was the reminder of why I had to move on. Why Calamity wasn't my stopping place.

Why Wilder would never be home.

The wedding photo should have been the hardest to take. But it was the last photo in the box that felt like the final dagger through my heart.

Wilder had his hands on her cheeks, framing her face. Amie had her eyes closed and a smile ghosted her mouth as she waited for him to kiss her.

It had to have been early in their relationship. They looked younger than any of the other pictures, but God, they'd been in love. The emotion all but radiated from the paper.

They were totally consumed with each other. Oblivious to whoever had the camera pointed their way. Maybe Danny had taken this one. He'd been a witness to their love story.

My eyes flooded. but I blinked the tears away and started the tedious process of returning the photos to the box. One by one, reversing the order I'd lifted them out in, I tucked Wilder's past away.

When the wedding photo was once more on the top, I refolded the box's flaps and stowed it away. Then I plopped down on the floor again, my body too drained to even manage leaving the closet.

What was I doing? How could I have just invaded his privacy like that? Wilder had invited me into his home, his life, and I'd just betrayed his trust. Regret crawled over my skin like a million spiders making me squirm.

The front door opened and the sound of Wilder's boots thudded on the floor. "Iris?"

I stayed quiet.

He'd find me.

It only took him a minute.

He stood in the doorway of the closet, dressed in his usual work attire of jeans and a button-down shirt. A crease formed between his eyebrows as he stared at me on the floor. "What are you doing?"

"I went through a box," I blurted. "The top one that wasn't taped. The one with the photos. I'm sorry."

Wilder rocked back on his heels like I'd slapped him. "You what?"

He'd heard me. He didn't need it repeated.

I dropped my chin. "I'm so sorry."

His shock vanished quickly enough. In its place, a cold fury zapped any warmth from his vicinity.

Wilder took that chilly rage with him as he stormed out of my room.

I swallowed the lump in my throat—I refused to cry over my own epic fuckup—and shoved to my feet, following him to the living room.

He was standing exactly where I'd expected him to be: at the windows, his glare aimed through the glass at the towering mountains in the distance.

"I had no right." My voice cracked.

His hands fisted and his shoulders bunched. He stayed quiet. Time to collect my suitcases. I was about to be evicted.

"I'm sorry, Wilder. I was curious. That's no excuse. You let me into your home, and I betrayed your trust. She was the love of your life, and what I did—"

"She wasn't."

My brain screeched to a halt. "Huh?"

Wilder didn't move, he didn't breathe, then all at once the tension left his body, like his very bones had melted away. His shoulders dropped. He hung his head. And then he spoke, so quietly I was certain I'd heard him wrong.

"She wasn't the love of my life."

CHAPTER TWENTY

WILDER

SHE WASN'T *the love of my life*.

It was true and untrue. Right and wrong. Speaking those words was equally freeing and condemning.

Amie hadn't been the love of my life.

Maybe if I'd admitted it before now, she'd still be alive.

"W-what do you mean?" Iris whispered.

I couldn't turn around. Coward that I was, I couldn't face her. I wasn't ready to see the disgust on her face. So I kept my gaze aimed forward, toward the view beyond the windows that had been my sanctuary for so many years.

But the mountains, the blue sky, those golden plains and miles of evergreen forests didn't provide a hint of relief from this crippling guilt.

"I loved Amie." Loved in the way of two people who'd spent years together and grown comfortable. Loved in the way of two people who'd shared memories and adventures. Loved in the way that once, she'd been my friend.

I hadn't loved her the way I was supposed to love her. Not in the way a husband should love his wife.

"But I wasn't in love with her." Not in the end. So much had faded from the beginning.

After years of replaying our relationship—from those easy, early days in college to the angry, hard days in our marriage—I remembered the affection. The fondness. The friendship.

It was love. Just not the kind that she'd deserved.

My throat felt too thick, my lungs straining to expand. There was a brick sitting on my chest and had been for nearly a decade. I'd grown so accustomed to its weight, now that it was shifting, now that the truth was wiggling free, I'd forgotten just how heavy it was.

Maybe it would have been easier to keep quiet and carry these secrets to the grave.

But hearing Iris say that I'd loved Amie, hearing the conviction and vulnerability in her voice, had been so wrong that I couldn't stop myself.

Iris really believed I'd loved Amie, didn't she? That was fair. So did the rest of the world.

Except I didn't want her lumped in with everyone else. Iris stood apart. She was special. And whatever she'd conjured in that beautiful mind was simply incorrect.

If there was one person on this earth who should know the truth, it had to be Iris.

Even if she hated me for it. Even if it drove her away.

"We started dating in college," I said. "You know that."

From the corner of my eye, I caught her nod.

"Being with Amie was never easy. Maybe that's life. Maybe being with someone is never easy."

Though in the time that Iris had been here, easy was exactly how I'd describe it. Sure, she asked thousands upon thousands of questions. She'd upended every single one of my routines. But still, it was easy. Like breathing. When she was here, it felt right.

"I don't know how to describe it. I guess . . . it was like riding a roller coaster. There was always an up. Always a down. At first, it was exciting. I chalked it up to us getting to know one another. I thought that was just how relationships worked themselves into steady. You had to suffer the storm for the calm waters. Does that make any sense?"

"Yes." Iris's voice was quiet, barely audible, like she was afraid to be too loud for fear that I'd stop.

"I thought if we just stuck it out, we'd be fine. It wasn't like we were miserable. We just fought." Too often. Too loud. "I chalked it up to us still figuring each other out. And I knew it would break her heart if I ended it. It would have hurt me too. So I took the coward's way out. Instead of calling it quits, I proposed."

When I looked back at our relationship, my mistakes were so clear, it baffled me that I hadn't seen them at the time. That I'd been so blind. But the scales of our love had been unbalanced. At least, that was how it seemed now. Amie had loved me more than I'd loved her. And in the end, it had cost her everything.

"Wilder, you're not a coward."

I finally risked a glance to my side.

Iris's eyes were full of understanding and sympathy. It would have been easier to stomach judgment.

"Don't look at me like that."

"You're not a monster for marrying a woman you cared about and dated for years."

"Are you sure about that?"

Iris raised her chin. "Yes."

I wanted to believe her. "I should have ended it. Let her go."

"You were friends. Lovers. You had a history. Is that really such a horrible foundation for a marriage?"

Yes. No. "I don't know," I murmured. "I guess it doesn't matter now."

There was no changing the past. There was only suffering its consequences.

Iris could make excuses and arguments and justifications until she was blue in the face. It wouldn't make the regret go away.

"I knew that first year after we were married it was a mistake. We were both unhappy but too deep in denial to admit it."

Iris slid closer. She didn't touch me or say anything, just shifted a few inches. She was here. She was listening.

"We coexisted. More like roommates than lovers." We'd slept in the same bed but hadn't touched often. Sex, on the rare occasions we'd both been in the mood, had lost its passion.

The progression from intense to mundane had just happened over those four years. Amie and I had never talked about it. We'd both seemed to accept that our sex life was boring and there wasn't anything to do about it. We'd drifted apart.

Day by day. Hour by hour. We'd fallen out of love.

Even friendship had felt impossible at times.

"We'd get in these stupid fights over nothing," I said. "God, they were stupid. I'd load the dishwasher wrong, we'd argue about it, and then I'd sleep in the guest bedroom for three days. She'd run her car out of gas, I'd lecture her on checking the damn gauge, and she'd cry for a week."

Our marriage of four years had become misery for us both, but we'd been too stubborn to admit it.

"I liked coming home from a hectic, loud day at school to peace and quiet. Amie would have the music turned up so loud I couldn't see straight. Everything I did seemed to make her cry. Everything. It was the tears that finally shoved me over the edge."

"What do you mean?"

"I realized one day that I saw her cry more than smile. And I just . . . couldn't do it anymore. To her. To me. I didn't want to look back on my life and have the memories be of tears. So finally, I told her I wanted a divorce."

Not a soul in this world knew about this. Not one.

"Oh," Iris whispered. "I didn't realize."

"No one does." I swallowed hard. "The night I told her it was over was the night of her accident."

The night Amie died.

Iris gasped, her hand flying to her mouth.

The ache in my chest was so fierce I pressed a hand to my sternum.

"I loved Amie. But I wasn't in love with her." My voice cracked. "And that's the reason she's gone."

"No, Wilder." Iris's hand wrapped around my forearm. "It was an accident."

I shook my head. "It was my fault. I broke her that night. I think she would have gone on pretending we were happy

241

for the rest of our lives. But she'd been starting to talk about kids and I just . . ."

The idea of having a baby simply because that was what married couples did next had been grating on me for months. It was part of the reason for all of Amie's tears. I'd told her I wasn't ready and every time, she'd cry and cry.

Rightly so. What kind of a man didn't want children with his wife?

"Do you not want kids?" Iris asked.

I gulped, hating myself for what I was about to say. "Not with Amie."

This was when Iris left. When she told me I was a sorry son of a bitch and never wanted to see me again. I'd help haul her suitcases to the Bronco.

But her grip on my arm didn't falter.

I waited, my heart thundering, for her to let me go. Any minute now, she'd rush out of this house and be gone forever.

But Iris stayed at my side, holding fast.

"She must have been crying. Maybe she would have seen the truck otherwise." Crying, because of me. Gone, because of me.

"What happened? The accident?"

"She was on the freeway. A guy driving a truck came flying across an onramp. He was drunk at four o'clock in the afternoon and slammed right into her. Rolled her car five times. He broke his arm. According to the police, she died on impact."

"Oh, Wilder." Iris sniffled. "I'm so, so sorry."

Me too. For Amie, I would always be sorry. She'd left the house because of me. She'd died because of me.

As long as I lived, that would always be the worst day of

my life. When the police had come to tell me she'd been in an accident, I hadn't believed the two officers. I'd actually stood in the doorway at my house and told them they had the wrong address.

But as they'd told me more and more details—her car, name and license plate number—it had started to sink in. Denial was a powerful adversary, and I'd still been skeptical, so I'd called her phone over and over again. Each time it had gone to voicemail.

That phone was in a box somewhere in the closet. Iris must not have found it today.

Instead, she'd just found photos of a life gone too soon.

"If I had waited, if I had told her differently, if I hadn't told her at all, if we hadn't gotten married . . . she'd still be here."

"You can't think like that," Iris said, shaking my arm. "It's not your fault. It's the drunk driver's fault."

No, the fault was mine.

That was not something she'd ever convince me of otherwise. That guilt would never end. It was as infinite as the stars in the night sky.

"People fall out of love," Iris said.

"Do they?" Or had it not been there to start with? "My parents are madly in love. You'll see when they're here on Friday. They can't be apart for more than a day at a time. They kiss and touch like my teenagers at the high school. That's what I grew up around."

The idea of falling out of love was entirely foreign to me.

Though maybe I wasn't built for the kind of love my parents had. Maybe it was so rare, it wasn't in my cards.

Amie and I had never had that sort of infatuation with each other.

But Iris? There was potential here. A possibility that was terrifying and electrifying.

Would this constant need to be close to her fade? It was pointless to worry. She was leaving at the end of the month. Soon, she'd be gone.

And I wouldn't have to fall out of love with another woman.

"Tell me about her. What was she like?" Iris asked.

"Why?" Why did she seem so interested in Amie?

"Because I don't think I'll be able to convince you that her death wasn't your fault. But maybe if you talk about her, it won't hurt as much."

It did hurt. I wasn't going to deny it. It had been hurting for nine damn years.

It had been a long, long time since I'd talked about Amie. It was easier to keep her inside. To keep her locked away with the regret for all I should have done differently.

"No."

"Please?"

"Iris."

"Please, Wilder. Just . . . try."

"Why?"

"So that maybe seeing Larke Thatcher won't bother you so much. So that maybe you'll look through those boxes your-self one day. So that you can move on."

With her?

Was that why she was asking? Because she didn't think I'd be able to move on?

Maybe Iris was right. Maybe this had to stop.

"She would have hated this house." I let my gaze rove the walls and windows as I spoke. "It would have been too quiet for her and too far from town. She wouldn't have liked Calamity either. It's too small. But she wouldn't have complained about it either. She didn't complain. She always said she didn't want to be that negative person who brings the people around her down."

Amie had been the sugar to my sour.

"She always needed to be doing something. Shopping. Meeting friends. Trying a new restaurant. She couldn't sit still. We'd watch a movie together and she'd get up ten times for a snack or water or to change a load of laundry. It used to wear me out just watching her."

I used to ask her to sit with me on the couch and just chill. Like the way Iris would sit with me while I was reading. Amie never lasted more than three minutes before she'd get bored and irritated with me for not wanting to *do something*.

But her energy had been contagious at times. We'd gone to concerts I would have skipped but was glad I hadn't. We'd experimented with restaurants I never would have chosen for myself.

"We were opposites," I told Iris. "I think it works for some couples. It didn't for us."

Our differences had become more and more noticeable over the years. Until they were a wedge forcing us apart.

She'd resented always having to shove me out the door. I'd gotten tired of fighting her to just stay home.

"We put up a good show to the world. To each other. No one knows this. I don't think Amie even told her family we were struggling. I sure as hell didn't tell mine. It was just easier to pretend."

And after she'd died, I'd been swallowed in grief and guilt. I'd come to Montana desperate to escape that house we'd moved into after our wedding. I'd needed a place where the echo of her crying didn't greet me each morning and haunt me every night.

I'd needed to get away from the people who'd thought we'd been the perfect couple.

"Danny never knew?" Iris asked.

I shook my head. "I told him once that we were fighting a lot. He told me it was just a rough patch. That after we had kids, we'd get through it. When I told him I wasn't sure we'd have kids, he told me to just wait another year."

Iris huffed. "That's Danny. Any other lifestyle beyond his doesn't quite compute."

I hummed. A month ago, I wouldn't have considered that the reason for Danny's advice. But now that I knew Iris, now that I'd heard her take on her family, well . . . she was right.

"Thanks." She leaned into my shoulder, resting her head against my arm.

"For what?"

"For telling me."

I shifted and tucked her into my side.

"I'm sorry for snooping too."

"I'm not."

She'd been right to do it. She'd been right to push. She'd been right to ask all those questions over the past month.

The darkest corner of my heart, the place where Amie and those memories lived, wasn't quite as black today. Like a door had been cracked, letting just a flicker of light inside.

"I haven't gone through her things," I told Iris. "I just packed everything into boxes. Sold the house furnished, empty picture frames included."

Too many memories. Too much regret.

In every room, there'd been a fight. So I'd just shoved that life, my marriage, into cardboard and hidden it in a closet.

It wasn't fair to Amie. This was something, another thing, that would have made her cry.

"I need to go through her things," I said, more to myself than to Iris.

"Okay." She wrapped her arms around my middle. "Want some help?"

A month ago, I would have told her no. I would have said I'd do it after she left. Except we both knew I wouldn't. I'd find a reason to delay and avoid the pain.

But Iris wasn't gone yet. And I was man enough to admit, I needed her.

"Please."

CHAPTER TWENTY-ONE

IRIS

errands

I SAT behind the wheel of the Bronco outside the post office and let out a long breath. My fingers skimmed the corner of the envelope on my lap, taking in Wilder's neat script. His address in the corner. Her parents' address on its face. The red, white and blue stamp.

I had no idea what he'd written to them—I wouldn't ask, not about this. If he told me, I'd listen. But otherwise, I was only here to help. And he'd asked if I'd take this letter to the post office with the last of Amie's boxes to ship to her family.

Rolling down my window, I slid the letter into the mailbox's slot. It dropped to the bottom with a whoosh. The boxes were already inside, destined for Utah.

I'd spent the better part of the past three days helping Wilder with the task of clearing out that closet.

He'd work each day at the school until midafternoon. While he was gone, I'd run errands and tidy up the house for his parents' visit. And after he came home, we'd sort through box by box.

The closet in his guest bedroom was empty. It looked massive without the rows of boxes.

Wilder had been deliberate and methodical with her things. He'd studied each item for a few moments, whether it was a sweater or a photo or a trinket, either replaying old memories or memorizing it for the last time. Then he'd given it to me to sort into one of four piles.

Most of the clothes had been given to the local Goodwill. Her college papers and textbooks, some miscellaneous junk and two worn pairs of shoes had gone to the trash. There was a small collection of photos that Wilder had opted to keep.

But the largest pile had taken up nearly the entire expanse of my bed. It had been the items for Amie's parents. There'd been mementos from her high school and college days. A handful of shirts that she'd worn often and he'd thought they might want. Photos. A stuffed teddy bear. Yearbooks.

My job was dealing with the piles once they'd been sorted. I was the errand runner, taking items to the trash or local charity drop so he wouldn't have to. If all I could really do for him was chase around town, I'd be the best errand runner in Montana.

Those errands for today were done. Or, mostly done. I'd even snapped a selfie to post on Instagram today. In the photo, I was here, behind the Bronco's steering wheel, wearing a new pair of sunglasses and my favorite straw hat. Makeup was minimal today and my lips were a pale pink.

No smile. I didn't really feel like smiling, even on this gorgeous day.

First Street was crowded and the sidewalks bustled with happy tourists. The June sun was shining in a cloudless blue sky. But a strange, sinking feeling plagued me as I headed for home.

It had been a heavy three days, and not just for Wilder. It hadn't been easy going through Amie's things. For a woman I'd never met, I'd had to fight tears more times than I could count.

It wasn't fair that she'd died in that accident. It wasn't fair that someone had decided to drink and get behind the wheel and Amie had paid the price. It wasn't fair that Wilder had lived with such guilt over her death.

He'd convinced himself he was at fault for Amie's death, not the drunk bastard who'd crashed into her car.

It wasn't fair.

Not only did I ache for his pain, but I hurt on Amie's behalf.

I was sleeping beside her husband. I kissed him each morning and had his body beneath my hands each night. And maybe I'd even taken a piece of his heart that had once belonged to her.

How was it possible to betray a woman I'd never met?

Going through her things, pushing so hard for Wilder to talk about Amie, had backfired. Now that I knew her—not well, but enough—I felt like I'd stabbed a friend in the back by taking her husband.

Amie and I wouldn't have had much in common. The more boxes we'd sorted through, the more I'd seen those differences Wilder had mentioned.

They really had been opposites. In more than one photo, where Amie had been laughing and smiling at a party,

Wilder had been at her side, pretending. His smiles hadn't reached his eyes. His broad frame had been so stiff.

If I could see it in an old picture, how had she missed it in real life?

Maybe she hadn't seen his misery. Maybe she had, but had ignored it. Or maybe she'd simply hoped he'd stay.

Wilder Abbott was not a man you gave up easily.

The icky feeling kept me company on the drive to his house. I'd expected to have a few hours alone before he came back from work, but when the house came into view, so did Wilder's truck.

I parked beside it and headed for the door. It whipped open the moment my feet hit the first flagstone on the patio.

Wilder filled the threshold, his hands braced on his hips. The angry scowl on his face halted my footsteps.

"Um . . . hi?"

"Your room is clean."

"Yes," I drawled. "Your parents are coming to town."

This morning, after he'd left for school, I'd packed Amie's last box. Then I'd scoured that room and bathroom, making sure it was spotless for his parents. And since we'd been busy each night with the closet, Wilder hadn't had time to clean the house. So I'd tackled that next.

The drive to town had been my last task for the day.

Well, not quite.

I still needed to check into the hotel.

"Where are your suitcases?"

"In the Bronco."

His scowl deepened. Without a word, he stomped out of the house and blew past me. The back door of the Bronco popped open and then came the crunch of his boots on the gravel as he passed me again, a suitcase in each hand.

"Hey, put those back. I'm going to the hotel this weekend." In Bozeman. A detail I kept to myself for now because I knew he'd do exactly this. But there weren't any vacancies in Calamity.

Wilder ignored me and went inside.

I followed, hurrying to catch him before he made a mess of that pristine guest bedroom. The carpet had the vacuum lines, and if his mom or dad noticed that sort of thing, then I wanted them untouched.

But Wilder didn't go down the hallway to my room. He veered down the hallway toward his own.

"Nope. No. Stop right now, Wilder."

He kept walking.

"Give those back."

His long strides, nearly twice the length of mine, meant I'd have to run to keep up. And I was not chasing him down like a child.

"Wilder."

Nothing.

"Some days talking to you is like talking to a brick wall."

That earned me a smirk over his shoulder.

"It's not funny."

He headed into his bedroom and when I made it to the door, he was just disappearing into the walk-in closet.

"You do realize I'll just take them back outside later."

A zipper's click filled the space. A drawer opened. And *plop*.

By the time I made it to the closet's doorway, another scoop of my clothes landed in an empty drawer.

"Wilder," I scolded. "What are you doing?"

"What does it look like?"

Another handful of shirts was dumped into that drawer. His sock drawer.

"Wait. Where are your socks?"

Wilder rapped a knuckle on the top drawer. That was where he'd had his boxers. Either those had moved somewhere else, or he'd made room.

He'd made room so I could have a drawer.

And not just one. He opened the bottom drawer, yanking it open to toss in more of my clothes. He didn't bother keeping anything folded.

"Your parents—"

"Will be here in an hour. Dad called as I was driving home."

"I was going to stay at a hotel. Give you time with them."

Wilder frowned and rezipped the now empty suitcase. Once it was closed, he hefted it to the shelves at the top of the closet, tucking it in tight.

That shelf was so tall I'd have to get a chair or stool to reach it.

He moved for the next suitcase but I shot out a hand.

"Stop."

He stood tall and crossed his arms over his chest. "No hotel."

"But—"

"No. Hotel."

I sighed, the weariness of the past few days weighing on my bones, so I leaned into the door frame. "Have you dated? Since Amie?"

"No." His gaze narrowed. "Why?"

"Have there, um . . . been other women?" Ugh. I'd been thinking about that question for days. And still, I wasn't sure if I wanted the answer to be yes or no.

Yes, because I didn't like the idea that he'd gone nearly ten years alone.

No, because the idea of another woman touching his body coated my vision in red.

He gave me a single nod.

No. Definitely no. I did not want to think about him with anyone but me.

I fought the urge to grimace. "Have your parents met any of those women?"

"No."

"Then they'll be expecting you to be alone. I don't want to intrude on your time with them or make them uncomfortable." Or give them ideas that I'd be staying when I had no idea if that was even an option.

As much as we needed to *have* that conversation, it wasn't the time. I still hadn't showered today, and if I was meeting his parents today, I was not doing it with bleach-scented hands and a white tank cropped so short the band of my black sports bra was showing.

"Do you want to unpack this suitcase?" He pointed to it on the floor. "Or should I?"

"I'll do it," I muttered. "But it will have to wait until later. I need to take a shower and change."

He grinned. "Then I'll get your other suitcase."

"Don't act so smug."

With a low chuckle, he came to me and bent, brushing a kiss to my temple. Then he strode for the door.

But before he could leave, I called to his back, "I'm not having sex with you while your parents are here."

He scoffed.

"Smug bastard."

We both knew I wouldn't deny him, whether his parents were under the same roof or not.

I stripped off my clothes and tossed them in the hamper. Then I went to the shower, giving the water a minute to warm up before I stepped under the spray.

I'd just wetted my hair when Wilder strode into the bathroom, his large hands full of my toiletries. The makeup was set on the counter along with my brushes and a bag of skin care products. He opened the shower's glass door and handed me my shampoo, conditioner, body wash and razor.

It had taken me an hour to pack. That time and energy he'd dismantled in less than five minutes. So I didn't say thank you as he tossed me my shower puff.

Wilder's gaze raked down my naked body. He stood in the doorway, staring unabashedly with that gleam I'd seen night after night. The gleam that said he was going to get creative later.

I turned to hide a blush. "You're letting out all the steam."

"Need me to come in there and warm you up?"

"Go away." I tried—and failed—to hide my smile. "If you come in here, I'll never be ready in time."

He lingered, his roving gaze hotter than the water, until finally the door closed, and I dove under the spray to shampoo my hair.

My fingers shook as I hurried through my routine, drying and curling my hair. I kept my makeup simple with a pale pink lipstick and a few swipes of mascara. Then I dug through the mess in my new drawers, picking out the plainest, most demure outfit I could assemble.

It was an outfit I would have worn to my parents' house. Something, maybe, Amie might have worn.

Damn it, I wasn't supposed to be here. I wasn't ready to meet Wilder's parents and answer questions about who I was and why I was here. Or worse, see the disapproval in their eyes when they realized I was his lover.

Would they hate that I was here? Would they feel like I was stealing Amie's place? Would they want him with someone, anyone, else? My stomach was in a knot by the time I spritzed my wrists with perfume.

Wilder was in the kitchen, twisting the top off of a beer bottle, when I emerged.

"Want—" He did a double take when he spotted me, then set his bottle down and braced his hands on the countertop. "What the fuck are you wearing?"

"They call these clothes." I rolled my eyes. "They're fairly popular amongst the human race."

He shook his head and shoved off the counter. When he stopped in front of me, he braced his hands on his hips. But instead of explaining, he just stood there with that signature Wilder Abbott frown and a clenched jaw.

"What?" I finally asked. "Stop it. You're being weird."

"I'm trying to decide how to say this."

"Can you decide faster? Your parents will be here any minute, and I'm nervous enough as it is without you glowering."

"You're nervous?"

"Uh, yeah. These are *your parents.*"

"Why are you nervous?"

"Because I want them to like me. Wouldn't you be nervous if you were meeting my parents?"

"I've already met your parents."

"That's not the point and you know it. What are you trying to decide to tell me?"

"I hate your outfit."

My jaw dropped. And with it, my gaze as I took in my clothes.

I'd chosen a pair of gray, pinstripe, wide-leg trousers. Normally I'd wear them with a cropped shirt to show off some midriff. But instead, I'd paired the pants with a fitted black turtleneck, the sleeves so long they ran to my knuckles. It was a shirt I'd bought for the sole purpose of wearing to family functions whenever I visited Mount Pleasant.

Maybe it wasn't my normal attire. Not a single tattoo was on display. But it wasn't like I'd come out dressed in a garbage sack.

"Well, you're wrong," I told him. "I look nice." *SO. THERE.*

His eyes softened and crinkled at the sides. "You look beautiful. You're always beautiful."

"Then why are you criticizing my outfit?"

"Because you got dressed for my parents. Not for yourself." Wilder's hand came to cup my cheek, his thumb caressing my skin. It was a light touch so he wouldn't smudge my makeup.

"I wanted them to like me."

"Just be you. Just be Iris. And they will." He swept me into his arms, practically smothering me against his chest. "I never once dreamed of telling Amie I hated an outfit."

Strange, but I liked that he was comfortable enough with me to be sincere.

I was used to the critiques. Strangers on social media told me they hated my clothes every day. And Wilder wasn't saying it to be mean or rude. He only wanted honesty between us. An honesty he hadn't had with Amie.

With me, he could always speak his real, raw truths.

I sighed, sagging into his chest. "I hate turtlenecks."

"Need me to help you take it off?"

"No." I laughed. After a quick kiss over his heart, I hurried back to the closet, swapping out the sweater for a satin, lace camisole. I stacked my favorite bracelets on both wrists and loaded each finger with a ring. Then I returned to the living room, just as a car door slammed outside.

Wilder's gaze scanned me head to toe. When I came to stand at his side, he ran a finger over the thin strap on my top. "There she is."

I summoned a fortifying breath.

Then we went to the door.

And I met his parents.

CHAPTER TWENTY-TWO

WILDER

A WEEKEND SPENT with Iris and my parents was the best time I'd had in years. We'd spent every waking moment together, laughing and sharing stories.

There hadn't been a doubt in my mind that Mom and Dad would love Iris. And as expected, they'd embraced her immediately. We'd all glued together without seams.

The only sour note of the weekend was that it had gone too fast.

"Always great to see you, son." Dad held out his hand as we stood on the porch, having just loaded their luggage to his car.

"You too." I took his hand and pulled him in for a hug.

He was just as strong and tall as ever. Since I'd seen him last, there were more grays speckled into his black hair. But Dad had passed his fit and healthy physique down to me.

All my life, I'd resembled my father. Mom used to call me his clone. I only hoped I'd take as good care of my body as he had his.

"Drive safe." I clapped him on the back, then let him go.

"Oh, we will." He turned toward the view, drawing the cool morning air into his lungs, holding it for a moment. "We didn't get a chance to talk about it, but I'm thinking about retiring."

"Really?"

Dad loved his job as an electrician and this was the first he'd ever mentioned retirement.

He shrugged. "Your mom and I have been talking about it. Sure would be nice to see you more than a couple times a year. Maybe travel a bit while we've still got the chance."

"No arguments here. I'd love to see you guys more often."

He put his hand on my shoulder, giving it a squeeze. "We'll have to get travel recommendations from Iris."

This was the segue into the conversation I'd been expecting since they'd arrived. But it was one of the only moments we'd been alone.

Mom was inside with Iris, finishing the breakfast dishes. So it hadn't come as a surprise when Dad had asked me to help load suitcases.

"I don't know how to say this." Sadness crept into his gaze. "You know we loved Amie."

"Yeah."

"It's been hard to see you alone since she died."

Mom and Dad didn't know that Amie and I had been struggling. Not even my parents had gotten the whole truth. The only person who knew was Iris.

"You're different around Iris," Dad said, studying my face. "Lighter. Happier. And I don't just mean recently. You fit with her, better than you ever did with Amie."

He voiced the words I felt too guilty to say.

"She's special," he said.

"She is."

His gaze drifted over my shoulder to inside the house. "Your mom spent an hour last night scrolling through her Instagram."

"Mom has Instagram?"

Dad chuckled and nodded. "She kept showing me Iris's photos from all over the world. Her two months in whatever city. That's quite a way to live."

The pressure in my chest that had been missing all weekend returned. The pressure that came whenever I thought about Iris leaving.

"You don't need advice," Dad said. "You already know what I'd tell you to do."

Don't let her go.

I turned, following his gaze through the windows to where Mom and Iris were hugging in the living room.

It wasn't a brief embrace. They clung to each other, like lifelong friends about to say farewell.

Or a mother with her daughter.

Mom had never hugged Amie like that.

When they finally broke apart, both women dabbed at the corners of their eyes. Then they came toward the door, joining us on the porch.

It was Dad's turn to hug Iris while I pulled Mom into my arms, kissing her hair.

"Love you, Mom."

"Love you too." She gave me a smile, her eyes glassy with tears, then took Dad's outstretched hand.

He held it all the way to their car, where he opened her

door. After she was seated, he bent inside to fasten her seat belt, Dad's way to steal a kiss. Then he closed her door and felt the seams to ensure it was shut tight.

I'd been watching my father buckle my mother into a seat for years. It never got old.

With one last wave, Dad slid behind the wheel, and sooner than I was ready, their car disappeared past the trees.

I hauled Iris into my side, pressing my nose to her hair to breathe in that vanilla and citrus scent.

She buried her face in my chest like she was breathing me in too. "What are we doing?"

Her question was so quiet and muffled against my shirt, I barely made it out. As much as I wanted to take her inside, to spend my first official day of summer break buried inside her body, this was a conversation that couldn't be ignored. Not anymore. Not after a weekend spent as a family.

Iris had been a part of that family, like the fourth leg to a table or chair.

"What do *you* want?" In the end, it didn't matter what I wanted. If her wings took her flying to the other side of the world, then I'd find a way to grow wings of my own.

I'd miss Calamity like a limb, but if she wanted to travel the world, she'd have company.

Iris shifted, loosening her hold to look up at me. "I feel restless."

Wings it was.

"It's not the same as it used to be," she said. "It's a different restless, and I can't tell if I want to travel because I actually want to travel or because it's expected. Or because if I stop, then in some small way, they've won."

"Who?"

"My family," she admitted. "I know that's ridiculous. But I've worked so hard to prove myself to them, that I don't need a fancy degree or office job to be successful. And I know I don't need their approval."

"But you want it."

"I do."

Part of me wanted to tell her they did approve. That they loved her. But it had been a long time since I'd seen Iris's parents. And other than a shallow reply to his latest text about how it was going, I was still avoiding Danny.

"It's more than just my family. I've built this whole persona and . . ." She sighed, trailing off.

"And what?"

"I'm tired, Wilder." Her body sagged against mine, like she could finally admit it and didn't need to stand so strong anymore. "I'm too young to be this tired. I'm tired of not having a place that's mine. A home. An address. But I don't want to lose who I am if I stop."

She was worried that she'd find her way back to the shy, quiet girl from Mount Pleasant.

"You won't," I promised.

"How do you know?"

"Because I won't let you."

Her blue eyes locked with mine. "What are you saying?"

"You love to travel?" It was a question and a statement.

Iris nodded.

"Then travel." I brushed a lock of hair off her temple. "You love this house?"

Another nod.

"Then stay. You can have both."

"And what about you?"

"You can have me too."

She blinked rapidly. Then in a flash, she put her hands on my face and pulled my mouth to hers. "I'm not leaving."

The air rushed from my lungs. "Thank fuck."

"And I'm keeping you."

I dropped my forehead to hers. "Good."

"And your mom and I decided that we're all going to Jamaica together this fall."

I chuckled. "Just tell me what days to take off work."

Iris's arms looped around my shoulders and she jumped, wrapping her body around mine. "Is this really happening?"

I pinched her ass.

"Ow!" she yelped and shot straight. "What was that for?"

"Now you know you're not dreaming."

She giggled, bending to drop a kiss on my mouth. The smile on her lips faded fast. "We'll have to tell Danny."

I spun for the door and carried her inside. "Not today."

Today, we were celebrating.

So I stalked to the bedroom, grateful for the empty house. We'd been quiet while Mom and Dad had been visiting. Right now, I wanted to hear her scream.

I set her on the edge of the bed, letting her unwind her limbs from my body. Then I took her chin in my grip, holding it firm, as I bent at the waist and sealed my lips over hers.

She reached for my face, probably to thread those fingers in my beard, but with my free hand, I batted her away and broke the kiss.

"Lie back."

The corner of her mouth turned up in a sly smile as she did as ordered.

"Put your hands above your head. Don't move them." If she did, I'd find something to tie them to the bedpost.

The idea of her trussed to this bed, entirely at my mercy, sent a wave of lust through my veins. My cock strained against my jeans.

Iris scooted deeper into the bed, falling back on the pillows. Then as instructed, she raised her arms until her palms flattened on the headboard.

She'd dressed in my favorite frayed denim shorts this morning and a white T-shirt of mine that she'd worn to bed last night. The neon green bra beneath peeked through the cotton.

"Close your eyes," I ordered.

Her breath hitched as she obeyed.

I stared at her, savoring the sight of her on my bed. Her blond hair spread in long tendrils. The beautiful tattoos on her smooth skin.

Mine. She was mine. Now I just had to keep from fucking this up.

I loosened the button on her shorts, flicking it open. With slow, lazy precision, I undressed her. My fingertips skimmed the sensitive spots on her thighs and ribs. I drew it out, turning it into foreplay, until her breaths were coming in short pants.

When I pushed her knees apart, her pussy gleamed. "Always so wet for me."

"Wilder—"

"Keep those eyes closed."

"But I want to watch."

"Closed, Iris."

She huffed but didn't argue. And her hands stayed exactly where instructed, above her head.

That first lick through her center was so fucking sweet I nearly came.

"Yes," she whimpered.

I flicked her clit with the tip of my tongue and her hips jerked. "Don't move those hands."

She loved to tug and pull on my hair but right now, I wanted her at my mercy. I wanted her to feel every lick. Every kiss.

I dragged my lips across the flesh of her inner thigh, leaving a wet trail nearly to her knee. When I found her core again, she was already trembling.

My body ached to sink inside hers, but first, I wanted the sweetness of her orgasm all over my tongue. So I devoured her until she rocked and writhed beneath my mouth. I gripped her hips, keeping them pinned as I feasted.

"Oh my God." Iris's hands were clawing at the headboard, her body quaking. "I'm—"

The warning was cut off as I sucked her clit, hard, and she exploded.

She screamed. It was a gasping, achingly beautiful sound of sheer pleasure as her back arched off the bed.

I kept at her until her orgasm ebbed and she collapsed, boneless and breathless. Then I climbed in bed beside her, still fully clothed, to memorize the faint smile on her lips.

Sparkling azure pools swallowed me whole when she finally opened her eyes. Then she giggled.

I loved her. Damn it, how I loved her.

If all I managed to accomplish for the rest of my life was keeping her, I'd consider it a success.

"My turn." She pounced, faster than I'd expected, and planted both hands on my shoulders, shoving me to my back. And just like I'd done to her, she undressed me with lazy, torturous movements.

I sank into the bed, letting her play, until those sensual lips wrapped around my cock. "Hell," I hissed. *Heaven.*

She sucked and licked, the flat side of her tongue stroking my shaft. Her hands gripped my thighs as I rocked my hips, fucking her mouth.

I didn't bother restraining or holding back my release. Iris's mouth was too hot, too perfect, and when I came shooting down her throat, she swallowed every last drop.

After wiping her lips dry, she crawled up my body and nestled into the crook of my arm. Her finger found my nipple, toying with it. Iris was as infatuated by my nipples as I was hers.

"Careful," I warned.

"Why?"

"I was going to give you a minute to rest. Keep that up and I'll change my mind."

She flicked my nipple.

And we started all over again.

It was dark by the time we finally succumbed to exhaustion. We'd stolen naps throughout the day. We'd snuck to the kitchen, naked, and raided weekend leftovers from the fridge. But otherwise, our day had been spent beneath the sheets. Always touching. Always wanting more.

This was the first time I'd ever spent an entire day in bed with a woman.

Not just a woman.

My woman.

It was something I wanted to do again and again. For the rest of my life.

If I didn't fuck it up. If I didn't fail her like I'd failed Amie.

"I'm scared."

Iris lifted up, propping her chin on her hands as they folded over my sternum. "Of what?"

"I don't want to fall out of love with you."

Her mouth opened. Closed. Opened. Closed. When she finally spoke, her voice cracked. "You love me?"

I cupped her cheek, my thumb running across that smooth skin. "Is it really that surprising?"

Her face softened. "You won't fall out of love with me. I won't let you."

If there was a woman who could will me to love her until my dying day, it was Iris.

Iris wasn't Amie. Maybe if I reminded myself of that enough, the fears would ease. I wasn't the same man I'd been all those years ago either.

"I love you," she whispered.

My chest was so full it hurt. I sat up, bringing her with me, crushed my mouth to hers and kissed her with everything I had to give.

When we broke apart, she nuzzled against my chest. "This feels monumental, but I'm too tired for more sex. That's your fault."

I chuckled as she poked at my ribs. Then I spun us into

the pillows, curling her back into my chest and holding her close.

It was a fresh start. I wasn't sure I deserved one.

But damn it, I was taking it anyway.

"Goodnight, Wilder Abbott," she said on a yawn.

I kissed her hair. "Goodnight, Iris Monroe."

CHAPTER TWENTY-THREE

IRIS

theif

"WHAT DO you want to do today?"

Wilder shrugged from his end of the couch, where he was drinking a cup of coffee. "Whatever you want."

He sipped from his mug, gaze aimed toward the windows. Those dark eyes were shining this morning. His frame was relaxed and he seemed . . . at peace. Maybe it was because he was officially on summer break. Maybe because we'd had such a nice weekend with his parents. Or maybe it was because of everything we'd talked about yesterday.

His hair was damp from the shower he'd taken after going on a run and lifting this morning. He'd invited me along to work out but I'd stayed in bed to sleep.

"Did you hear from your parents?" I asked.

"Mom texted yesterday afternoon when they got home."

"I like them."

"They like you too." He glanced over with a smile.

"You're right. They are madly in love."

He hummed his agreement, taking one of my ankles to drape it across his lap.

I'd lost count of the number of times his parents had shared a look or a knowing smile. They were always touching and often kissing. In twenty years, I wanted that too. I wanted to be as obsessed with Wilder then as I was now.

He traded his coffee mug for the paperback on the end table.

I snuggled deeper into the couch and took out my phone. As usual, I alternated swipes on the screen with chaste glances at Wilder.

It still hadn't quite hit me yet, that he was mine. That I could stay. That I *was* staying.

That he loved me.

I wanted to scream it from the rooftops, but first, we had to tell Danny.

My brother had texted me this morning—*How is Montana?* His curiosity must be running rampant since Wilder kept blowing him off. I'd replied back with a string of emojis. Thumbs up. Sunshine. Mountains. And a heart.

"We need to talk to Danny."

Wilder sighed, setting his book aside. "Yeah."

"Want me to tell him?"

"No, I need to be the one."

"Okay." I gave him a sad smile. That wouldn't be a fun phone call. "After you talk to him, would you care if I posted about you?"

His attention returned to his book and he lifted a shoulder. "Whatever you want, baby."

Baby. My heart was so full it hurt. "From now on, only call me baby."

Wilder put a hand on my foot, giving it a squeeze.

I turned my attention back to my phone, fighting a smile.

It dropped the moment I opened my notifications and found a string of comments on a video that Kim had posted.

"Oh, shit." I launched myself from the couch, not believing what I was seeing.

The latest video on my feed was the video from weeks ago. The video of Wilder holding my phone hostage.

"What?" Wilder's book closed and he was on his feet. "Did someone say something?"

"Oh my God." I shoved the hair from my face, then let my fingers fly across the screen.

"Iris."

My heart raced as I hit the option to delete. Delete, delete, delete.

Why was it that when I wanted to remove a video there were so many checkpoints?

Are you sure? This cannot be undone.

YES! I'M FUCKING SURE.

The moment it was gone, my shoulders sagged. I refreshed ten times, just to make sure it was gone, then I switched over to TikTok. Sure enough, Kim had posted it there too.

With the same caption that she'd used on Instagram.

thief

Wilder was a thief. The man who'd stolen my heart.

And if I had to pick a caption for that video, *thief* was perfect. Except we were not ready to tell the world. So the video was deleted too before I sent a frantic text to Kim that I'd screwed up.

"Iris." Wilder's voice had a panicked edge.

"Sorry." I turned to face him, worrying my bottom lip between my teeth. Then I threw my phone aside. "Gah."

"What?"

"I messed up. I batched a bunch of content and sent it to Kim. Remember that video you took of me when we were outside taking photos? You held my phone away from me. I must have included it with the rest on accident. She just posted it."

It was innocent. When I'd told Kim about Wilder, I hadn't mentioned that we were keeping our relationship a secret. And she must have seen the magic in that video. She knew that when I gave her content, she had free rein to post it whenever she wanted.

Damn it. How could I have been so freaking stupid? My own obsession with that video had come back to bite me in the ass.

"Hell," Wilder muttered, dragging a hand over his beard.

"You can't see your face or anything. But your voice is in it. And your body. It was only up for a few minutes, so that's something. I just took it down. Danny doesn't even follow me but . . . someone could have seen it. My mom maybe."

Wilder's eyebrows came together. "Danny doesn't follow you?"

"No." I shook my head. "Mary might."

His scowl deepened. "I can't exactly get pissed since I don't follow you either, but that still pisses me off."

"Not the biggest issue at the moment, babe."

"Yeah," he grumbled. "I'll go make a phone call."

With that, he strode out of the room, swiping his phone from the counter.

I rushed to my phone too. A string of panicked replies and apologies from Kim popped up. Rather than type back, I called her.

"Oh my God. Iris." She sounded on the verge of tears. "I'm sorry."

"Don't apologize. It's my fault," I said. "This is all on me."

We talked for a minute, then I ended the call and strained my ears for Wilder's voice.

But he came walking out of the hallway, shaking his head. "Voicemail."

"Damn." My shoulders fell.

"Hey." He came to stand by me and put his hands on my shoulders. "Maybe this was a good thing. This was the push we needed to stop hiding."

"I like our bubble." And knowing my family, they'd do their best to pop it.

"I do too. But it's time."

"Yeah," I muttered. "Sorry."

"Don't worry about it. I'll talk to Danny whenever he calls me back."

" 'Kay."

This was a good thing, right? Wilder was important. It was time for my family to know. Effective yesterday, my life was going to be different.

Maybe it should have freaked me out that I was giving up the lifestyle I'd built since high school. But I didn't feel a flicker of fear or panic.

This was *right*. This was home. It was time to stop chasing all over the world.

Or maybe the reason I'd been traveling the globe was because I'd been finding my way here. To Wilder.

"It's going to be okay," I said, more for myself than Wilder.

He tugged me against his chest. "Don't let this wreck our day."

"Okay." I drew in his scent and closed my eyes, my heart climbing out of my throat. "I love you."

"Love you too."

"Baby. Love you too, *baby*."

He chuckled. "Love you too, baby."

"Much better."

We retreated to the couch, and while we both tried to relax, we were on edge, waiting for Danny to call. When he still hadn't returned Wilder's call hours later, and I hadn't heard a peep from anyone else, I blew out a sigh of relief.

They must have missed the video. *Phew.*

But a hint of adrenaline still lingered in my veins and when I couldn't sit still any longer, I took a shower and dressed in a yellow mini sundress.

"Will you take me out to lunch?" I asked Wilder when I emerged from the bedroom.

"Sure."

"Baby," I corrected.

He shook his head. "Sure, baby."

"You're catching on."

We ate lunch at the White Oak Café before setting out along First for a stroll.

It was different today, seeing Calamity as home. I didn't

need to memorize everything or memorialize it in photos. I had time. How many years had it been since I'd given myself more time?

"I want to get a post office box here," I told him.

"Today?"

"No, but maybe tomorrow."

"All right." He took my hand, lacing our fingers together. He'd pulled on a baseball hat to shield his face and he looked as handsome as ever. He looked like mine. "I need to grab some cash from the bank. And I should probably get a birthday card to send your brother."

"You send Danny birthday cards?" I didn't even send him birthday cards. The last card I'd given him had been homemade from when I was in middle school.

Wilder shrugged. "I like sending cards."

Of course he did. No texts or calls for Wilder Abbott. He'd mail a physical card. "Where do they sell the best cards in Calamity?"

"I usually just grab one from the grocery store."

"When there are all these cute shops?" I scoffed. "Let's do more than window shop."

Wilder groaned, but I clamped harder on his hand, refusing to let him go as I dragged him into a gift shop.

It was teeming with tourists and local shoppers, but we browsed, shuffling through the cramped space until we found a wall of greeting cards. Three different people bumped into Wilder and with each, he grunted and shot them a glare.

He chose a blank card with a scenic painting on its face, and after we paid, he practically carried me outside to the sidewalk. "Are we done?"

"Are you done?"

He looked over my head at the people swarming around us. "Yes."

"Okay." We'd take the busy Calamity outings in stride. So we headed toward where we'd parked three blocks away.

We were just passing a law firm when its door opened and a couple stepped outside, nearly colliding into us. The man had a little girl on his shoulders. And behind him was Larke, her pregnant belly stretching the cotton on her own sundress.

"Oh, hi." She nodded to Wilder as she took us in. As she followed the line of his arm to his hand, linked with mine, she smiled. "Iris, right?"

"Good to see you again."

"You too." She put her hand on the man's arm. "This is my husband, Ronan. And our daughter, Wren."

"Nice to meet you," I said.

Ronan gave me a kind smile but as he looked at Wilder, his jaw flexed. "Abbott."

"Thatcher." Wilder dipped his chin and took a step, like he was about to flee these two faster than we had the gift shop. But then he stopped, so abruptly I nearly slammed into his back. He looked to Larke, holding her gaze. "In case I don't see you beforehand"—he waved to her belly—"congratulations."

She blinked, her jaw dropping as she looked up at Ronan, who appeared equally as puzzled. "Um, thanks, Wilder."

"Have a nice summer break."

"You too." She stared between the two of us but before I

could say anything, Wilder tugged on my hand and towed me behind him.

"What was that about?" I asked.

"It's not as hard to see her as it used to be." His quiet words were almost swallowed up by the noise from the sidewalks. Almost, but not quite.

Maybe he'd never get over everything that had happened with Amie. Maybe he'd always carry the guilt of how they'd ended and her death. But maybe in time, he'd be able to put it behind him. Maybe I could help a little.

Maybe I already had.

"I'm glad."

He loosened a breath. "Me too."

"What are your thoughts on PDA?"

"Not against it." He lifted up our linked hands.

"Good." I gripped his hand with both of mine and stopped walking, forcing him to stop too. "Kiss me."

He bent, angling his face so the brim of his hat wouldn't smack me in the face as he brushed his lips to mine. When he pulled back, he threw his arm around my shoulders and hauled me into his side, pressing his mouth to my hair.

I leaned into his side, tucking my hand into the back pocket of his jeans. Then faced forward to cross the street.

And froze.

Ten feet away, standing with her hands fisted and tears swimming in her eyes, was Sadie.

"Shit," Wilder muttered.

I took a step but Wilder's grip on my hand tightened. "Sadie—"

She spun around and ran, weaving past people until she was gone.

"Damn it." Today was supposed to be a good day. A day for Wilder and me.

But even though the sky was clear and blue, there might as well have been a gray storm cloud over my head.

That cloud followed me all the way home.

"I feel like I messed that up," I told Wilder as we walked inside.

"You didn't know," he said, tossing his keys on the table beside the door. "She'll get over it."

"Yeah," I mumbled. "I just wish I could have talked to her. Told her I was sorry."

"You didn't do anything wrong."

Wilder was right. I'd had no clue about Sadie's feelings. But why did it feel like I'd betrayed her? "I guess I just relate to her. I thought maybe I could help her if she wants to be an influencer. Encourage her to follow her heart. Now she can't even look at me. This sucks."

"If it makes you feel any better, I expect Danny to disown me once he finds out about us."

"He'd better not. You don't disown friends who mail you birthday cards. Why isn't he calling you back?"

Wilder shrugged. "Payback probably, since I've been ignoring him for weeks."

"Brat," I muttered.

Wilder held out his hand. "Come on."

I placed my palm in his. The minute he had a hold on me, he bent and hefted me over his shoulder. "Wilder!"

He smacked my ass, then carried me to the bedroom, where we blocked out the world until long after dark.

"Would you ever shave your chest hair?" I asked as I nuzzled into his arms. Our legs were twined beneath the covers and the heat of his body warmed my naked skin.

"No."

"What if I didn't like it?"

"You do like it."

"But what if I didn't?"

"You'd be shit out of luck."

I smiled against his heart and yawned. "Do you know how to fish?"

"Yes."

"Will you teach me? That's always been Dad and Danny's thing to do together. I never got invited. But what if I like fishing?"

"I'll teach you how to fish."

"Tomorrow?"

"Iris," he warned.

"Baby," I corrected.

"Baby, stop asking questions and go to sleep."

"Thanks."

"For the orgasms?"

"No, for making me feel better."

"You're welcome, baby."

A smile tugged at my mouth as I began drifting off, cocooned in his large body. I breathed in the masculine scent of his skin and snuggled closer. I was seconds away from sleep when Wilder's body tensed.

He shoved up to a seat, his gaze on the window's blinds.

"What?" I sat up beside him, clutching the sheet to my breasts.

He cocked his head, like he was trying to hear something.

Then I heard it too.

Voices.

My heart leapt into my throat. "Is someone outside?"

He pressed a finger to his lips and flung the covers off his legs, climbing out and swiping his sweatpants from the floor. "Stay here," he whispered.

Not a chance.

I ripped the covers from my legs and nearly tripped on the T-shirt I'd pulled on earlier for dinner. I yanked it over my head as I hurried down the hallway, hanging back as he went to the cabinet above the fridge to pull out a black box.

A gun box.

I gasped.

His eyes narrowed when he spotted me. "Stay inside."

"You can't go out there."

"Iris," he clipped, then tiptoed toward the door, peering through its small window. Even in the dark, I could see the flex and tension in his muscles.

He slunk away from the door, and when he was away from the glass, he turned and rushed to the island, setting the gun aside.

"Wilder," I hissed.

He held up his finger to his mouth. Then pointed to where my feet were on the floor.

Stay here. Got it.

He crouched and made his way to the side door, slipping outside without a noise.

Oh God. Who was out there? There'd definitely been voices, right? Or had I heard an animal?

Leave it to my man to go outside in bare feet if there was a grizzly bear or mountain lion roaming around.

My arms were shaking and I shifted my weight from foot to foot. I held my breath, trying to hear anything. But it had gone eerily quiet.

I inched forward, freezing in place. My eyes stayed locked on the door. Surely Wilder would come inside now and tell me it was just his imagination. But there was nothing, so I took another step, crouching like Wilder had done as I made my way toward the front windows.

By the time I reached the glass, I was nearly crawling. I peered over the base of the window, squinting through the dark to try and see something. Anything. But beyond the area illuminated by the porch light, there was nothing. The night was so black I couldn't even make out the treetops.

He was okay. He had to be okay. He'd be back in a minute and tell me that a rogue squirrel had gone on the roof to make some noise.

But as the seconds passed and my heart pounded inside my chest, my stomach churned and churned.

Until finally, there he was, stalking along that flagstone pathway with . . . a teenager.

Two teenagers.

Wilder had a boy by the arm. Ryan? That was his name, right? And behind them, with her arms wrapped around her middle, was Sadie.

I stood tall, my hand coming to my mouth, as Wilder shoved the boy onto the bench seat. Then I rushed for the front door, flinging it open and stepping outside into the light.

Sadie was crying, her face splotchy and her eyes glassy. She took a step and swayed slightly. Was she drunk?

"Explain," Wilder barked at Ryan.

He kept his gaze on the ground.

Wilder dragged a hand through his hair. "Iris, call the cops."

"No." Ryan's eyes bulged. "Please, Mr. Abbott. No cops."

"Tough shit, kid."

Sadie whimpered, the tears streaming faster down her face.

"What happened?" I asked Wilder.

His chest was rising and falling with angry pants. His fists were balled at his hips as fury turned his expression to stone. It softened, slightly, when he looked at me hovering beside the door. "They vandalized your car."

"What?" I flinched, then before anyone could stop me, I was racing across the patio, my eyes adjusting to the dim light as I reached the gravel.

And there, on my white Bronco, the car I'd saved and saved to buy after coming back from Europe, was a word spray-painted in ugly black letters.

WHORE

CHAPTER TWENTY-FOUR

WILDER

THE DOORBELL RANG.

Iris was at the island, making sandwiches for lunch. Her grip on the knife tightened until her knuckles were white, but she didn't look to the door. She kept her gaze on the bread and condiments laid out on the counter because she knew exactly who was outside.

"I'll get it." I slid off my stool and walked to the door.

Sadie spotted me through the window and dropped her gaze to her feet, a bucket of cleaning supplies beside them. Behind her stood her father, his arms crossed and his expression granite.

I opened the door. "Done?"

She nodded. "Yes."

It had been three days since Ryan and a drunk Sadie had vandalized the Bronco. I'd come close to making a call to Sheriff Evans countless times. Every time I remembered the way Iris had cried, I regretted leaving the authorities out of this matter.

Though judging by the furious stare on Sadie's father's face, he would punish her far more than the cops.

"What else do you have to say?" he asked Sadie.

She gulped and lifted her quivering chin, meeting my gaze. "I'm sorry, Mr. Abbott."

It was one of many apologies she'd made, and deep down, I knew I'd let this go. Eventually. But right now, I was so fucking pissed. Three days hadn't been enough to erase the mental image of that word on Iris's car.

Even if they'd spent the past three days taking off the spray paint, I wasn't sure when I'd stop seeing it.

Ryan rounded the corner of the house, looking as sullen as Sadie. Though she was actually upset over what she'd done. Ryan was just angry that he'd been caught.

It had been Iris who'd ultimately decided not to turn the teens in to the police. She hadn't wanted it to mess up Sadie's future. Ryan, well . . . I hoped that kid grew the fuck up someday. Maybe college would straighten him out. Maybe not.

"We're finished, Mr. Abbott." He cast a wary glance at Sadie's father as he stepped up beside her. There was a rag in his hand, one he'd used to polish and wax the Bronco. "Do you want to take a look and make sure it's okay?"

I jerked my chin for them to lead the way. As I stepped outside, I glanced over my shoulder to find Iris's eyes waiting. "Back in a sec."

"Okay." She stayed on her side of the island.

Of all the words for Sadie to use, *whore* had been the absolute worst. It was the only insult that seemed to slice straight through Iris's confidence.

I hated seeing her sad, but I knew she wouldn't be able to

move on until this was over. So I blew her a kiss and closed the door behind me.

The kids were standing around her Bronco, Sadie's father putting their cleaning supplies in the back of his rig.

Without a word, I rounded the car and inspected every inch. Then I opened the back door to check out the inside.

Iris hadn't wanted the cops involved, but I sure as fuck wouldn't have let her clean this up. So I'd insisted on Sadie and Ryan getting the paint off and told them that Iris's car had better be spotless, inside and out, within three days.

They'd done a decent job. The interior smelled like citrus and glass cleaner with a hint of Iris's perfume.

I slammed the door, then leveled a glare at Ryan.

He gulped.

The little shit had yet to apologize. So I crossed my arms over my chest and waited.

"Sorry," he muttered.

The night we'd caught them, the whole story had come pouring out of Sadie's drunk mouth. She'd been bawling and hysterical, but she'd told us how she and Ryan had been at a party when she'd made some underhanded comments about Iris.

Ryan must have jumped at the chance to win her over again and get back at me for riding his ass that last day of school. Or maybe he'd learned of her crush on me. Whatever the motivations, the two of them had come up with a plan to "decorate" Iris's car.

He'd been the sober driver, bringing her out here. They'd parked about half a mile away, and under the cover of darkness, armed with phone flashlights and a bottle of black spray paint, they'd crept up to Iris's car.

Had we not still been awake, I doubted I would have heard them outside. But damn, I was glad they'd been caught. And now, it was over.

"Get off my property," I barked.

Ryan flinched, then bolted for his truck.

Sadie took a step but stopped, turning back. "Can I talk to Iris?"

"She doesn't want to talk to you."

Someday, Iris would forgive Sadie for this too. Probably sooner than me. But for now, she'd made up her mind and wanted some distance. We both wanted distance. But I'd promised to oversee the Bronco's cleanup and give Iris time to mend her wounded heart.

"I just want to tell her that I'm sorry," Sadie said.

"She tried to help you, Sadie." Hell, she'd given Sadie her favorite necklace. "And this is how you repaid that help? You hurt her."

"I know." She sniffed and dabbed at the corner of her eyes. "Would you tell her I'm sorry?"

I nodded.

"Sadie, let's go," her father clipped.

Ryan's truck was already down the lane, about to disappear from view.

Sadie slunk off to her father's truck as he came over to me, hand extended.

"Sorry, Wilder. Nothing like this will ever happen again."

I believed him. "Appreciate your help," I said, shaking his hand.

Ryan's parents had been livid when they'd come to pick him up the night of the vandalism. And while they'd been furious at their son, they seemed angrier that he'd put his college athletic scholarship at risk, rather than upset for the damage he'd caused. They, like their son, had nearly forgotten to apologize. And they hadn't been out since to help him fix this fuckup.

Sadie's parents had been devastated and embarrassed. And her father had been the one to research exactly how to clean up the spray paint to ensure the Bronco was as good as new.

"Can't thank you and Iris enough for leaving the sheriff out of this," he said. "We'll see you around."

I dipped my chin. "Bye."

He joined Sadie and waved one last time before backing away from the house.

Iris was in the doorway when I turned to head inside. Her arms were crossed as she watched them disappear. "Done?"

"Done," I said, following her inside. "You okay?"

She shrugged and went back to our sandwiches. "I really hate it when people call me a whore. They assume because I look like this, that I dress the way I do, I'm less."

She wasn't less. She was everything. "We should have called the cops."

"No." She gave me a sad smile. "It's over now. I just . . . she reminded me of myself at that age. I wanted to help."

"I'm sorry, Iris." Fuck, I was sorry. I hated seeing any of that light dim in her eyes.

"Baby," she corrected.

"Baby." I rounded the island and hauled her into my arms.

She relaxed into my hold, sinking into my chest. "I want

to go somewhere today. Just get out of here. Drive the Bronco and pretend like none of this ever happened."

"Where are we going?"

"Anywhere with you."

"Let's go to Prescott. It's about the same size as Calamity. We'll explore."

"Can we shop?"

"I'd love to shop."

She giggled. "Liar."

To put a smile on her face, I'd shop all damn day. "Let's eat." I smacked her ass and let her go. "Then we'll head out."

"Okay." She picked up the mustard, squirting some on her sandwich but not mine.

I liked it enough on burgers but not with turkey. Then she put pickles on mine, leaving them off hers. Tomato slices and lettuce for both. When she put the pieces of bread on top and plated my sandwich, she glanced up and caught me staring.

"What?"

"Nothing." I waved it off. Except it wasn't nothing.

Amie had never taken the time to learn how I liked my sandwiches. She'd make two of the same, assuming I liked them the way she did. And since I wasn't picky, I'd just eat them without comment.

But Iris had been quizzing me on my food choices since she'd been here. All those questions she'd asked, questions that had felt so pointless and endless, and now I realized why she asked them.

She knew me. Maybe we'd only been together for a short time, but she knew me.

"I love you."

"I love you too." She cut my sandwich on a diagonal because somewhere along the way she'd mentioned how triangles were prettier than rectangles.

I'd just lifted half of my sandwich off the plate when the crunch of gravel echoed from outside. "What now?"

Ryan or Sadie had probably forgotten something. I hadn't had this many visitors in years. It was annoying.

I took a bite, chewing quickly, then headed for the door. Through the window, I watched a black sedan park beside the gleaming Bronco.

"Do you know anyone who drives—"

Before I could finish my sentence, the driver's door opened.

And Danny stepped outside.

My stomach plummeted. "Fuck."

"What?" Iris was at my side in a flash, standing on her toes to look outside. When she spotted her brother, she gasped. "Oh my God."

Damn it. He hadn't returned my call, and after three days, Iris and I had both assumed we were in the clear. That whenever he called back, I'd break the news.

Today. Apparently, that was today.

Danny glanced around, having only been here years ago, then marched for the patio. The look on his face said this wasn't a friendly visit.

"He knows," Iris whispered. "He saw the video or something."

"That was days ago. Why the hell didn't he call me back?"

"So much for our trip to Prescott." She positioned herself

in front of me, steeling her spine, then opened the door. "Hey."

"Hey?" Danny scoffed. He stopped a few feet away, planting his hands on his hips. "I drive all the way up here from Utah and you say 'Hey'? Explain yourself."

She tensed.

"Danny—"

He silenced me with a hand slicing through the air. "Now, Iris. Explain yourself now."

Wait. What?

He was livid, but not at me. At Iris. He wasn't even looking at me.

Danny had always been the calm, collected one of the two of us. Most of the time, he was the guy who could keep a level head. But this? I'd never seen him this keyed up.

"How could you do this?" His face was red. He raked a hand through his brown hair before flinging his arms out at his sides. "I asked you to come up here to keep Wilder company. Not climb into his bed."

Iris flinched. "That's not fair."

"So you're not sleeping with my best friend?"

"I didn't say that," she muttered, her shoulders curling in on themselves.

Meanwhile, my head was spinning.

He'd barely glanced in my direction. He hadn't even told me hello. No, he'd just channeled all of his fury and frustration at Iris. I might as well not have even been here.

And she didn't seem at all surprised. Iris wasn't shocked that he'd directed his anger at her.

What. The. Fuck?

"Do not yell at her." I wrapped an arm around her shoulders, hauling her against me.

"Wilder." Danny's gaze flew to mine and his expression was like a punch to the gut.

Not condemnation. Not accusation.

Guilt.

He looked as guilty as Sadie's father had looked fifteen minutes ago.

"I'm sorry," he choked out. "I'm so sorry she did this."

Iris stiffened beneath my hold.

I blinked. "You're sorry?"

"I sent her here because I was worried about you. I didn't realize she would—"

"Stop." I let go of Iris, shifting her out of my way. Because I didn't want her in the middle when I pummeled her brother. "Did you come all the way to Montana to scold your sister for sleeping with me?"

Danny grimaced. "I can't believe she went this far. Knowing about Amie and all that you've been through. I've been sick about it for days and just couldn't do this over the phone. I'm so sorry. I never—"

"Shut the fuck up."

"Wilder—"

"Both of you shut the fuck up." Iris's nostrils flared as she shot me a glare, then put her hand on my shoulder, shoving me out of the way.

Rage had coated my vision and I hadn't realized that it paled in comparison to Iris's own. She stood in front of Danny, stepping onto the porch in her bare feet.

He was smart enough to take a step back.

"How dare you?" she snapped. "How fucking dare you?

What happens between Wilder and me is none of your business. But since you drove all the way up here to scold me like I'm some child, let's get a few things straight. You don't get to treat me like I'm the deviant here, seducing your friend. Who, by the way, is a grown man and capable of making his own decisions."

Danny's face paled. "Iris—"

"I'm not done." She mimicked his gesture from earlier, slicing her hand through the air to keep him quiet. "I love this man. I love him with my whole heart in a way I will never love another person. Never. But even if this was just us having a fling, why am I not good enough for him?"

"That's not what I'm saying."

"Isn't it? Fuck you, Danny. You and your judgmental bullshit can go to hell. I'm not going to fit into this mold you've decided is appropriate. I'm going to get tattoos because I like them. I'm going to dress in clothes that I love, whether you think they're scandalous or not. I don't need to go to college, nor do I want to. That has nothing to do with my success as a person. And if I want to be with Wilder, then I'm going to be with Wilder. Whether you think I'm good enough for him or not."

The way she spoke that last sentence was like a knife to the heart.

Did she think she wasn't good enough?

"Baby," I murmured, knowing it would get her attention.

"What?" She whirled, the unshed tears in her eyes another knife stabbing deep.

"You are more than I could have ever dreamed of."

She swallowed hard. "Tell your friend."

I looked over her head to Danny.

293

All this time, I'd been worried he'd come after me for chasing Iris. That he'd have my head for taking his sister to my bed. Not once in a million years had I expected him to get upset with her.

"You're an asshole," I clipped. "You talk to her like that again, and I'll break your goddamn jaw."

"I just . . ." He shook his head. "I know how much you loved Amie. How long you've been grieving."

"Amie and I were a wreck. We were getting a divorce." If not for that crash, we would have been divorced for nearly ten years.

"W-what?"

"You don't know what you're talking about. But you know who does? Iris." I put my hand on her shoulder, making sure everyone today knew exactly whose side I was taking. "She knows everything there is to know about me."

"She's been here for weeks."

"So? She's been your sister her whole life and you know fuck all about her. Not that you ever seem to try."

Danny opened his mouth but closed it, his gaze alternating between the two of us.

"I'm sorry we didn't tell you," Iris said. "I assume you saw the video. That's not how I wanted to share. I didn't even think you followed me."

I should probably watch that video.

"Well, yeah, I follow you. You're my sister."

"Here's the thing, Danny. You say that and I have no idea if you mean it as a source of pride or embarrassment. You don't know me. And you don't try. You just want me to fit into a box of your making."

She might as well have slapped him.

And the way the color drained from his face, he'd felt that strike.

"Iris . . ." He shifted his weight from foot to foot, his gaze dropping. Then he rubbed both of his hands over his face. "I don't know what to say."

She rolled her eyes, and any hint of tears vanished. "How about an apology?"

"I'm sorry."

"Then you tell us how happy you are that we're together."

He stared at us for a long moment, like he was still trying to figure this out. Then it must have clicked. Danny cocked his head to the side and narrowed his gaze in my direction. "Fuck you for sleeping with my sister."

The corner of Iris's mouth curled up. "That's more like it."

CHAPTER TWENTY-FIVE

IRIS

"I FEEL LIKE AN IDIOT," Danny said as he held a coffee mug between his palms. His eyes were bloodshot and his face had a gray-green pallor.

"For drinking too much last night?" I asked.

"Not so loud." He winced. "Yes, for drinking too much. And for coming up here without calling first. I saw that video and overreacted. I started stewing on it. Started thinking about all the texts Wilder hadn't answered. Why he was calling me. So I finally told Mary I had to get to Montana. Probably should have just called first."

"You think?" I deadpanned, nudging his elbow with mine as we sat side by side at the island. Good to know I wasn't the only Monroe to have a streak of impulsivity.

Wilder was at the stove, cooking breakfast. The scent and sizzle of bacon frying filled the air. Two pieces of bread were loaded into the toaster. And he was whipping a bowl of eggs to scramble.

"Sorry." It was another in a string of Danny's apologies since arriving yesterday. "But I'm actually glad I came."

"Me too."

Danny and I would never be best friends. Wilder had a claim on that title, and I wasn't going to fight him for it. But the past day had gone a long way to closing the gap between my brother and me.

Yesterday, after the confrontation on the porch, he'd come inside and given Wilder a half-hearted lecture about crossing a boundary. But Wilder had just shrugged him off, refusing to feel guilty for our relationship.

And I was tired of seeking approval from people who hadn't tried hard enough to get to know me.

But I would give my brother credit. He'd stayed yesterday and tried. It had taken him about an hour to get over that initial shock. Maybe to let everything we'd said sink in. But then he'd started asking questions.

Hours upon hours of questions. All directed my way.

One day wasn't enough for him to get to know me. For us to bridge that gap. But it was something.

The whiskeys Wilder had poured us all at dinner had definitely helped. By the time Danny had called Mary, he'd been slurring. Then he'd stumbled to bed in the guest room and passed out still in his jeans and shoes.

"You don't come home very often," Danny said.

"No, I don't."

"Is that because of me?"

"Partly." There wasn't a question he'd asked since yesterday that I hadn't answered honestly, even when the truth was brutal. "Mom and Dad don't understand me and they don't try. Mary makes too many underhanded comments about my tattoos, and I swear to God, the next time she gives me the side-eye, I'm going to lose my shit. It's not fun for me to come home, so is it really shocking that I stay away?"

"No." He sighed. "I'm sorry about Mary. I'll talk to her."

Did I think it would change his wife's opinion of me? No. But he could deal with her.

While Wilder cooked, I slid from my stool to get plates and silverware, setting the table for our meal. Then we sat together eating, mostly in silence, other than the occasional groan from Danny as he fought to keep his breakfast down.

"I'm never drinking again," he said.

"You okay to drive home?" Wilder asked.

"I'm afraid I'll puke all over the car. Mind if I crash in the guest bedroom for another night?"

"Not at all."

He slid off his stool, taking his plate to the sink. "I think I'm going to go take a nap."

"I'll probably head to the grocery store in a while," I said. "Want me to get you some ginger ale?"

"Yes, please." Danny started shuffling out of the kitchen, but before he could disappear to his room, the doorbell rang.

All eyes whipped to the front of the house, none of us having heard a car approach.

Wilder went to answer, but whoever he saw outside made his shoulders stiffen. Then he opened the door to Sadie. She was holding a bouquet of yellow roses.

"Hey, Mr. Abbott." She tucked a lock of blond hair behind her ear as her gaze darted inside, right to where I was still seated at the table wearing one of Wilder's T-shirts and a pair of scrunched, fuzzy socks.

"What do you need?" he asked her, his voice sharp enough that she dropped her gaze.

"I was just hoping to talk to Iris. Please."

It was the pleading in her voice that forced me from my seat. I went to stand beside Wilder, taking in Sadie's splotchy cheeks.

She'd been crying for days, hadn't she?

"Hi, Sadie." My voice held the gentleness that Wilder's lacked.

"These are for you." She held out the roses. "I'm sorry. I'm so, so sorry."

I took the flowers as Wilder's hand found the small of my back. Just a slight touch to show he was there.

Yesterday, he'd been so ready to battle Danny for me. But that fight had been a long time coming. A stand I'd needed to make on my own.

There was no fight with Sadie. She was punishing herself enough for us both.

"Thank you," I said.

"And this." She moved to unclasp the compass rose necklace from her nape, but I held up a hand.

"Don't."

"You should take it back. You were so nice to me, and what I did was unforgiveable. I'm the worst kind of person. I don't deserve this necklace."

"You're not a bad person," I told her.

"Really? Because I feel like dirt."

The remorse would fade in time.

"I just . . . I want to be like you. You have everything I want." Her gaze flicked to Wilder, then away. "I told my parents I didn't want to go to college. I told them I wanted to do something different, even if I don't know what different means right now."

"Good for you."

"Anyway, I'll leave you alone. I just wanted to apologize. I'm really sorry. And you're probably leaving soon so I didn't want to miss my chance."

To the world, my two months in Montana were nearly over. But Sadie could find out with the rest of them that I wasn't leaving.

Maybe my friendship with her hadn't lasted, but I wasn't giving up. I'd make friends here in Calamity. Good friends. I could feel it down to my bones.

"Are you sure about the necklace?"

"I'm sure." I gave her a soft smile. "Good luck, Sadie."

"Bye, Iris."

Wilder ushered me inside and closed the door. Then he took my face in his hands. "You okay?"

"Yeah." I fell into his chest, breathing in that spicy scent.

His lips came to my hair. "Proud of you."

"I'd better get these into some water." I pulled away and turned, only to stop. Danny was just a few feet away, listening to every word.

There was a strange expression on his face, almost confusion.

"What?" I asked.

He stared at me for another long moment. "She said she wants to be like you."

"Yeah," I drawled.

"Not even my own children have said that to me before." Danny shook his head. "I'm an idiot, aren't I?"

Wilder chuckled. "Yes."

"I'm proud of you too." Danny didn't wait for me to respond. He turned and trudged to the guest bedroom, closing the door behind him.

Wilder plucked the bouquet from my hands and took it to the sink, trimming the flowers and putting them in a vase.

I grabbed my phone from where I'd left it on an end table and took it to the windows.

It had been almost two months since I'd come to Montana. Two months since my first photo taken in this exact spot.

Opening the camera, I snapped another picture. The grass was a bit greener. The sky just as brilliant of a blue. But so much had changed in those two months. For the first time in a long time, with my feet planted firmly on the floor, I didn't feel like moving. Not an inch.

"Hey." Wilder came up behind me, his arms wrapping around my waist.

"Hi." I leaned into his chest and flipped the phone's camera to the other position. Then I held it up, smiling up at the screen while he nuzzled his face in my neck.

His eyes were closed in the photo, but there was no mistaking the affection on his face. The love in mine.

So while he held me tight, I let my fingers fly across the screen. And posted a photo I'd be getting framed for this house.

My house.

two months in montana wasn't enough

EPILOGUE

IRIS

TWO YEARS LATER...

There wasn't an empty seat at Calamity Jane's. Tourists and locals were crammed into the bar to watch Lucy Ross sing with the band.

Lucy Ross. My friend.

How was it that I was friends with a woman I'd once idolized? It didn't seem real. But there she was, standing at the end of our booth, chatting with me while Duke was visiting with Wilder.

"When do you guys leave?" she asked, tucking a lock of blond hair behind her ear. She was in a flowy tank top tonight and a pair of distressed jeans, an outfit we'd shopped for together.

"Three days. I really need to pack." I groaned. "I'm currently wading through a mountain of dirty clothes. For such a small person, Blakely creates so much laundry."

"Want me to lie to you and tell you it lightens up as they get older?"

302

I laughed. "Yes."

A click of the mic stole her attention and she glanced at the stage. The band was moving back into place after their set break. "I'll have to lie to you later. That's my cue to get back up there."

"Good luck." I waved as she weaved through the crowd, smiling as she made her way to the stage.

Duke shook Wilder's hand and hurried to catch Lucy at the stage, giving her a kiss before he took his usual stool at the bar.

"Before they start up again, I'm going to head outside and call the house," Wilder said.

"Babe, she's fine. We both have our phones." I tapped mine where it rested on the table beside my glass of water and half-empty basket of french fries. "They'll text if they need anything."

"No, they won't. They'll just try to figure it out and not bother us."

"So? Let them try to figure it out." My argument was pointless.

Wilder slid out of the booth, his phone in hand. "Be right back."

I rolled my eyes as he walked to the door and slipped outside.

His parents were staying with Blakely tonight, and it was the first time we'd left our nine-month-old daughter. Leading up to this date, I'd been a nervous wreck. Wilder had practically shoved me in the truck earlier to make me leave.

After an hour at Jane's, I'd relaxed, knowing she was in good hands with his parents. Yet Wilder's anxiety had only grown. He'd already checked in with his mom twice.

This was our trial run with his parents babysitting. We were all heading to Cozumel in three days for our summer family vacation. His parents wanted to give us a chance to spend time alone and would be watching Blakely so we could go on a few dates during our two-and-a-half-week trip.

I'd expected to be the parent who insisted we leave the second our cheeseburgers were finished. But with the way Wilder kept checking the time, I could tell it was coming.

He loved our daughter beyond measure. And I wouldn't care a bit if we cut tonight's date short so he could be there to rock her to sleep, just like he had every night of her life.

We hadn't planned on starting a family so soon, but the winter after I'd moved to Calamity, Christmas had been spent hovering over the toilet, retching my guts out. When the nausea hadn't stopped, I'd gone to the doctor, sure I'd picked up a virus. Nope, just pregnant.

My parents had expected us to dash to the courthouse for a quick wedding. Wilder wouldn't have minded, but I'd insisted on more. I wanted to get married on the beach. So we'd waited until this summer, when the school year was done and Blakely was old enough to travel, to have our dream wedding.

Maybe we'd gone about this a little out of order, but order was overrated.

The simple solitaire diamond ring on my finger gleamed beneath the table's light. I'd been wearing this ring for nearly two years, and in less than a week, there'd be a wedding band on that finger too. Soon, Wilder's hand wouldn't look quite so naked.

We'd planned a small destination wedding. Both of our families were traveling and staying a week. Then most of the guests would leave and his parents would stay to help with Blakely over our honeymoon.

At long last, we were going on a long overdue vacation.

My pregnancy had thwarted most of our travel plans these past two years. I'd been miserably sick for the first five months, and by the time I'd finally felt like myself again, my doctor had warned against any extensive trips in my last trimester.

So Wilder and I had explored closer to home. We'd gone on countless weekend road trips. We'd spent endless hours in the Bronco, Wilder behind the wheel while I rode shotgun and peppered him with questions. I had a lot of friends in Calamity these days, but Wilder would always be my best.

"She's fine." Wilder slid into his side of the booth. "They just gave her a bath."

"Feel better?" I teased.

"Yes." He smirked and stole one of my remaining fries since his basket was empty.

While he chewed, I snagged my phone and pulled up the camera. "Smile."

He didn't smile. He rarely smiled for staged pictures. Not that it mattered. Wilder smiled so often that I was able to catch it in plenty of candid photos. But I took a picture tonight anyway and posted it to my Instagram stories.

Whenever I posted about Wilder, we got flooded with messages. Kim expected that no matter what wedding photo we posted, we'd hit our new record.

It had been the most successful year I could have imagined for my business. My followers hadn't minded a bit that my two-month stints in various places had stopped. They'd gobbled up content of Wilder and our life in Montana instead. And my pregnancy had been wildly popular, bringing in new followers and the chance to expand my brand outreach to family products.

My content had shifted with my lifestyle, and though there were still days when nasty comments burrowed through my thick-ish skin, mostly, I was grateful that people still seemed interested in what I had to say.

Even my family had taken more of an interest in my career. On their last trip to Calamity, Mom and Dad had spent an entire dinner asking questions about what I did and how it was done. They'd all stopped pushing me to conform to their idea of a normal life.

Either that was Danny's doing—a lot had changed since he'd driven to Montana to yell at me for sleeping with his best friend—or this newfound acceptance was because of Wilder. Everyone adored him and credited him for keeping me in the country.

But what they didn't understand, and probably never would, was that he'd pack up everything in an instant if he thought a life of travel would make me happy. He'd follow me around the globe if I asked.

Not that I would. Our life was in Calamity and I wouldn't have it any other way.

"I love you," I told him just because I could.

"Love you too, baby." He checked the time on his phone.

"Do you want to leave?"

"We can stay."

He'd stay for me. But yeah, he wanted to go. "Let's go home."

That was all it took for him to dig out his wallet and

leave enough cash on the table to cover our tab. His hand found the small of my back as we made our way to the door.

He broke every speed limit on the way home, but we made it in time for him to sweep Blakely from his mother's arms and rock her to sleep.

They were a perfect pair. She fit against his broad chest like a key fit a lock. And with their dark hair and dark eyes, she was his in every way.

So while they cuddled, I trudged to the laundry room and started the long task of packing for Cozumel.

———

THREE DAYS LATER, with our daughter buckled in her car seat, we climbed in the Bronco at five in the morning, ready to drive two hours to the airport to catch our first flight.

Wilder's hand took mine, his finger touching my engagement ring. "Ready, Iris Monroe?"

To become his wife? More than ready. "Abbott," I corrected. "Iris Abbott."

ACKNOWLEDGMENTS

Thank you for reading *The Brood*! Writing stories in Calamity, Montana, always feels like a treat. I'm so grateful for readers who love this series as much as I do.

Special thanks to my editor, Elizabeth Nover. My proofreaders, Julie Deaton and Judy Zweifel. Thank you to Sarah Hansen for the covers. Thanks to Vicki and Nina for all you do. To my Vegas Party Bus crew for keeping me smiling every day. To my loving husband and sons, who fill my heart.

And lastly, thanks to Logan for your all-around amazingness. Also, I love that you loathe capital letters.

ABOUT THE AUTHOR

Devney Perry is a *Wall Street Journal, USA Today* and #1 Amazon bestselling author of over forty romance novels. After working in the technology industry for a decade, she abandoned conference calls and project schedules to pursue her passion for writing. She was born and raised in Montana and now lives in Washington with her husband and two sons.

Don't miss out on the latest book news.
Subscribe to her newsletter!
www.devneyperry.com

Made in the USA
Coppell, TX
20 November 2024

40624841R00187